Schrodinger's Cottage

A Comedy of Quantum Proportions

First Published in Great Britain 2013 by Mirador Publishing

Any reference to real names and places are purely fictional and are constructs of the author. Any offence the references produce is unintentional and in no way reflects the reality of any locations or people involved.

A copy of this work is available through the British Library.

ISBN: 978-1-909224-49-0

Mirador Publishing
10 Greenbrook Terrace
Taunton
Somerset
UK
TA1 1UT

Schrodinger's Cottage

A comedy of quantum proportions

By

David Luddington

~ Other books by the author ~

Return of the Hippy
The Money That Never Was
Schrodinger's Cottage
Forever England
Whose Reality is this Anyway?
Camp Scoundrel
The Bank Of Goodliness

Chapter One

FOR MANY WRITERS THE HARDEST part of writing is the opening line. I wish. I have hundreds of opening lines. I have a file on my laptop dedicated to nothing but opening lines. I have enough opening lines to fill two complete volumes, if only I could find a way of joining them all together. Nor is my problem the famous 'Writer's Block'. Tania always said I suffered the exact opposite, she used to call it 'Writer's Diarrhoea'.

No, for me it's the voices. The incessant voices that clamour for my attention, jabbering, making demands. To which ones do I listen? Do I listen to the characters in my comics who all seem to have their own opinion as to how they see my plots unfolding? Or do I listen to the ones that tell me to take all my clothes off in the Bluewater Shopping Centre and sing Bohemian Rhapsody from the upper balcony? In retrospect it seems such a simple choice but at the time I was slightly confused. Or mildly bewildered as I prefer to call it and not the alcohol induced borderline schizophrenic the therapist insisted on labelling me. Such an unfriendly label I feel.

Anyway, a year of therapy and a nice box of rainbow pills

and I'm all sorted. Or at least I would be if only the voices would shut up. In an effort to make them I opted to move house.

Tinker's Cottage hides in a forgotten corner of the Somerset village of Trembly, not two miles from Glastonbury. It had been left to me by my aunt Flora some four years previously but the excitement of the big city meant I had ignored its charms and only ever visited it once. I'd tried to rent it out but the local agents seemed oddly reluctant and the place had remained empty.

After an exhausting drive down the M5, I nudged my car up the overgrown drive until nature completely overpowered us both and I had to abandon it and walk the last twenty yards. I pushed my way through a variety of bushes until the front door of the cottage peeped out between the hollyhocks and roses that fought for control of the porch. I only know they're hollyhocks and roses as that was the description given by the letting agents on the particulars, my knowledge of botany extends to bluebells and primroses, neither of which appeared to be resident in this garden.

I brushed the cobwebs clear of the lock and wriggled the key in the rusting hole. It turned easily and I pushed at the door. It gave a short squeak and then meowed. That was odd. Another meow and something brushed my leg. A large black cat pushed and weaved between my legs, tail proudly held high. I'd never really been a cat person, in fact I'd never done very well with pets in general. I tried tropical fish once complete with underwater castle and canons. But they kept eating each other so I gave up that idea and filled the tank with a set of model soldiers re-enacting the battle of Agincourt.

The cat purred and nudged my leg again. It wasn't an easy

cat to look at. Its fur was so black that one's gaze seemed to disappear into it. More like a cat shaped hole in space rather than an actual cat. A sort of an anti-cat I suppose. The cat shaped hole sat down and looked up at me. Two brilliant green eyes stared from the blackness. Another short meow, cat speak for something vitally important no doubt. I pushed the door open and ducked into the hallway. At five ten I'm not exactly tall but I could see a few bumped heads were likely to be coming my way.

My eyes attempted to compensate for the gloom as I fumbled for a light switch. My fingers located it just where it should have been and I clicked it on. Nothing, even repeated switching on and off had no effect. Damn! I pushed the door further open to allow maximum light then fumbled my way to the kitchen. I only tripped over the cat once. The light from the front door failed to reach the kitchen but my eyes were adjusting and I could just make out the cupboard which held the mains switches. I pushed the trip switch. Still no lights but a radio hissed and crackled into life from the next room. Woman's Hour by the sound of it, extolling the virtues of a home birth with an Indian Head Massage as an alternative to drugs.

A bit more fumbling, another cat collision and I finally found the light switch. The kitchen flooded with light. Well, maybe not flooded but at least trickled. The forty watt bulb pushed bravely at the shadows lurking in the corners of the kitchen. I'd half expected inch thick dust and cobwebs everywhere but the place was remarkably clean. The letting agents had insisted I pay for a regular cleaning service to keep the place attractive for potential tenants, I'd always thought I was being taken for a ride, but maybe not.

I found the cause of the gloom. The bright June morning was being defeated by green wooden shutters on the outside of the kitchen window. I reached across the sink unlatched the window and pushed at the shutters. They didn't move. Either age had embedded the catches or they were fastened from the outside. The cat slinked in and out of my feet, giving short meows followed by loud purrs. I glanced down and the luminescent green eyes caught my soul, demanding I do something with the empty silver cat bowl near my feet. My eyes scanned the room looking for anything I could drop into the bowl to keep this creature quiet so I could continue my explorations. I noticed a carton with a picture of a happy cat on it and emptied some of the contents into the bowl. The eyes looked at the bowl then back at me. They blinked in and out of existence a couple of times.

"Don't ask me," I said. "That's all there is."

The anti-cat seemed to understand and started crunching at the food. I turned my attention back to the window. I needed to let some light and fresh air into this place. I made my way back to the front door, switching on lights as I went. The path to the rear of the property was completely overgrown and I had to do battle with brambles and stinging nettles before I finally located the kitchen window. The shutters were latched on the outside by a small wooden lever. I swung the shutters open then headed back round to the front, opening two other sets of shutters on the way.

There was no sign of the cat when I returned to the kitchen but the bowl was empty. And the kitchen was still in gloom. I stared at the window not quite understanding. The shutters were still closed.

"Idiot!" I cursed. I must have opened the wrong shutters.

Another battle with the garden and I found my way back to the window I had mistaken for the kitchen. I wondered to which room this window belonged and peered inside. It was the kitchen. That didn't make any sense. I looked again, maybe there were two kitchens? No, it was the same kitchen, complete with one black cat staring at me from the worktop. Perhaps the shutters had swung shut in the wind or something. I pushed the shutters back against the wall and located them in the securing clips.

I returned to the kitchen only to find the gloom remained and the shutters still in place. If I didn't have a certificate in my suitcase from the Ealing Psychotherapy centre testifying to my sanity I would have been having severe doubts about now. As it was, the niggly voices whispered at the door of my pre-conscious. They spoke of goblins.

Grasping my sanity in a sudden act of decisiveness, I pushed hard at the window, forcing the catch on the shutters to give. The windows and shutters swung open and daylight poured into the room. I peered cautiously through the window, half expecting to see some teenage hoodie with a peculiar sense of humour, or at the very least a leprechaun or something. The garden was peaceful and apparently leprechaun free. The wind, of course that was it, just the wind. I'd heard Somerset was windy.

I went through the rest of the cottage forcing open the windows and shutters in each room. Sunlight followed me as I went from room to room, chasing my feelings of unease back into the dark corners. The cat was waiting for me when I made my way into the lounge and offered its help with the shutters. Well, maybe not help as such, more like stroll along the window ledge pushing the various ornaments to the floor.

As soon as I had the window open Anti-cat slid through it into the garden and disappeared into the undergrowth outside. There was a lot of undergrowth out there, in fact the garden seemed to be mostly undergrowth interspersed with a few small less dense patches of what had probably once been lawn. I'd enjoy trying to bring that lot under control. The garden in my Ealing flat had consisted of a huge Torbay Palm in a Chinese pot set in the middle of a four foot square patio. I also had a barbecue and deck chair for sunny days, although the high buildings all around meant the sun only reached my patio in late June. I always felt a sort of kinship with the builders of Stonehenge as I awaited the coming solstice each year.

I glanced around the lounge. Most of Aunt Flora's personal belongings had been taken into storage and replaced with an IKEA 'Instant Home' kit in readiness for the expected tenants. The blue and yellow striped curtains were slightly too long and ruffled on the floor. A glass coffee table and matching sideboard combined TV unit took over most of one end of the lounge. Against the rear wall, a blue futon served as both seating and extra sleeping facilities if bookings demanded it. They never did. The only booking I'd ever had was from a couple of American tourists who wanted to investigate the mysteries of Glastonbury. They disappeared after three days leaving behind a large pink suitcase, a wooden walking stick with a wizard's head and something ominous in the refrigerator.

I sat back on the futon. Not bad. Comfortable enough for short breaks. I wondered again at the lack of bookings. The price was low enough; I'd reduced it twice, and the location perfect for exploring the Somerset levels and ancient stuff.

There was a lot of ancient stuff round here I'd been reliably informed. Apparently King Arthur is buried near here along with the Holy Grail, and I believe several caches of Roman gold. Although I do think the gold was just a myth put about by the locals to boost tourism. The cat purred on my lap as I stroked it. I hadn't even noticed it arrive, how do they do that?

I wondered if Anti Cat had belonged to Aunt Flora or if it was a stray. A black cat would have suited her perfectly though, she always had been a bit odd. My eyes drifted to the huge stone fireplace half expecting to see a broomstick in the hearth but there was only a plastic imitation wicker log basket. I wondered if IKEA did logs. She hadn't been a proper aunt of course, just one of those adopted ones that some families seem to pick up along the way. We had always visited her at Christmas and I was often left with her for the summer break when I was kid. I remembered looking forward to her presents with excitement and usually a slight degree of trepidation. Certainly not the usual socks or pencil set from Aunt Flora. Fossilised spiders, a strange green stone that glowed in the dark and one year a plant that ate flies. And left over bits of turkey as I'd later discovered. Even until quite recently she'd continued to send me random gifts, not two months before she'd died I received a CD with John and Julian Lennon playing a selection of old Beatles songs together, apparently recorded in 1987. It sounded remarkably authentic although these pirates really ought to get their dates right.

I glanced at my watch, but I needn't have bothered as my internal timer is more precise than any atomic clock. One minute past twelve. That meant I was allowed a lunchtime drink. Since deciding that I would never be able to maintain a life of abstinence I'd set myself rules. No alcohol until midday was Rule One. I left the windows open but locked the front door then fought my way back down the jungle path.

The Camelot was a small village pub in the great Somerset tradition. Eighteenth century whitewashed walls struggled to support a sagging thatched roof. A small garden in the front contained two wooden tables and the now obligatory smoking gazebo. The sign, the newest part of the building, depicted an image of a twelfth century castle. Until recently this place had gone under the identity of 'The King's Head' but had changed its name in an attempt to pick up passing trade from any off-track Glastonbury pilgrims.

"You're that fella what's movin' in to Flora's cottage aren't you?" the barman greeted me. Ah, the rumour mill of a Somerset village, fastest known force in the universe. Einstein had got it all wrong. Sod the speed of light. A Somerset rumour would have time to stop and ask for directions and still be there at the other end with a cup of tea waiting for light to catch up.

"Thinking about it," I said. "A pint of that please." I pointed at a beer pump bearing the picture of a goblin hiding in some long grass. I hadn't the faintest idea what it was but the picture was cool.

"One pint of Old Grumbler's coming up." He pulled the beer slowly and with the care of a master craftsman. "You a relative or something? Didn't know she had any relatives."

"Sort of." I took the beer from the counter and sipped cautiously. It was thick, almost syrupy but with a sharp bite. Not bad. "She was my aunt."

I carried my beer to a wooden table in the bay window. The table wobbled as I set the glass down, spilling drips of

Old Grumbler's across the dark oak surface. I mopped at it with a beer mat. Bright sunlight streamed through the window glinting off the damp surface. Apart from my table, there were six others and four stools arranged along the bar. All were empty, although it was still early I guessed.

"Funny old stick, Flora." The barman seemed determined to engage me in conversation.

"One of England's great eccentrics," I conceded.

"Regular as clockwork for her morning sherry, she was. Although sometimes it wasn't until the afternoon. Then other days we wouldn't see her until late evening." He paused and thought for a while. Then, "Of course there were often times when we wouldn't see her for weeks."

"More of an irregular regular then?"

The barman slammed both hands flat on the bar. I jumped and the table wobbled, spilling more Old Grumbler. "You must be, Ian!" he announced as if this had just been revealed to him in a vision.

"That's me," I said mopping at the puddle with the soggy beer mat.

"She told me all 'bout you one time. You're that fella that writes comics."

"Graphic novels actually." I bristled. I hated the term 'Comics'. Made it sound like I spent my life creating inane stories for Tommy The Cat or some such pointless scribbling.

"Oh, right," he said. "Name's Albert by the way. But everybody calls me Arthur."

"Okay," I said. "I'm Ian. Although of course you already knew that." I pulled deep on the beer. The golden liquid ran round my veins. It was surprisingly strong and the day suddenly became more relaxed. I think I'll move to Spain, twelve o'clock comes an hour earlier there.

"On account of the name of the place you see," he continued. "Pub's called Camelot, so everybody took to calling me Arthur." He beamed proudly, obviously pleased with his nickname.

The door at the far end swung open and a man in green overalls entered catching Arthur's attention. I thanked the stars for the interruption.

I stared out of the window and watched the village go about its daily business. A couple of hippies with tatty rucksacks ambled past. The female, an attractive dark haired woman in her early thirties, carried what appeared to be a sandwich toaster. I enjoyed people watching. They often gave me ideas for characters. I could create a whole back story in an instant when I spotted an interesting looking character. Observing people was fascinating. It was actual people contact that I hated and tried to avoid wherever possible.

"Been here seventy two years, I have", a raspy voice informed me. I turned to find the source was a small man in a blue suit three sizes too large. He sat at a small table near the fireplace. I hadn't seen him arrive. "And my father before me. Sixty two years." He turned to look in my direction. The turning of his head resembled that of an owl as the suit didn't follow his movement. His walnut face glowered at me and he continued. "I've still got his ladder."

"I'm so pleased," I said. "A good ladder is always worth hanging on to." I hoped that gave an air of finality to this strange discourse. No such luck.

"He was given it when he left The Railway."

"Unusual retirement present?" I lifted the beer glass only to find it was empty. My soul sank a little.

"You're that Londoner taking on Flora's cottage." It was more statement than question.

"For a while, at least." I studied the empty glass. Nope, it was definitely empty.

"Need to cut those trees back. Some of them are hanging over the lane." His head rotated on the top of the suit again until it faced his beer. He took a long sip. "Had another Londoner here once. Didn't stay long though. Added all sorts of conservatories and pergolas and stuff to his house and then fifteen years later he was up and gone."

Only one pint at midday, that was my rule. "Village life doesn't suit everybody I guess."

"I hope you're not going to build a pergola, are you?"

The beer glass glistened with condensation and felt pleasingly cold to the touch. I briefly closed my eyes as I drank half of it down in one. Ah... Now, where had that come from? It's never a good sign when that happens.

"Don't want to pay too much mind to George," Arthur said. I realised I was standing at the bar and I had no recollection as to how I'd got there.

"What?" I said.

"George, he's lived here all his life and generally won't even talk to somebody who hasn't buried at least two grandparents in the graveyard."

"I feel honoured indeed." I finished my beer, waved Arthur goodbye and set off to buy some essentials.

Chapter Two

I STRUGGLED TO MANOEUVRE THE shopping past my car which remained trapped in the drive. Eventually I piled everything on the roof and slid the bags forwards towards the bonnet then retrieved them from the front. I would need a better system. On second thoughts, what I really needed was a chainsaw.

Anticat weaved through my legs as I struggled up the overgrown path leading to the front door. I slipped the lock and pushed my way past the cat to dump everything on the kitchen table. 'Everything' consisted of some milk, coffee, bread, frozen pizza, a case of Budwieser and more 'Happy Cat''. I had no idea how much cats ate.

I gazed through the window as I put the kettle on. The early afternoon sunlight brought out the colours in the jungle. The bright orangy coloured flowers on the big bushy thing contrasted beautifully with the pale blue that seemed to cover the prickly one. I couldn't see the end of the garden from here. I'd been told it was over an acre. I hadn't the faintest idea what an acre was and when I'd asked Google I'd been helpfully informed it was the amount of land an ox could plough in a day. I'll have to explore.

Anticat gave one of her short squeaky meows which I'd come to understand as meaning 'More Happy Cat please'. I emptied the last of the original packet into her bowl. She sat and looked at the bowl for a moment then crunched furiously at the little nuggets like she hadn't eaten for a month. I finished making my coffee and made my way through to the small dining room that linked the kitchen and the lounge. My laptop lay on the centre of the pine table. I switched it on and plugged in the internet dongle. I couldn't get a signal so I carried the laptop around the house until it picked up one bar on the small landing at the top of the stairs. As long as I held the laptop at a thirty degree angle up against the little window.

I downloaded my emails and returned to the dining room table to deal with the flurry of electronic correspondence that suddenly overwhelmed my inbox. By the time I'd deleted all the offers of improving my manhood or rescuing a Nigerian King's money from the nasty bank, the 'flurry' had turned into five emails, all from Tania demanding to know why I'd 'Gone Off Radar' and when could she expect the final copy for issue 172 of 'The Falconer'. I shut the lid of the laptop and stared out of the window. I'd been stalling on the latest story and Tania knew it. I'd been writing the adventures of The Falconer now for twenty one years. 171 issues of superhero daring-do. And I'd had enough. There's only so much you can do with a Super Hero with extendable talons and the ability to command birds of prey. But the fans never cared. They just demanded more and I churned out copy after copy. Essentially the same half dozen stories reworked issue after issue. I'd grown tired of him and I wanted to try something different. So issue 172 was where I planned to kill him off. If I could bring myself to write the words.

Anticat walked across the laptop several times before climbing on the window ledge and pawing at the glass. I pushed the window open for her and she slid through like a shadow disappearing under a bright light. I watched as she reappeared briefly from some yellow flowery stuff then slid out of view completely.

I pulled open the laptop and started typing an email. 'Dear Tania, I have decided that the time has come to kill off...' Delete. 'Dear Tania, after much thought about the journey I have been on all these years with The Falconer, I have decided it is time to move on and...' Delete. Anticat tried to help by walking across the keyboard typing random letters for me. I pushed her off several times then looked at her offering. Although her version of my email seemed to make more sense than mine I still deleted it and closed the laptop. I'll do that tomorrow, I'm not in the mood today.

Anticat used my lap as a springboard then sat expectantly by her empty bowl. I suddenly realised I hadn't seen her come back in. No wonder these things are such good hunters. One just can't see the buggers coming. I emptied more nuggets from the new packet of Happy Cat into her bowl and she ate happily. I wonder if cats are like goldfish. Will they just keep eating everything you give them until one day you find them bloated on the surface of the fish tank?

This time she left half the food and headed off through the lounge. Presumably to do more cat stuff out the front door this time.

I watched through the window as a large magpie swooped into the garden and settled onto a small wooden platform that hung from a rather sparse looking tree. He looked all around before flying off again. I realised the wooden platform was supposed to be a bird table of sorts and no doubt the magpie had come for lunch. I'd heard that magpies are spooky birds and it's probably best not to upset them. There's a rhyme somewhere in the dark corners of my childhood memories that warns of the dangers of not treating them with due respect. Having no idea what magpies eat I decided to try him on a little Happy Cat. Although apart from a frozen pizza or a can of Budweiser, it was about all I had.

I still hadn't found the key to the back door yet so I went out the front door and round to the rear garden. I sprinkled a handful of Happy Cat on the little hanging platform and returned to the kitchen. I watched for a while then the magpie returned to settle on the table. I waited to see if my sacrifice of Happy Cat would suffice. Evidently it wouldn't. The magpie skittered around the little table for a moment before taking off once more. Okay, so Happy Cat is not the preferred menu item for magpies. A little brown bird fluttered onto the platform. I peered through the window trying to see if it would take the food. The table appeared to be bare. How odd. The little bird padded about for a moment before hurtling off into the undergrowth like a stone from a catapult. I looked again at the table to see if I could see the food. It was definitely empty. I guessed the magpie must have eaten it all in the time it took me to walk back round through the front. Perhaps I hadn't upset the magpie clan after all. That's a relief. But I had disappointed the little brown one though. I took a small handful of Happy Cat and headed back to the rear garden.

The platform already had the original nuggets on it. Neither of the birds had taken it, I had obviously just not been able to see it clearly from the kitchen window. I returned to the kitchen and dropped the nuggets into Anticat's bowl.

I thought I probably ought to eat something so I pulled a frozen pizza from its box and set about trying to understand how the oven worked. After close investigation I deduced that in order to make the oven work I first needed to cut down several trees and fill up one side of this beast with logs, set them on fire and wait several hours for it to heat up to a temperature where it could cope with pizza. I returned the pizza to the freezer. I could see 'Instant Food' might have its difficulties in Tinker's Cottage.

A noisy chattering drew my attention from the garden. The magpie danced around the little wooden platform. I squinted my eyes and peered at the table. It was empty. Of that there was no doubt. One empty bird table and one very irate magpie. Another handful of cat nuggets and I once more circumnavigated the cottage to the rear garden. The bird table already had cat nuggets on it, just as it had last time I'd come round. So why could I not see them from the window? I didn't think my eyes were that bad. After all, I was The Falconer with fifty mile vision and talons of steel. I should be able to see a bird table not five metres from my window!

I returned to the kitchen and looked out through the window. The bird table was empty, apart from unhappy magpie in full telling-off mode. I gave up and threw the handful of Happy Cat through the window to land just underneath the platform. The magpie flew off at this obvious attempt to kill it by throwing cat nuggets in its direction. A few minutes later several of the little brown ones gathered underneath the platform to investigate the offering.

I opened up the laptop and penned a bland email to Tania

explaining I was just putting the finishing touches to the artwork for issue 172 and clicked send. It didn't send of course. I took the laptop to the sweet spot at the top of the stairs and aligned it to the perfect angle required and eventually my email slid off into the ether. From this upstairs window I had a better view of the area. Tinker's Cottage was indeed isolated. Nothing but trees and fields, apart from the small lane to the east. The fields rolled upwards to some woods at the top. Halfway between the end of my garden and the woods, a huge oak tree stood proud and alone. I know it's an oak as I used to play in one just like it when I was a small boy. Mine was hollow and held the secrets of the elves and goblins.

I returned to the kitchen to find Anticat sat by her bowl. "You can't be hungry again!" I looked down at the bowl. It was still half full of cat nuggets. By the side of the bowl lay the fresh corpse of one of the little brown birds. Ah, now I see why the platform is raised.

"And just what am I supposed to do with that?" I asked the cat shaped hole in space. "Do you want me to lightly sauté it in a little olive oil and garlic for you?"

The cat's eyes blinked in and out of existence several times. I picked up the little bird by its tail and took it out to the dustbin. I felt sorry for the little mite. I'd led it to its demise with the temptations of Happy Cat and now it was going to an unceremonious internment in a black wheelie bin. I shut the bin lid and headed back to the kitchen to discuss with Anticat the rules of the house. Anticat was nowhere to be seen.

* * * * *

The village of Trembly consists of one small general store that seems to be a conversion of somebody's front room, The Camelot Pub, and a church the size of Westminster Abbey. Also on a Wednesday morning Badger's Farm opens its Farm Shop and this being Wednesday morning I decided to explore.

"Good morning, Mister Faulkener," I was greeted by a tall woman who was busy organising onions in a display box. "How are you settling in?"

"Er, fine." Clearly I was the news topic of the week.

"What can I do for you?" She straightened up and dusted her hands on her blue striped apron.

I panicked. "Cheese," I announced randomly. "I was looking for some cheese."

"We've got a lovely Somerset Tangy." She held up a packet of Somerset Tangy to prove her point.

"Okay, I'll have one of those and..." My eyes drifted around the shop looking for food I didn't need to cook. "And a Cornish pasty and I'll have one of these." I picked up a packet of bird food that had a picture of little brown birds on it so I assumed it was alright for the ones in my garden. Maybe the reason Anticat had killed the bird was because they were eating her food. My eyes lighted on a net bag of split logs and thoughts of pizza returned. "And I think I need some of these for my cooker," I said hefting the bag onto the counter.

I returned to Tinker's Cottage and struggled once more past the jammed car. I was really going to have to do something about that. I dropped the food and logs by the front door then went straight round the back in order to leave a little of the bird food out whilst I had it in my hands. I felt a need to appease the birds for the senseless slaughter of their brother I appeared to have caused. I opened the packet and sprinkled some of the seeds on the hanging platform and turned towards the cottage. The back door was open.

My first thought of course was of giant goblins with pitchforks. I pushed that to one side and the slightly more rational fear of axe wielding drug crazed hoodies came to mind. I pressed myself against the wall and sidled towards the open door the way I'd seen it done on CSI. Except of course they had guns and I had a packet of bird seed. On the bright side though, at least whoever the intruder was had managed to open the bloody door for me. I peered around the edge of the door. The intruder, clearly female had her back to the door. She wore blue jeans and a tight white T shirt contrasted the jet black hair that tumbled down her back. I was about to burst in and threaten her with the bird seed when I realised she was doing a strange silent dance. My fears which had briefly subsided in the absence of masked maniacs once more rose. I'd seen The Wicker Man. I understood young women performing strange dancing type rituals in isolated villages.

I moved closer to the door and just at that moment she turned to face me. She screamed and I think I might have screamed too but I wasn't sure. I raised the packet of birdseed over my head. She threw her hands across her face and dropped to the floor in a crouch. I waited to see if she was going to metamorphosise into some hideous creature. She didn't. She pulled a set of earphones from her ears and threw them to the floor, sobbing and jabbering in some strange language. Next to her lay a discarded can of spray polish and a duster. Okay, I suppose I just might have got hold of the wrong end of the stick here.

The strange jabbering language reminded me of Spanish.

Very much of Spanish come to think of it. She stared up at me, eyes wide in terror. I realised I still held the birdseed over my head. I put it down and crouched in front of her, holding my hands out in a friendly gesture. She pushed herself back towards the cupboard she had been polishing when I'd arrived.

"What you want?" she asked with a touch of defiance in her voice.

"My cottage," I said, waving my arms around the room. "Mine."

"No," she said. "Senora Flora. This is her house."

"Aunt Flora? Senora Flora is... She died ten years ago. I'm Ian, her nephew. Well, sort of nephew."

She pulled herself to her feet but still kept her distance. "Why you say this?" She tugged a mobile phone free of her hip pocket. "I clean house for Senora Flora every week." She waved the phone at me. "You go now or I telephone the Police."

"Ah, you work for Hunter and Parks? The estate agents?" Maybe they hadn't told her Aunt Flora had died. After all, why should they?

"No! No estate agents!" She was getting more confident as I grew more confused. "Senora Flora lives here. Not you... not estate agents. Senora Flora."

"But I've just moved in. Didn't they tell you? Didn't you see my car in the drive?" It should have been difficult to miss, I thought.

"What car? No car in drive!" She started jabbering in Spanish again. I presumed it was a string of insults directed at my sanity. A subject about which I was beginning to have increasing doubts.

"Come, I'll show you my car." I started towards the door. At least I could prove that I'd been here before she'd arrived. Although how she'd managed to not notice I couldn't imagine.

She started walking behind me and just as I got to the door she gave me a shove in the small of my back and I stumbled into the garden. The door slammed shut behind me. I turned back towards the door to see her turning the key in the lock.

"Idiot!" I cursed and pushed at the door. It didn't shift. Damnit. She continued jabbering from the other side although I could no longer hear what she was saying. She waved the phone towards then pulled the curtains closed.

I stood outside for a moment replaying all that had happened. It still didn't make sense. My car? It must still be there. I'd had to squeeze past again on the way back. Hadn't I? Of course I had. She must be wrong. I couldn't miss a car. What if the car had really gone but my imagination had somehow retained it in my conscious? Knowing it was ridiculous, knowing I was going to find the car just where I'd left it, I had to check anyway.

It was there of course. Just where I'd abandoned it yesterday. That meant I had a crazy woman loose in my cottage. A crazy woman who thought Aunt Flora was still alive and who could walk through cars. With a sense of righteous indignation I set off back up through the front garden and in through the front door. My righteous indignation weakened into timid trepidation as I approached the lounge. All was silent. I pushed the door open and looked around the empty room.

Oh hell! She must be hiding somewhere. I moved cautiously from room to room. I felt a bit like Clouseau waiting for Kato to jump out of a wardrobe at him. The two upstairs bedrooms were completely devoid of mad Spanish women. In the main bedroom, my overnight bag still sat on the floor where I'd left it and my clothes spread haphazardly on the double bed. The second bedroom consisted of two single beds and a simple dresser. The pine wardrobe was empty.

Downstairs I checked the lounge again it was still empty. I pushed at the back door, it was locked. A quick search for the key failed so I assumed she had her own keys. Although of course that didn't make any sense at all. I could almost understand a crazed woman with a desperate need to break into people's houses and give them a spring clean, but one with her own keys?

Satisfied that the house was empty, she must have slipped out the back, I headed for the kitchen to make a nice sane pot of tea. That's one thing I did learn from Aunt Flora, when the world is going mad, a nice cup of tea puts it all back into focus again.

Anticat greeted me with one of her single, sharp meows. She was sat by her empty bowl. I glanced down. Next to the bowl were the neatly arranged head, body and entrails of a small rodent. All beautifully removed and separated. A top surgeon couldn't have done a better job.

"Now what?" I asked. Anticat pushed in and out of my legs then returned to her bowl. "Is that for me?"

Perhaps this was in exchange for the Happy Cat I'd been providing. Although had I ever had a desire for filleted rodent I would have asked the butchery counter of Waitrose to prepare it for me. And how can this one cat eat so much?

I gathered the remains of her gift up in some kitchen roll

and deposited it in the dustbin, which at this rate was soon going to be full of what used to be the wildlife of Trembly. I picked up the packet of Happy Cat. I noticed it was beef and tuna flavour. As I poured it into her bowl I wondered why they don't make bird flavoured cat food. Or rodent cat nuggets. Beef or tuna were hardly natural prey for a household moggy. I had this mental image of Anticat trying to bring down a calf.

I sat at the kitchen table with my cup of tea and Cornish pasty staring at the big green oveny thing in the corner. I was really going to have to get the hang of it sometime soon. And keys. I needed keys to the back door. I decided I would have to pop into Glastonbury to see the letting agents. They also might be able to shed light on mad Spanish women.

Chapter Three

I PARKED THE CAR IN the car park next to Glastonbury Abbey. I pulled yet another twig from the rear wiper, I thought I'd got them all when I'd disentangled the car from the drive. Hunter and Parks Estate Agents were located halfway up the hill between a Wiccan Bookshop and a Fairy's Crystal Grotto. I pushed on the green painted door. They were closed. A notice on the door informed me they didn't open until ten. I checked my watch, half past nine. I looked up and down the street. It appeared that most of the shops were still closed. Obviously Glastonbury has its own time zone that doesn't entirely agree with Greenwich. I moved down a few doors and found an open bookshop that was displaying one of my graphic novels in the window. Issue 168, The Falconer faces Steel Wind. I was particularly proud of that one. Steel Wind had been one of my best villains, a creature that morphed into a wind capable of cutting through anything or anyone in its path. I went inside.

The shelves were stuffed with books on Druids, Fairies, Witches, Stonehenge, Camelot and every conceivable permutation thereof. 'The Fairies of Camelot march on

Stonehenge'. One complete section was given over entirely to alien abductions. I leafed through one book that explained how Buddha had been abducted by aliens as a child which explained his profound wisdom. There were maps and birth charts, family lineages and even the results of a DNA test on some hair found in his hut that had just been discovered. All very scientific, meticulous research, and as far as I could tell, complete and utter bollocks.

As a writer of fantasy, I do try to keep an open mind on these things but some people are just taking the piss. 'Aliens Have Secret Base Under Stonehenge' another book informed me in bold print and underneath, 'Government Covers Up Invasion'. I checked my watch and continued browsing. A section at the far end attempted to deal with slightly more grounded subject matter. Stephen Hawking nestled alongside Brian Cox and Michio Kaku. I picked up a copy of 'A Brief History of Time' which I had always meant to read but had never seemed to find the time. Maybe now I'd find time to catch up on all the things I'd promised myself over the years. Learn to play the guitar or take up fishing. I took the book to the counter and paid for it.

Although it was now just after ten, the estate agents door remained closed. I continued up the street and wandered through the first open shop doorway. My nose was immediately assaulted by the heavy musky scent of burning incense. A woman in a long stripy caftan stopped arranging exotic birthday cards to greet me.

"Welcome to The New Dawn," she said. I assumed that was the name of the shop and not an announcement of some apocalypse I'd missed by not listening to the 'Today Programme' this morning.

"Thank you," I said and meant it. She seemed genuinely pleased that I was in her shop. The simple wooden shelves held an astounding selection of the most esoteric and downright bizarre items I had ever seen in a single shop. Twisted wooden wands and tarot cards jostled for shelf space alongside boxes of crystals and porcelain fairies. One shelf held simple Ordinance Survey maps of the area and guide books and another held leather bound spell books and ceremonial daggers. A large blue crystal on a silver chain caught my eye. It flashed brilliant shafts of colour in the morning sunshine. I picked it up and it felt oddly familiar in my hand.

"That belongs to you," the woman said.

"How much is it?" I asked, feeling its smooth surface under my fingers.

"I can't sell it to you," she said. "But if you would like to donate... say fifteen pounds as I've been looking after it for you for all these years then that would be in balance."

It was certainly the strangest sales technique I'd ever encountered, and I frequented Camden Market regularly so I thought I was wise to every ploy going.

"Oh, okay. Thank you." I kept hold of the crystal and continued to browse. I found some sandalwood joss sticks, a book of local folklore and guide to the wildlife of the Somerset Levels.

"Your aura is badly damaged," the woman said as she bagged up my purchases. "You need to take care."

"I'll try," I said. I watched her as she rang my purchases and donation through the till. Her hair was long and sun streaked and accented her tanned skin. I guessed her to be in her early forties.

"Take some of this with your morning tea." She dropped a tiny brown bottle into the bag.

"How much is that?" I asked reaching for my money again whilst admiring her sales ability.

"Take it," she said. "I can't take money for healing. It doesn't work."

"Not even a donation?" I asked with what I hoped was light, humorous cynicism.

"Not even a donation." Her smile told of mischief. She handed me the bag.

* * * * *

By the time I had ambled back down the street again, Hunter and Parks had finally deigned to join the rest of the world of commerce and opened their doors. Two desks faced the front door, each with a chair in front. I sat at the desk behind which a slightly balding man in a blue striped shirt and red tie did his best to ignore me. I pushed some leaflets around the desk and eventually he looked up. "How may I help you?" he asked

"My name's Faulkener, you're managing a property for me?"

"Oh, what's the address?" He sat with fingers poised over his keyboard. I gave him the address and he tapped the keys. "Here we are, Tinker's Cottage. What can I do for you?" He slid his half moon glasses down his nose so he could look at me from across the top of them.

"I want to take it off your books," I said.

"Oh dear. Why is that?" He seemed genuinely hurt.

"Well, firstly you haven't managed to secure me a single

long term let in three years and secondly, I'm moving in there anyway."

He clicked more keys and pushed the mouse around a bit. "Hmm, we do appear to have had some difficulties with that particular property. Strange place."

"What do you mean?" I felt defensive all of a sudden. Which was silly really as I'd only had the place a couple of days.

"Well, one has to wonder what became of that American family. And then there's the previous owner, a miss... Taverstock?. Strange business." He pushed the mouse to one side and studied me over the screen.

It was true, nobody had ever been quite sure what had happened to Aunt Flora. The milk had piled up outside the door over nearly a week until the police had been summoned to force an entry. The place had been deserted and all had seemed as it should be except the back door had been forced. At first it was assumed to be a bungled robbery and then perhaps a kidnapping. Although why anybody would want to kidnap a sixty five year old recluse with no real family was beyond any sense of reason. But the end result was she never turned up. After the statutory seven years the coroner declared her dead and the will was actioned. Which is how I'd come to be the current owner of Tinker's Cottage.

"Contrary to what Agatha Christie may posit, rumours and mystery never really help the letting potential of a property, you know," the estate agent continued.

"I'd have thought mystery was just what most folks came to Glastonbury in search of?" I said. He was beginning to annoy me and I felt an overwhelming desire to staple his tie to the keyboard.

"Not usually our client profile. The ones who come looking for mystery, in my experience mostly come in tents." He moved to a large filing cabinet and flicked through the racks of folders. "Here we are." He dropped a large brown envelope on the desk as he sat down again. "I think you'll find everything in order."

I picked up the envelope. A small typed label at the top read; Tinker's Cottage HP0023421.

I opened it up and peered inside. Two sets of keys and various bits of paper.

The man stood and held out his hand. "We shall send our account in due course, mister Faulkener."

I stood but ignored his hand. Just as I reached the door I remembered the mad Spanish woman. "The cleaner," I said. "Will you arrange to stop her?"

The man looked puzzled. "We haven't had the cleaners in there for over two months."

"But I met her yesterday, Spanish woman?"

"You must be mistaken, mister Faulkener. We use Eco Angels cleaning services and as far as I know they are all English. And anyway, as I said, we terminated their contract two months ago with regard to Tinker's Cottage."

I left Glastonbury in a bit of a daze, wondering if the place always had that effect on people.

* * * * *

I thought that with a bit more caution I might just manoeuvre the car up the drive this time. I thought wrong but I did succeed in getting it jammed a bit further along. That was going to be a pig to get out tomorrow. I pushed my way through the undergrowth and unlocked the front door. The phone was ringing as I entered. I dumped my bags on the kitchen table and grabbed the phone.

"Hello?"

"Ian? Are you all right?" asked Tania, my full time Literary Agent and one time lover.

"Of course, why the worry?"

"I've been trying to ring you all morning. Tried your mobile as well."

I pulled my mobile from my pocket and studied it. "Ah, sorry. Battery's dead."

"I was worried. Your email yesterday sounded odd." Tania had a sixth sense that often unnerved me. We had spent two glorious years together until I had finally trashed our relationship, along with most of her kitchen, in a fit of alcoholic temper that would have made The Incredible Hulk look cuddly. Shortly after that I started seeing goblins and from there it was a short run to the Ealing Hospital Special Unit for the bemused and bewildered.

"I'm fine," I said. "Just been into Glastonbury to sort out the paperwork for the cottage. Some confusion over cleaners... and cats. But mostly alright." I pulled the crystal from the paper bag as I talked. It felt friendly in my hand.

"Why the delay with number 172? Why are you stalling?"

"I might be... I was thinking about..." How could I tell her I wanted to kill off The Falconer? I know she's moved on now and living with somebody called Aaron but The Falconer kept us talking. And in some perverse corner of my pre-breakdown brain I still held on to a twig of hope. "I thought I might take a break for a couple of months... er... weeks." I finished lamely.

"Well just as long as you're alright. I still worry you know."

We finished with the usual banal pleasantries that only ex lovers can do and I switched the off phone. I found I'd been holding the strange blue crystal. It seemed to glow ever so slightly in my hand. Hippy nonsense. I placed the crystal on the table.

Loud chattering outside the window snagged my attention. The magpie sat on the empty bird table and was in full telling-off mode. I emptied the envelope from the estate agent and picked up the keys. After trying every key of both sets in the back door at least twice I gave up and threw them on the table. "Sod it!" Still no back door key. I looked for the bag of birdseed and realised I'd left it in the lounge when I'd been confronted by mad Spanish woman. I went through into the lounge to retrieve it but it was nowhere to be seen. I was sure I'd put the packet on the coffee table when she'd started screaming at me. I looked around again. No, definitely a birdseed free zone. That meant that not only had the crazy woman broken into my house to clean it for my dead aunt, but she had also stolen my fucking birdseed!

Back in the kitchen I crumbled some bread onto a plate and headed out the front door and round the back. The magpie had disappeared by the time I'd got there, probably lurking in the bushes waiting for me to leave the food and go again. I piled the bird table high and went back inside. I returned to the kitchen and looked through the window. The magpie was still nagging and pattering around on the now empty bird table.

"Look, I don't know what you keep doing with it." A loud meow drew my attention to the corner of the kitchen. Anticat sat by her empty bowl. "Or you!" I said as I emptied more cat nuggets into her bowl. "You've either got an eating disorder or there's more than one of you."

I left Anticat to her munching and Magpie to his chattering and turned my attention to the oven. Pizza. I stared at the big green beast. Fill it with wood, set it on fire, put pizza in. How hard can that be?

After an hour I discovered just how hard that could be. The big green monster had eaten all my wood and had barely defrosted the pizza. I removed the warm soggy mess just as the flames from the oven died away. I stared at the pizza for a moment before consigning it to the rubbish bin and heading off for The Camelot.

* * * * *

The chalkboard behind the bar informed the world the special of the day was Locally Sourced Meat Pie and Seasonal Vegetables. I ordered the special and carried my pint of Old Grumbler over to the table by the window. The early afternoon sunshine forced me to squint as I watched the comings and goings of Trembly folk. A pair of large German Shepherds were taking a petite woman in a pink trouser suit for a walk up the main road. The trio nearly collided with a small red faced woman in blue dungarees coming the other way. They stopped as they met and there followed such animated chatter as to make Magpie look positively laconic. My mind played with the image of the woman in the pink trouser suit. A fiery valkyrie from hell on a chariot drawn by two demon wolves bursts free from the underworld. She'd make a great villain.

My Locally Sourced Meat Pie and Seasonal Vegetables arrived. The pie appeared to be one of the Cornish pasties from the farm shop and I'm sure the sweetcorn and peas were seasonal when they were frozen so I'll have to give The Camelot credit at least for creative advertising copy. But then again my knowledge of what's seasonal or local is somewhat confused by the fact that at home I can pop down to the corner shop on Christmas Eve and find fresh mangoes and kangaroo meat. I took a long draft from my Old Grumbler, I was developing a taste for that, and placed the glass on the small table. A large brown handbag appeared next to it and wobbled the table slightly. I gazed up in the direction from which the handbag had appeared.

"You'll be that comic man from London what's got Flora's place," the owner said.

I smiled my best 'nice' smile and tried to keep the calm in my voice. A year of therapy taught me to keep the calm in my voice. "Yes, she left it to me in her will. And it's graphic novels, not comics. And you'll be...?"

"Miss Timkins, Tabitha. Everybody calls me Beth."

I placed my knife and fork on the side of the plate and studied the woman before me. She looked to be about sixty with flushed cheeks that hid in the shade of a large brown hat that appeared to match the handbag. "Nice to meet you, Beth," I said. "I'm Ian, but I expect you knew that already."

"Funny business, Flora. One moment she was there and the next... whoosh. Gone like as you please." She pointed at my beer. "You not going to offer a lady one of those?"

"Pardon my manners," I said. "I can't think what came over me." I waved my arm and caught the attention of Arthur at the bar. "Can I have a half..." I glanced at Beth and read the look. "Sorry... a pint..." I looked at my own drink, still nearly full. To hell with it. "Make that two pints of Old Grumbler."

"You know she was kidnapped by the gypsies up on the hill, don't you?"

"No, I'd not heard that one." I'd heard many other equally ludicrous stories attempting to explain Aunt Flora's disappearance but I could honestly say I'd not heard the one about the gypsies on the hill. I speared a potato on my fork and was just raising it to my mouth when her hand grabbed my wrist, stopping the potato two inches from my mouth.

"They keep people in their caravans and then claim the social for them. What's a graphic novel when it's at home then?"

Her hand let go of mine and the potato finished its journey. Quite tasty. But I was so hungry I don't think I'd have cared if it was raw. "A graphic novel is an art form. A comic is a kid's temporary amusement."

"Never went much on art. I expect you'll be doing the place up to sell?"

I'd had conversations with dope heads high on amphetamines who had better skills in staying on the point. "No I plan on staying there. It seems like a nice area."

"You'll need to get that garden under control then."

"So I've been informed. But that comes some way down the list behind cooking facilities and doors."

"My boy knows all about doors." Arthur planted the two pints of Old Grumbler on the table and sat down with us. Great, this was turning into a village meeting. "Been on a retraining course he has," Arthur continued.

"A course on doors?" I stared from Arthur to my meal and

wondered if I'd ever get to finish it. I reached for my beer and pulled deep.

"One of these government courses. Retraining for The New Millennium or something I think."

"Doors?" I asked. "A government training course in doors?"

"They do these courses in all sorts now," Beth said. "My sister did one in oyster farming once."

"Is that your sister Alice?" Arthur asked.

"No, Daisy. You know, she lives in Birmingham now."

I finished my second beer in one, picked up what remained of my Cornish pasty and headed for the door. "Got to dash," I said. "I left something on the... er... green thing... cooking machine." I realised I was probably being rude but if I stayed any longer there was a high likelihood of blood and a return visit for me to the nice people in the Ealing Special unit. I paused momentarily at the door and looked back at the table to see how much offence I'd caused. My seat had already been taken by George and all three seemed deep in conversation, apparently my departure unnoticed. I slipped through the door and into the late May sunshine.

I made my way back to Tinker's Cottage and clambered across the roof of my stranded car. As I opened the front door to the cottage I realised Postie had been. Reader's Digest have allocated me a prize, British Telecom seemed genuinely upset because I'd left them and the estate agents had already sent a bill for their services. 'Services' seems such an optimistic word in relation to what they actually achieved. I thought I'd tell them that and decided to write them a note to go with the cheque. Paper, there must be some paper in this place. I went through the kitchen drawers and opened all of the cupboards.

As soon as I opened the cupboard containing the cat food I heard a 'Meow' and felt something rubbing around my ankles. The cat food cupboard door obviously has a silent alarm that registers only in the cat frequency. Another meow and I found myself holding the box of cat food and realised I had no conscious memory of taking it out of the cupboard. Remote psychic programming or something. These things had powers we humans can't even begin to comprehend. I bent down to feed Anticat some of the dried nuggets. Only it wasn't Anticat. This was a pure white cat. Pink nose, pink tongue and the most remarkable blue eyes.

"Where did you come from?"

The cat circled and nudged in exactly the same way as Anticat. I wondered if they were twins. I dropped some nuggets into the bowl and watched as the white version of Anticat wolfed them down. I'd have to try to find out who owned these cats. There'll be some poor widow somewhere wondering where her beloved moggies had gone. I hoped.

The search for paper took me upstairs to the small landing between the two bedrooms. This obviously served Aunt Flora as a sort of office area. The view was stunning from here, looking out across the field with the oak tree and to Glastonbury Tor in the distance. A wooden desk sat underneath the window and I sat in the chair and searched the drawers. I couldn't work out whether the various pens, pieces of string, rubber bands and other assorted desk drawer detritus had once belonged to Aunt Flora or had been placed there by the agents for use by tenants. It didn't matter I supposed, but it felt somewhat comforting if I believed they were Flora's belongings. A sort of connection. I found what I was looking for, at least partly. The drawers gave up a pad of lined paper but unfortunately no envelopes or stamps. That would have been expecting too much. I did however find a bunch of keys. I tossed them into the air and caught them triumphantly then headed downstairs to do battle once more with the patio doors. My short-lived triumph soon faded though as each of the four keys would not even fit the lock. Giving up I dumped the keys on the window ledge.

I returned to the desk on the landing to pen my reprimand to messrs Hunter and Parks. But first I had to persuade the white cat I could actually write a letter without his help and that sitting on the pad did little to endear it to me and might in fact even threaten future Happy Cat supplies. White Cat seemed to understand and set off downstairs. I returned to my missive to the letting agents and explained at length how their use of the term 'Service' could be construed as misleading under the Trades Description Act then went on to give them two pages of advice on customer relations. It never does to piss off a writer. I folded the paper around the cheque which I'd already made out for a sum exactly ten pounds light of what they'd requested, embuggerance factor charge.

I made a list of essentials, envelopes, stamps, birdseed. I glanced out of the window and thought for a moment then added chainsaw to the list. Another moment's pause then included microwave. Hmm. this list might be beyond the resources of Trembly but I'd start there at least.

The village general store doubled as a Post Office. It also seemed to double as a bookshop, an off-licence and a haberdashery. From the outside it looked quite small but once inside it extended through a rabbit warren of rooms and annexes. I eventually managed to locate everything I needed with the exception of the microwave and chainsaw. Although

I wasn't convinced I wouldn't find those in here if I looked hard enough.

The man behind the counter was tall and rotund with a pair of red braces stretched taught over his stomach. "Afternoon, Mr Faulkener," he greeted. "I tried to order some of your comics when I heard you was here but the wholesalers said they don't stock them. That'll be five pound seventy please."

"Thank you," I said. "And they're graphic novels, not..." Oh sod it. I could be having this conversation for the rest of my life. "Do you know if anybody has lost a pair of cats? A black one and a white one?"

"Old Flora used to have cats. Strays I think mostly. Not of a mind as to anybody losing one though. You could put a notice on my board." He waved his hand towards a notice board near the door.

"Thank you. Do you have a postcard to write it on?"

I bought a pack of blank postcards, wrote the note and paid for two weeks. That should cover it.

"Just pin it to the board as you go." he said.

My advert joined a dozen others on the board in amongst prams for sale and babysitting services. One notice in what looked like very neat child's handwriting caught my eye. It advertised general repairs, gardening and locksmith. The postcard suggested I call Wayne for all my odd jobs and gave a mobile phone number. I wrote the number down on one of the postcards.

After dropping my shopping inside I pulled out Wayne's number and gave him a ring. He answered quickly and seemed quite confident when I explained my problem with the patio doors. He said he'd be round dreckly, which threw me at first until I realised he meant 'Directly'.

As I made myself a cup of tea I remembered the little brown bottle the woman in Glastonbury had given me. I tapped a couple of drops of the liquid in my tea and settled down at the kitchen table to await Wayne. The green cooker stared at me from the corner reminding me I'd forgotten to get fuel for it. Although I wasn't sure what the damned thing ate as it had gone through my bag of wood in no time. The tea tasted slightly sweet, I never used sugar so it was noticeable but not unpleasant. I watched through the window as evening drew in and the colours in the garden changed with the fading light. The little brown birds fluttered around the empty bird table so I opened the new packet and went out through the front door and round the back to the bird table. They were gone by the time I got there, probably hiding again. There were certainly plenty of places for them to hide in this garden. I sprinkled seeds on the table and headed back to the kitchen. I checked through the window and as earlier, they appeared to have eaten the lot in the time it had taken me to get back to the kitchen. They would have to make do. I could see I could keep this up all day. My eyes scanned the kitchen. It seemed slightly odd that there was no back door. It would seem to have been an obvious thing for a cottage kitchen to have a back door to the garden.

The sky outside darkened and there was still no sign of Wayne. I rang his number and he said he hadn't forgotten and he'd be along directly.

"But it's dark outside now, Wayne," I said. "Won't it be difficult to see to work?"

"I'm not coming tonight," he said, sounding surprised. "I'll be along tomorrow, like I said, dreckly. Can't do doors in the dark!"

"Okay," I said. "I'll see you then." I switched the phone off and realised I hadn't sorted out a time with him. It seems the word 'Directly' has a different meaning in Somerset. I supposed I was going to have to get used to a slightly different pace of life here. I felt strangely calm and briefly wondered why I hadn't given Wayne a slice of my usual acerbic anger that I usually kept in reserve for idiots that stole my time. My eyes caught the little brown bottle on the table.

Chapter Four

I struggled with the thumping in my head. The total silence of the Trembly night had made it difficult to sleep and I'd enlisted the aid of a rather large gin and tonic. The thumping continued and I forced my eyes open. I stared around the little bedroom wondering for a moment where I was. The thumping came again and I realised it wasn't a particularly loud hangover but was actually coming from downstairs. I grabbed some jeans and pulled them on then headed downstairs. As suspected the thumping was coming from the door. I opened it and daylight attacked my eyes. I squinted and made out the shape of a man against the brightness.

"Morning, guv!" the shadow cheerfully greeted. "Said I'd be along directly."

"Oh, yes. Wayne, good morning. You're here to do my lock?" I stepped aside to let him in. Wayne was a big, well built man probably in his mid twenties. He wore oil stained jeans and a T-shirt with holes in which had probably once been an England supporter's shirt. I wasn't sure I wanted an England supporter in my house before coffee. No matter how relentlessly cheerful he appeared to be.

"Do you want to see my certificate?" he asked dumping

his tool box on the hall carpet while he rummaged through his pockets.

"No, Wayne. Thank you. I'm sure it's fine." I showed him through to the lounge and pointed at the patio doors. "I need the lock changing. Idiot estate agents lost the keys."

"Locks... Ah...yes I do locks." Wayne's face gave the appearance of being slightly less convinced than the words he uttered. Which didn't exactly fill me with confidence. "I've got a tool for that," he continued.

"Would you like a coffee?" I asked.

"Tea would be good, Guv. Thanks. White with four sugars please." He opened the top of his toolbox and started spreading various strange looking artefacts across the carpet. I headed into the kitchen to make the drinks and by the time I'd returned he had the door open and the lock removed. With surprisingly little mess. He took the tea.

"That was quick, Wayne."

"Nothing to it." He took noisy slurp of his tea. "Got a special tool for that." He gazed around the mess of implements all over the floor. "Somewhere," he added.

"Soon have it done then?" I was feeling slightly more human as the Gold Blend kicked in.

"Well, I would do if I had a new lock to put in there."

"You haven't got a new lock?" I thought this was going far too smoothly.

"Might have one back in the yard." He dumped his empty cup in my hand and picked up his keys. "I'll just go see. Be back dreckly."

I stood in the lounge feeling somewhat bemused. The patio door was at least open now, although it might never close again. And it did have a hole in it where the lock lived. I took the empty cups back to the kitchen, made myself a refill then went upstairs to shower and dress properly.

An hour later and there was still no sign of Wayne's return. There was however plenty of coming and going of cats. Both the black one and the white one seemed intensely curious about something at the back of one of the units in the kitchen. As I sat there with my third coffee, the one that usually finally kick-starts me, I watched them slipping in and out through a small gap I'd not noticed before. I decided to call the white one Possicat, at least until its owners turned up. They slipped out of the gap and through the kitchen then back again as if playing chase with each other. At one point I lost track of which was where and could have sworn there were two black ones.

I wanted to go into Glastonbury to see if I could find a microwave oven as I was not going to be able to survive on Cornish pasties forever. I decided that with the patio doors being currently lockless there probably wasn't much point in worrying about security. I left a note pinned to the front door for Wayne saying that if he returned while I was out just to carry on. I wouldn't be long. I was tempted to add I'd be back 'dreckly' but thought better of it.

A remarkably successful visit to B&Q yielded both a microwave oven with grill and bake facility and an electric chainsaw. For good measure I also bought an extension lead that should see me as far as the oak tree in the field. I returned home, it seemed like home already, this time leaving the car in the lane next to Wayne's van as I was intending to do battle with the drive and the chain saw.

There was no sign of Wayne as I carried the microwave into the kitchen but a quick glance in the lounge revealed that he'd been back and made quite a neat job of the door. He'd left the doors open and the keys in the lock. And several of his tools still across the floor. Probably gone off to collect some other vital component. I played with the door briefly, all seemed okay. Finally I locked the doors and placed the keys on the window ledge along with the other mystery ones. I returned to the kitchen and tested the microwave. All seemed okay. I'd need to nip down the shop later for some microwave suitable food. I heard a banging noise from the lounge, probably Wayne returned. I looked in but there was no sign of him. The doors were still shut. Just as I turned to leave the banging returned. It sounded just like somebody knocking on the patio doors. I walked cautiously to the doors and peered through the glass. I caught a glimpse of somebody disappearing round the side of the cottage and opened the doors to look. Nothing, just the usual jungle. Mind you there could be the lost tribe of the Amazon living out there for all I knew. I just hoped my chainsaw was up to the job.

It took me an hour to assemble the chainsaw. Never had much use for mechanical gardening implements at my flat in Ealing. Very little need for rotovators or sit-upon mowers with a potted Torbay palm and four square feet of concrete patio. There was still no sign of Wayne, maybe he's gone for lunch or something. I trailed the extension lead down the drive as I figured that was probably the best place to start. It would make life a lot easier if I could get the car closer to the cottage instead of climbing over the roof.

Once I'd got the hang of it, the chainsaw made light work of the bushes that encroached into the drive. Along with a portion of a trellis fence, an apple tree and half the house sign. I also now had a pile of debris that would have served as the

Guy Fawkes bonfire on Hampstead Heath. I dragged the pile onto the centre of the front garden and checked my watch. Five minutes past twelve, time for lunch. I'd have a quick pint at the Camelot then pick up a sack of microwavable food.

The chalkboard declared the menu of the day to be local cod and fresh fried potatoes with Somerset beans in a delicious tomato sauce.

I ordered the special at the bar and collected my pint then settled myself at the window table. The only other occupant was George and I purposely sat facing the window which meant I had my back to him. Hopefully that would forestall any conversation. I thought wrong

"Cutting down your hedges I see," he said.

I twisted in my seat to face him. "Yes, trying to clear the drive a bit."

"You're going to need to do the stuff overhanging the lane as well," he reminded me. "Brambles nearly had my hat off on the way to church."

"I might have to buy a longer extension lead for that."

Arthur placed my lunch on the table rescuing me from further inanities with George.

"Getting your doors done then," he said as laid my knife and fork carefully each side of my plate.

"Locks, actually. How did -."

"My boy, Wayne, told me he was going there to do it. Did I tell you he'd done a course in doors?"

"Ah yes." The penny dropped. "I remember. Retraining course or something you said."

"That's right, he got made redundant from the cider farm when the French bought it. Or it might have been the Americans. But he does a good job in doors."

"Yes," I agreed. "He's surprisingly good."

Arthur left me in peace and I finished my fish and chips and ordered a second pint. The day drifted by outside in that lazy way that Somerset afternoons have. A couple of walkers headed briskly along the street complete with alpine walking sticks, always useful on the Somerset levels. I watched in bemusement as a caravan the size of a small village was being dragged through the tiny street by a huge four wheel drive Sanyoara Blitzkrieg or something. Why do people say they're going to 'get away from it all' and then take it all with them?

Warmed and relaxed by the sunshine and beer I popped into the shop for some microwavable supplies then headed back home. Wayne's van still sat in the lane outside. I thought about moving my car up the drive now it was clear but decided to do it next time I went out. Admiring my hedgemanship as I wandered up the drive I nearly tripped over Anticat as she hurtled out of a gap in the hedge and down the drive. I'd never seen her run so fast. A few seconds later and Possicat headed after her. Ah, cat games.

The house was deserted, even though he had no key I'd half expected Wayne to be there. His tools were still where he'd left them however. I gathered them up to place them in the hall cupboard. Just as I opened the door to the cupboard door Anticat slipped out and rubbed up against me, offering that pathetic little meow she does when trying to persuade me to feed her. I dropped the tools in the cupboard and she followed me into the kitchen. It was only when I was sprinkling the cat nuts in her bowl I realised I'd just passed her in the drive. She certainly hadn't slipped in the door with me, unless of course they had a secret entrance. I remembered them rummaging around behind the units at the back of the kitchen. That would be about the area that backed on to the hall cupboard. I fetched my torch and lay on the floor with my head between the units trying to see if there were any secret cat doors. Anticat came to help and walked over my head then sat in front of me so I couldn't see a thing past her. I pushed and poked at her but she just took that as affection and purred loudly. I drew myself out and decided to investigate later when I was more catless than I was now. It did however suggest that my hunch had been right, I seem to have more than one of the black ones.

I sat for a while in front of my computer which I'd laid out on the desk at the landing window. This was a pleasant place at which to work. The swallows swooped and balled across the Levels hurtling round the huge oak in the meadow before strafing my roof. I turned my attention back to my computer and the looming finality of issue 172, The Death of The Falconer. I'd written all but the final scene. At the moment he was trapped in a cave by the Bat People. This is usually the point where I'd concoct an outrageous escape involving a secret miniaturised laser or something. But not this time. This time there was no escape for The Falconer. I shut the computer down and decided to go for a walk across the meadow.

I found a gap in the hedge just up the lane from Tinker's Cottage and slipped through into the bottom of the field that led into the meadow. The grass had been newly mown and lay in lines across the field. The late afternoon sunshine made the hay smell sweet and a few butterflies danced before me as I walked. I was going to enjoy living here. Finding my way into the meadow from the field proved a little more difficult. As I pushed into a thick hedgerow I realised there was a small stream dividing the fields and I had to follow this for a while before finding a place to cross. I would need to buy wellington boots if I was intending to do much of this field walking business. The meadow stretched out before me, rising up a slight incline into the distance. I stood for a moment struggling with a slight sense of unease before I realised what the problem was. There was no oak tree. Stupid idiot! I cursed myself. How could I have got that wrong? I pushed my way back into the first field to reorientate myself. My sense of direction is not the best, especially when my usual points of reference are underground stations but even I could see this was wrong. I'd come in from the field at the edge of the lane, a narrow field that I knew from the landing window lay between the road and meadow. No, I'd been right. I pushed back through the hedgerow and across the small stream, quite expecting this time the oak tree to be there. It had to be.

It wasn't.

A vague sense of fear prickled through my veins. The same fear I'd felt when the goblins had first appeared four years ago. The goblins that brought with them paranoia and night fears. Locked rooms and multi coloured pills. I walked towards the centre of the field where the oak tree should be. I kept an eye on my cottage over the field. I could see the landing window where my desk sat so I knew I was in the right place. I wandered about the meadow for a while until my feet scuffed a rough area. I stopped and looked down. The grass was longer here and covering a slightly raised circle of about six feet in diameter. I paused. The raised area was wooden and clearly the remains of a hollow tree. I gazed across to my cottage. I was standing in just about the position the oak should be. I suddenly realised I was caressing the blue crystal in my pocket. It brought a sort of strange calmness to this very odd situation. I must have been mistaken. I don't see things that aren't there, or were there once but not anymore, or might not have ever been there in the first place. I don't see vanishing trees... or goblins. I definitely don't see goblins. Not anymore.

I turned and started back to the gap in the hedge. I needed a drink and I didn't care that my internal clock told me I still had another forty three minutes to go before I was allowed my afternoon beer.

Wayne's van was still parked in the lane, which was very odd. I retrieved my car and drove it carefully up my newly reclaimed drive. With a bit of gentle manoeuvring I even managed to navigate the tight right hand corner at the top. I parked it in front of another wall of nature which I think concealed a garage. I'd have a go at that sometime soon.

Anticat number one, or it might have been number two, greeted me as I opened the front door. I went into the kitchen and dropped food in the bowl, she had me well trained. I sat at the kitchen table with the cold beer in my hand watching the birds swooping in to investigate the empty bird table before chirping loudly and swooping off again. They'd have to wait. I broke the seal on the beer and sank half of it in one. A magpie settled gracefully onto the bird table and the last of the little brown ones disappeared. I was really going to have to get a bird book. Magpie seemed to stare straight at me, I'd had no idea how demanding nature would be. I picked up the packet of seed and thought about the previous games these creatures had tormented me with. 'Quick, let's eat it all before he gets back in!' I put the birdseed down and tore a chunk off a loaf of bread, broke it into bits and lobbed it through the window in the general direction of the bird table. Magpie looked at me with what appeared to be a scowl. Assuming magpies can scowl of course, of which I wasn't sure. Another reason to buy a bird book. He flew down from the platform and picked up a piece of bread then headed off across the hedges. Again it struck me as slightly odd there was no back door from the kitchen. I looked around and my eyes settled on a patch of wall where the plaster looked slightly raised. It certainly looked door-shaped. I wondered why somebody would block it up.

I replaced the empty beer and retreated to the lounge to search for a movie on the television. Three hours later I woke up to realise that was the second time I'd missed the end of Lord of The Rings. I made myself a quick supper in my new microwave, poured a good sized gin and tonic then watched a couple of old sitcoms on Channel Four before going to bed. Studiously avoiding looking out of the landing window as I went.

Chapter Five

I AWOKE THE FOLLOWING MORNING with a remarkably clear head and resolve to finish Issue 172 and perhaps tackle the jungle in the back garden. After copious amounts of coffee and toast I settled in front of the computer. But not before I'd closed the curtains on the small window that looked out over the meadow. And the nonexistent vanishing oak tree. I didn't want to think about that. I pulled up the storyboard for The Falconer 172 stared at it for a moment before opening a browser window and logging onto Amazon in search of bird books. There were over 105,000. This might take a while. I'd got as far as page ten, Garden Birds of Europe, when I heard a knocking from downstairs. That must be Wayne finally coming to pick up his tools. I headed downstairs and unlocked the front door. As I pushed the door open one Anticat slipped through my feet to go out and another slipped in, closely followed by Possicat. Apart from the random collection of cats the doorstep was empty. I stepped outside and looked around, there was certainly nobody there and I went back in and closed the door. I was just beginning to feel the touches of prickly panic when I heard the knocking again, this time I realised it was coming from the patio doors in the lounge. I scolded myself for my paranoia and took two calming breaths before heading for the lounge.

I hesitated as I stepped into the lounge. There was indeed somebody standing outside of the patio doors. My relief at finding that I wasn't imagining things was confused by the fact that somebody should choose to fight their way through the undergrowth to knock at the patio doors rather than the normal, and more accessible front door. Furthermore the shape outside the door was that of a big man. I thought for a moment that it could be Wayne but his build was wrong. He looked vaguely familiar. The man tapped lightly on the door when he saw me approach and gave a little wave and a smile.

I'd always been taught not to open doors to strangers and this was about as strange as it got but still I found myself opening the double doors.

"Hello!" the man greeted. "Do you know who I am?"

That's generally not the first words you expect when somebody just turns up at your patio doors. 'Excuse me, I appear to be lost,' or perhaps, 'I've just moved next door and would like to borrow a cup of sugar.' But not 'Do you know who I am?'

"Erm, yes," I said, hesitating for a moment. This had to be a strange dream or a television hidden camera stunt. "You're..." I studied the face for a moment. It wasn't quite right. "You're..." Could I bring myself to say it? "You're Stephen Fry?"

"Excellent! Yes indeed," The man seemed quite excited that I'd recognised him and gave a little clap. Although there was something not quite right. The nose, that was it. He had a straight nose and Stephen Fry's was most certainly not straight.

"At least, you look like Stephen Fry," I continued. "Are you his brother?" I suddenly realised this was a quite insane conversation to be having at ten in the morning at my patio doors. And all before beer.

"Oh no! I am he. Most assuredly. Do you mind if I use your front door? I've never really been keen on patio doors."

I stepped back to let him in then waved him towards the front door. He bustled through the lounge door then paused by the front door.

"Through here?" he asked.

"Yes." I opened the door to let Stephen Fry through I briefly thought I should be calling the police or something but I was feeling slightly dazed.

"Thank you. Jolly good!" he said. "Very nice to meet you... er..."

"Ian Faulkener." Although I was seriously beginning to have my doubts about that.

"Ah, of course you are! Flora's nephew. You write The Falconer. Well, jolly nice to meet you." He gave another little wave as he headed off along the path and into the drive.

I closed the door very slowly and walked upstairs. I sank into the seat by my desk with a feeling of complete bewilderment. Either I was rapidly losing my grip on reality again or Stephen Fry had just casually strolled through my house. He even seemed to know who I was. I turned to the computer and googled my uninvited guest. No reports of him going missing or doing anything unusual. In fact he seemed to be appearing tonight in a one man show in Sheffield. Okay, so, I'd let a Stephen Fry look-alike wander through my house. In fact a look-alike who actually believes he's the real thing. I really needed to work on my paranoia. It's not actually very clever to get all worked up over an oak tree and then go and let a delusional six foot three lunatic wander around my house.

I put it down to village life being a bit odd in general and decided he was probably related to George or something. That must be it. They're probably all related to each other round here anyway, possibly more than once. I opened up the storyboard on the computer and was just about to start work on the final scenes of The Death of The Falconer when I heard a knocking downstairs. My hands gripped the edge of the desk so hard I felt my nails digging into the wood. Who is it now? Terry fucking Wogan? I marched downstairs and into the lounge, ready to do battle with whatever idiot thought it a good idea to annoy the hell out of me before my lunchtime drink. The patio doors stared vacantly back at me and the knock repeated itself from behind me. The front door. I marched briskly to the door and yanked it open. One black cat out, one white one in.

"What now?" I snapped before I noticed the uniform.

"Are you Mr Faulkener? Mr Ian Faulkener?" asked the policeman.

"Er... yes." I answered hesitantly, my mind quickly trying to recall if I'd jumped any speed cameras lately.

The policeman glanced at his notes. "Mr Ian Faulkener of Tink Cot?"

"Tink Cot? Oh, no... It's Tinker's Cottage. I got carried away with the chainsaw." I wasn't exactly sure that was the best thing to which to confess to an officer of the law.

"I see. My name is PCSO Proudfoot." He held a card for me to take. It did indeed say he was PCSO Proudfoot of Glastonbury police station, closed on Wednesdays.

"How can I help, officer?"

"We're trying to locate the whereabouts of one..." He consulted his notebook. "Mr Took."

"I'm sorry, I don't know of anybody by that name," I said.

"I believe you contracted him to carry out certain repairs to your property?"

"Oh, you mean Wayne?"

He checked his notebook again. "I understand he attended your premises on Wednesday twenty fifth of May at approximately nine hundred hours in the morning for the purposes of effecting repairs to said property."

"He came to fix my door, if that's what you mean?"

"And when did you last see Mr Took?" He licked the tip of his pencil.

I explained how he'd gone to his yard and returned to complete the job while I was out, leaving his tools and van behind.

"All a bit odd wouldn't you say, sir?"

"You can come in and see if you like." I stepped back to let him through. "Left his tools in the lounge here." I showed him through.

PCSO Proudfoot gave the door a cursory examination and satisfied himself the lock appeared to have been recently replaced. Possicat rubbed himself along the constable's leg, leaving a trail of white fur on the black uniform.

"I see you're a cat person, sir. Prefer dogs myself. Never know where you are with a cat."

I knew exactly where I was with these cats. I was the butler. "They sort of came with the house," I said. Anticat tried to sharpen her claws on the constables leg and I shooed her off.

“Don’t know how you tell them apart,” he said.

“Er... one’s black and the other’s white?”

“No,” he said, pointing towards the corner of the room. “I meant between those two.”

I followed his gaze and with a slight start saw what he meant. Two white cats were playing tag around the curtains.

“Ah,” I said. “That’s a new one,”

PCSO Proudfoot insisted on having a wander about the house, I supposed just checking to see if I’d got Wayne locked in a wardrobe or something. He seemed happy and made his way to the front door.

“Well, let me know if anything untoward occurs, sir,” he said.

I was tempted to ask what he meant by untoward. Did that include disappearing oak trees, Stephen Fry or multiplying cats? Instead I just said, “You’ll be the first to know, officer,” and closed the door behind him. I stared at the computer for a good ten minutes before shutting it down and heading into the village for some light refreshment.

Chapter Six

ARTHUR GREETED ME WITH A degree reticence. “Morning, Ian,” he said. “Still no sign of my boy I suppose?”

“Sorry, no. His van’s still there, as are some of his tools. Has he done this before?”

“Not since he was ten,” Arthur slid the pint towards me without me having to ask. “That time he turned up at his cousin’s. And he didn’t leave a van behind him then.”

“Could he be there now?” I asked and took a restrained sip of Old Grumbler.

“I shouldn’t think so. His cousin’s in Afghanistan at the moment. You eating today? We’ve got something very special on this lunchtime” Arthur slid a photocopied sheet towards me. Bold letters in over elaborate word art announced ‘Menu Du Jour - Filet de bœuf en croûte avec petit pois and pomme frites.’

“It’s in French,” he explained. “We’re having a continental day to celebrate the French farmer’s market in town tomorrow. Only I couldn’t find out what the word for ‘Menu’ is in French, so I left that bit in English.”

I ordered the special and took my pint to the window table and tried to ignore everybody. It didn’t work.

"See you've been at your hedge," George said loudly from behind me.

"Yes," I said without turning. "It was either that or buy a smaller car."

"I've got a chainsaw," George said, then added thoughtfully; "And a small car."

I had a thought. "You've lived here a while, George. Was there ever a big oak tree in the field behind my cottage?" I turned to face him.

George thought for a moment then, "Little buggers burned it down in sixty five. Or was it sixty four? No it was sixty five. Sixty four was when they burned down the Post Office."

That was reassuring then. I wasn't going mad and seeing things that didn't exist, I was just seeing things that haven't existed for fifty years.

My food arrived with disconcerting rapidity. I studied my steak, chips and peas, failing to see any connection to France, farmers or markets. I really was going to have to get the hang of that beast in the kitchen, I wasn't sure how long I'd be able to survive Arthur's gastronomic adventures. I cut into the steak, it was surprisingly tender and bled just the right amount. Okay, not quite haute cuisine but not bad.

Arthur reappeared by my side balancing something ominous on a spatula. "Forgot the croûte," he said and dropped a piece of fried bread on top of the steak.

* * * * *

Anticat was waiting on the doorstep when I arrived home. I opened the front door and the cat slipped between my legs and into the hall. As soon as I entered she slipped back out again. Or it might have been the other one as there was still one of them in the hall.

In the kitchen I put the kettle on as I tried to ignore the magpie who had now taken to sitting on the window ledge. I took my tea upstairs and sat at the desk. The oak tree stood tall and proud in the middle of the field. I stared at my computer for all of three minutes before deciding to attack the back garden with the chainsaw. I opened my newly accessible patio doors and trailed the extension through them into the garden.

The undergrowth quickly succumbed to the machine and within a couple of hours I'd cleared an area in the centre of the garden twice the size of my patio in Ealing. I stood back to admire my handiwork. I still hadn't cleared back to the rear fence and I had a mountain of debris to do something with but I felt a warm glow of accomplishment. I needed tea.

I sat at the kitchen table and stared out of the window. From where I was I couldn't see the bit of the garden I'd cleared, only the jungle yet to be challenged. I felt slightly overwhelmed but also somewhat exhilarated at how much one could accomplish in a relatively short time. I looked around the kitchen mentally thinking about improvements I could make. Taking on the challenge of Tinker's Cottage might be just the lift I needed. I'd have to do something about the cooker, either tame it or change it for a gas one. I understood gas cookers. And the gloom, the kitchen always felt gloomy with just the one small window. In fact the whole house appeared to suffer from a shortfall of windows. I'd read somewhere that some king or other in the past had brought in a window tax and people had bricked up their windows. So maybe that explained it. I'd have to find out when that happened. However it didn't explain doors. I was sure there'd never been a door tax. I stared again at the area of raised plaster where it appeared there had once been a door to the side of the kitchen. A back door would be handy. I went over to it and ran my hand across the area. It shouldn't be too hard to open that up again. I might give that a try when I've finished clearing the back garden. Or maybe I should get somebody in to have a look at it. I remembered Wayne, I wasn't having much luck with local tradesmen. No, I'd have a go myself. How hard can it be? There must be a machine or something for that.

I turned back towards the window and froze. From this angle I could see the area I'd just spent the best part of the afternoon clearing. Or I should be able to. But I couldn't. The garden was all jungle from here. I moved closer to the window from where I should be able to see most of the garden. There was still no sign of the cleared patch. Either this was the fastest growing undergrowth on the planet or somehow I was seeing a different part of the garden. But that didn't make any sense at all. I went round to the lounge and out through the patio doors. My chain saw still trailed its lead out into the garden. My cleared patch hadn't overgrown whilst I'd been enjoying my tea break. I stood in the centre of the newly reclaimed garden and looked around. The kitchen window was clearly visible from here so it stood to reason I should be able to see this spot from the kitchen. Back in the kitchen I pushed open the window and poked my head through. From here I could see pretty much all of the garden and there was certainly no cleared area. Just the same surplus of nature that had always been there. With Magpie sat on his empty bird table. He chattered at me. Anticat seized the opportunity of the open window and slid out past my face and headed in the direction of the bird table. She sat poised underneath it staring up at Magpie, who in turn just stared back at her. He was obviously unimpressed with her display of fierceness and eventually flew slowly off across the bushes.

I sat down at the table and in somewhat of a daze I poured myself another cup of tea. Aunt Flora had always been a great believer in the recuperative powers of tea. I added the last few drops of the liquid from the small brown bottle as I reasoned tea alone wasn't going to cut it at the moment. I placed the empty little bottle on the table and stared at it while I stirred my tea. The bottle was a safer thing at which to stare than the view outside the kitchen window. I wondered what was in the bottle; the label simply said 'Rescue Remedy'. Wasn't there a law or something where they had to say what was in medicines these days? And usually twelve pages of instructions as to what to do in the event of accidently ingesting too much of the stuff. What would happen, I mused. Could one be 'over rescued'? I sipped at my tea and steadfastly refused to look through the window. Madness lay outside the kitchen window. And quite possibly goblins. I finished the last of my tea and exhausted all there was to study on the bottle. Of course there couldn't be a different view from the kitchen to the lounge. That was insane. I must have cut into some hallucinogenic bush or something. Who knew what strange foliage lay out there? Probably the cure for swamp fever for all I knew so it certainly wasn't beyond the bounds of possibility that I'd accidently drugged myself on the sap from some exotic plant or other.

I peeped through the window and immediately wished I hadn't. The garden still overflowed with the joys of nature and no sign that I'd spent two hours out there with a Vorkskraft 2000 four speed monster of a chain saw. I rushed through to the lounge, perhaps half hoping I'd catch the garden by surprise in mid change. The garden was just as I'd left it, complete with chainsaw lying in the centre of the clear patch. I looked at the kitchen window again and noticed it was closed and yet I clearly remember it being open as Anticat had gone out through it. I peered in through the window and saw my kitchen almost as it should be. Almost because all the surfaces were empty of the bits and pieces I'd been scattering around for the last couple of days. There was no packet of tea on the side and no tea cup or empty small bottle on the kitchen table. No loaf of bread on the breadboard where I'd left it this morning. It was my kitchen but it wasn't my kitchen.

I tried to prise open the window but it was latched from inside and wouldn't budge. I sat down in the centre of the cleared patch pulling my knees up to my chin. If this was a hallucination or delusion of some kind then it was remarkably consistent. My memories of the last time I'd lost my way from reality were that nothing at all was consistent. In fact lack of consistency had featured fairly highly in the list of indicators that the psychiatrists had been so keen on. Along with touches of paranoia and a healthy quotient of sociopathic tendencies. So applying Sherlock Holmes's logic that when all sensible options are eliminated then the one that's left, no matter how crazy, must be the one left me with the inescapable conclusion that there were two different versions of the garden divided by the kitchen window. Of course if that were the case then it also meant I had a second garden to clear.

Feeling only slightly reassured I tidied up the chainsaw, closed the patio doors and headed back to the kitchen. I looked around wondering idly how I'd go about clearing the second garden. It would probably involve me and the Vorkskraft 2000 doing some acrobatics through the kitchen window. I looked again at the badly plastered door shape on the side wall. That must have been the door to the 'other' garden. I also noticed that to the right of the window, just below a wall cupboard, another area of poor plastering was evident. It looked like there had once been a second window that had been blocked in and the cupboard hung on top of it. Perhaps whoever had done this had been too disturbed by the second garden and wanted to shut off the view as much as possible. I suddenly realised how well I was taking all this. I should by now be climbing the walls or sitting in a quivering heap in the corner clutching a gin bottle. My eyes lighted on the little brown bottle. Maybe that was why I was coping remarkably well, given the circumstances. I also realised that the bottle was now empty and that if indeed that was the glue holding the bits of my sanity together I should probably get a refill. I glanced at the clock; it was just after four which meant I just had time to pop into Glastonbury to pick up another one.

* * * * *

The woman wore a faded red cheesecloth shirt and low slung jeans that just displayed a small tattoo disappearing into her waistband. I tried to work out what it was without appearing to stare. A wolf?

"Hello again," she greeted. "Nice work on the aura."

"What? Oh right. Yes, hello. What do you mean about the aura?" I babbled.

"It's looking a lot healthier. The Somerset air must be doing you some good."

"I suppose it is, or it could be... How did you know I'm new here?"

"Last time you bought a couple of books on the area, folklore and wildlife, usually only incomers do that. How did you get on with them?"

"Haven't had chance to read them yet. Having a bit of an issue with windows."

"Ah windows, of course. What can I do for you?" She leant forward on the counter and tipped her head to one side.

"That healing stuff, the one I couldn't buy, I need some more. I've run out. I'll make a donation... or something."

"How did you run out? There was enough there for three months!"

I picked up a book on fairies to hide my slight feeling of discomfort. "I've had a sort of challenging few days."

"With windows?" Hers eyes sparkled with mischief.

"Windows and doors. Oh, and an oak tree that isn't there, or maybe was. But mainly windows."

"You're that writer that's just moved in to Flora's old place aren't you? Ian Faulkener isn't it? You write The Falconer. Thought I recognised you the first time. I love your work."

"Thank you. Yes, but how..."

"Glastonbury's small and Flora was a well known character. Here," she placed a small bottle on the counter. "Just a couple of drops twice a day. That's all you need."

"Can I buy it?" I asked, remembering the previous transaction here.

"No." Again that smile which started with the eyes and finished somewhere in my soul. It made me feel at once uncomfortable but also somehow connected for the briefest moment.

"What if I bought something else?" I glanced around the shop. There was such an eclectic assortment of items here I was bound to find something I needed.

"Then I could give you the healing as a gift."

I picked up a couple of vials of incense and a burner then my eyes settled on the bookshelf. Fairy magic, stone circles, Arthurian legends, even a recipe book for woodland foragers. I had a thought. "Do you have any books on..." I hesitated. "Things that don't look the same if you..." This wasn't going well. "Windows. Windows which are different from the other side. Sort of thing." I added.

"Ah, your windows again." She came over to the bookshelf and stood close enough for me to smell a faint scent of roses in her hair. She leafed through the books. "You know that Flora's... sorry, your cottage is on the intersection of three ley lines, don't you?

"No, I wasn't aware of that." I had only a very vague idea what a ley line was. I seemed to remember it usually involved strange men in hats, wellington boots and carrying a bent coat hanger.

"Try that." She handed me a small book entitled, 'Ley Lines and Earth Forces'.

"Thank you."

"Have you ever read Schrodinger's Cat?" She pulled a slim volume from the shelf and gave it to me."

"No, only Simon's Cat." I smiled.

She gave me the look I seem to remember my primary

school teacher giving when I'd drawn a picture of a penis on the chalk board.

"Try it," she said. "You never know, it might help you with your windows."

I paid for the books and the incense and she popped the brown bottle into the bag. "Now remember, just one or two drops. It's not whisky!"

I stopped off at the DIY centre on the way back and bought a drill with special attachment that the salesman assured me would cut through a wall like butter. I also bought a pickaxe just in case the butter turned out to be particularly tough. I couldn't spend the rest of my life trailing through the lounge every time I wanted to take the rubbish out. And if I could also add a cat door into this project it would save me a lot of butlering.

I left the drill and pickaxe on the kitchen floor near the 'soon to be door' and settled down with a beer to watch the sunset through the kitchen window. I felt a momentary pang of panic when I remembered that the view I was seeing here was not the same as that from the lounge and sank the rest of the beer in one. That helped. I retrieved the books and started reading 'Ley Lines and Earth Forces', intrigued with the notion of how the lines were conceived by joining ancient landmarks together and how the intersections disturbed the foundations of reality. Tales and anecdotes about strange happenings at these sites were interspersed with a supposed scientific explanation about magnetic forces due to the earth's core.

The phone ringing startled me out of my concentration. It was Tania.

"Hi, Tania. Look I'm sorry, it's not ready yet. I got side tracked."

"We need this one out, Ian. The publisher is pushing."

"I know. I'll get right on it. Promise."

"Are you alright? You sound a bit odd." Tania's sixth sense was clearly working overtime.

"I'm fine. Just having a bit of trouble with..." She wouldn't understand windows that go different ways. "Spot of bother with the garden."

"What sort of bother, Ian?"

"Oh nothing really. I got a chainsaw and cleared half of it." I'd been idly leafing through the book as I spoke and a section about somewhere called The Fairy Toot caught my attention. "Chainsaw... garden grew back while I wasn't looking." Fairy Toot was on a nearby leyline and the home of goblins. "Goblins!" And with horror I realised that had come out loud.

"Ian? Are you alright?"

"I'm fine, it's the television. They're doing a thing on goblins."

"I'm coming down."

"No! You don't need to do that. I'm fine. Just a touch tired. I'm okay, honest."

"It's no bother. I was planning on going to Cornwall to see my sister Emma at the weekend anyway. First National do two coaches a day that go via Glastonbury so I can catch the early one, drop in to see you and then pick up the later one."

"Are you sure? I mean... that's a lot of trouble to go to." I panicked.

"I'll see you tomorrow. Can you pick me up from the coach stop?

"Huh? Oh, yes... but—"

“Then you can show me the manuscript for 172.” The phone went dead.

“Fuck it.” I realised my hand had managed to find another beer without me being aware. Sneaky. I took beer and books into the lounge and pulled the curtains without looking outside. I settled into the sofa and began reading Schrodinger’s Cat. It was heavy going and before long I felt I was losing the battle with my eyelids and headed for bed. I’d get up early and hammer out the bulk of the story so I at least had something to show Tania.

Chapter Seven

THE FOLLOWING MORNING I POURED myself a strong coffee and settled down at my office area. I pulled up the storyboard and started work. The Falconer had been lured into a cave by his arch nemesis Starfire. I laid out the rough drafts of the images then glanced out of the window. The oak tree stood proud and challenging in its field. The bit I'd read in Schrodinger's Cat talked about things that could be in two states at once. Alive and dead. Was it possible for an oak tree to be both there and not there? Perhaps I should report this to somebody? I imagined for a moment the potential conversation with PCSO Proudfoot. No, that wouldn't work. They'd have me back in the Ealing Special Unit before I'd got to the end of my explanation. Perhaps Stephen Hawking would be interested? How would one go about approaching him? Especially with something that wild. They must get people trying to get to him all day with way out ideas and probably many of them more sane than mine.

I realised the view from the window was going to make it impossible for me to concentrate and took the laptop down to the kitchen table. Another coffee and I settled down, purposefully sitting with my back to the window. The

Falconer was faced with the impossible choice of staying behind in the cave to hold off Starfire in order to give the villagers time to escape but that would mean the cliffs would crumble and he'd be trapped. I glanced up in mid thought. On turning my back to the window I had of course pointed myself directly towards the blanked off door. If somebody had simply bricked it up, it should be easy enough to open again. The lintel should still be there so there was little chance of me bringing the wall down. It should be fairly straightforward. I glanced at the drill and pickaxe that were on the floor where I had left them last night. A simple pilot hole through the centre of the blanked off door wouldn't be too difficult or risky.

It only took a few minutes to unpack the drill and work out how to fix the huge bit the salesman had told me I needed. A couple of attempts with different settings and the drill did indeed go through the wall in the manner advertised. However it was only one hole and I seemed to have deposited a fine layer of dust over everything in the vicinity, including my laptop. I blew at the keyboard to get rid of the worst of it then closed the lid. I set about drilling more holes in a circle about the size of a dinner plate. After about twenty minutes the wall looked like a piece of scenery in a Bruce Willis movie, sunlight streaming through an array of holes shafting through the dust cloud in the dimly lit kitchen. I stepped back to admire my handiwork for a moment then set to work with the pickaxe with the objective of joining all the little holes into one larger opening. The relatively fresh brickwork gave way easily and tumbled onto the kitchen floor. I now had a hole large enough to put a football through. Or my head.

I pulled away some of the looser brickwork and peered

through, squinting into the bright sunlight. Only it shouldn't really be bright sunlight from that side of the cottage as there was a fairly narrow passageway between the wall and the log shed with a high hedge behind. My eyes adjusted to the light. There was no log shed, only an unkempt lawn running to a low stone wall along the edge of the road. That didn't make sense. I pulled my head back from the hole and glanced towards the kitchen window. Thick bushes and tangles of prickly stuff filled the garden out there. I returned to the hole to check my understanding of the view that way. Still unmown lawn and stone wall.

I sat down on the chair for a moment to collect my thoughts. I'd almost grown used to the idea of a different view from the lounge patio doors and the kitchen window, now I was being confronted with a third one. I needed to remind myself what it was supposed to look like from that side of the house. I went out the front door and round to the side where the blanked off kitchen door should be. It was all there, high hedge, log shed, tool shed. Everything exactly as it should be. Except... except no hole in the wall. Two hours work from inside had made no impact on the wall here. I could see the blocked off door's outline here as a disturbance in the rendering. But no hole. I peeped around the back corner of the house half expecting to see an alien landscape from Mars or something. But no, the garden was overgrown and tangly, pretty much how it looked out of the kitchen window. Only... no, it was close enough and I wasn't going to scramble my head any more. It looked almost the same and that would do.

I returned through the front door and back to the kitchen. My eyes caught the area of raised plaster around the cupboard. That was on the back wall, the same wall as the other window. So the view out through that should be the same as the one I'd been seeing every day. Shouldn't it? I emptied the contents of the cupboard onto the floor and in the absence of appropriate tools I prised it off the wall with my pickaxe. It tumbled to the floor and dismantled itself into three sections. There was a definite area of new brickwork here. The area behind the cupboard hadn't even been plastered.

I balanced on a chair and took my drill to the brickwork. My sense of growing panic and disorientation resulted in an almost random series of holes as opposed to the orderly ones I'd created in the door area. It would do. I balanced on the chair again, this time with pickaxe in hand and swung it at the drilled patch. The chair wobbled just as I'd started my swing and the pickaxe embedded itself in a virgin area of wall some eighteen inches away from the bit at which I was aiming. It took a fair degree of pulling and twisting to dislodge it and when it came free it came with a large chunk of plaster. My next attempt fared better as I used two chairs and within ten minutes I had a sizable hole. I peered through and immediately wished I hadn't. Gone was the garden, neither overgrown nor cleared. In its place was a forest. At least that's how it looked through the small hole. Tall trees, some thick enough that I wouldn't be able to wrap my arms around them, had I been so inclined. Which I wasn't. I was actually more inclined towards running upstairs and hiding. Probably with a bottle of something very alcoholic. The trees had obviously been there for many years. Even with my limited knowledge of forestry, which had so far extended to a potted palm tree, I knew a mature wood when I saw one.

I stepped carefully off the chairs and used my foot to clear a piece of floor space in which to place one of the chairs back by the table. I sat down and stared up at the new hole. If up until now I'd had even the vaguest notion of dismissing the whole business as just imagination, this latest view destroyed that option. There was something very odd here. I glanced over to the clock. It was twelve fifteen. My internal timer had failed me, obviously my sense of disorientation had disrupted my routine. I went to the fridge and removed a can of Budweiser. The new window hole was disturbing. I think I could possibly grow used to the other views, given time. One could almost believe they were just essentially all the same. But a forest where a garden should be was just too far away for even my skills in self delusion. I needed something to cover it.

As I still had a lot of my possessions in boxes finding something suitable to hang there proved problematic. Eventually I found a framed Luis Royo that showed a naked girl and an alien monster. It was one of my favourites but usually more suitable for an office wall rather than kitchen. But as it was the only one I could find easily it would have to do for the moment. Another bit of drilling for a hook, which I found surprisingly difficult to do whilst avoiding looking at the hole and resulted in another snowfall of plaster. I hung the picture and picked up my beer. The can was empty. How had that happened? I dumped the can on the table next to half a brick and pulled another from the fridge.

A knocking on the front door followed by a call of "Cooee!" startled me. I froze.

The "Cooee" repeated, followed by a "Ian? Are you there?"

Oh hell! Tania! I'd completely forgotten. I put my Budweiser on the table and brushed some of the dust off my shirt as I headed for the door.

"Look, Tania... I'm sorry. I completely forgot."

"Don't worry about it, Ian. I guessed you might so I got a taxi from the coach stop."

We performed the obligatory chaste hug and peck on the cheek then as she stepped back she realised I'd just covered her in brick dust.

"Lovely," she said as she brushed at her suede jacket with the back of her hand. "I take it this er... stuff..." she looked again at the dust."This is in some way related to The Falconer issue 172?"

"Not entirely. I sort of got distracted."

"I can see." She paused and stared at me for a moment and then, "Well? Aren't you going to invite me in?"

I recalled the chaos in the kitchen. "I thought it was just a flying visit. As you said, drop by on your way through."

"Don't be ridiculous, Ian." She pushed past me and headed for the kitchen. I followed quickly, half hoping to head her off into the lounge.

She stepped into the kitchen and stalled. I manoeuvred around her and brushed off one of the chairs for her. "Have a seat," I said lamely.

"Thank you." She sat in a sort of disbelieving daze.

"Can I get you a cup of tea, or something?" Act naturally and it won't arouse suspicion.

"Tea? Oh, yes, tea would be nice." Her eyes wandered around the chaos. "I have to say I love what you've done with the place."

"Yes. It's sort of in the... er... preliminary stages. Not

much more than, erm, constructive planning." I filled the kettle and flicked it on. "Exploratory feasibility studies."

"I see." Anticat slipped in through the new hole, padded around in the dust then jumped on her lap. She tried to push her off but Anticat just saw that as affection then purred loudly. "Never had you down as a cat person?"

"They sort of came with the house. I adopted them. Or they adopted me, not sure really."

Anticat spied Anticat number two, wriggled her bum slightly then pounced from Tania's lap, causing Tania to wince as the claws dug in for purchase. She tried to brush the dusty footprints from the suede skirt.

"Never been keen on them myself. I don't trust them." Her eyes settled on the closed, and by now dust covered laptop. "And how goes the writing?"

"Oh, yes. Good. Just taking a bit of a break, you know."

She drew a finger across the top of the laptop, leaving a line in the dust. "Yes, you need a break every so often."

I tried to ignore the edge in her voice. "I'm at a tricky bit in the story. Just needed to get away for five minutes." I poured boiling water on a tea bag.

"I can see." Again her eyes ran round the room. "Are you feeling alright, Ian?"

"Yes, I'm fine. Never better. Why?"

"Only, this is not the first kitchen you've done this to, if I remember rightly."

"Ah, yes. Sorry." I put the tea in front of her. "I was in a difficult place then."

"I see you've brought professional tools for this one though." She poked at the pickaxe with her foot.

"It's not the same. There used to be a door and window

here before." I wanted to tell her. I wanted to show her the different views. That would prove I wasn't going mad, if she could see it too. But what if I told her and then she couldn't see it? Could I risk that? That would prove I was heading for another breakdown. What did Schrodinger say? The state of the cat is not determined until it is observed.

"Do you think you ought to come back to London for a while?"

"No, really. I'm okay. Just settling in. Would you like something to eat?" I glanced around the kitchen. "I've got... pizza." I remembered my last attempt at pizza. "Only I'm not sure how to work that thing." I nodded towards the oven.

"Tell you what," she said as her eyes swept the chaos in the kitchen."Let's say we eat out. My treat. There must be a nice pub around here."

* * * * *

The Camelot was offering a lunchtime special of 'Pie and a Pint' for £5.99.

"This your lady?" Arthur asked as he took our orders.

"No," I said. "That is... A long time ago... Before..."

"We used to be lovers and now we're not," Tania helpfully clarified.

We took our drinks to a table near the fireplace.

"It's a bit basic," I apologised. "But they're friendly here."

"You going to clear up that pile of hedge cuttings?" George said from a nearby table. "It's started to spread onto the lane."

"It's on the list," I said to George, then I turned to Tania. "That's George, been here all his life. He likes to josh me."

Tania took a sip of her tea. "Are you ever going to finish that story, Ian?"

"Nearly done. Just filling in the fine details."

"You've been telling me that for three weeks. You can't expect them to wait forever you know. They'll pull your contract."

Might not be a bad thing, I thought. Take the decision out of my hands. "Tania, I've been meaning to tell you something about this latest issue."

Arthur placed two casserole dishes on the table. Steam escaped from under the pie crust sat on top of each one. "There you go. One steak feast special and one vegetarian moussaka pie."

"Which is which?" Tania looked up at him.

Arthur pointed to the one nearest him. "That's the steak one... or the vegetarian. One or the other. I've forgotten now."

I poked my fork into the pie in front of me. More steam escaped along with some brown liquid. "Looks like gravy so I suspect this will be the Steak Feast."

Tania repeated my experiment with her pie. Similar steam but this time with an off white sauce. "You were saying?"

"What? Oh, nothing. Just that I think this will be the best issue for a while. Got a few surprises."

"Well don't make them too severe. You know how fans dislike major changes."

We made idle small talk as we finished our meal. I came to realise that we had nothing in common any more. Maybe we never did. Just good sex, perhaps that's the best for which one can hope.

When we returned to the cottage she insisted on 'The

Tour'. I showed her around studiously avoiding pointing out any discrepancies through various windows.

"I suppose it will be nice when you finally get it the way you want," she said as we stood in the lounge. "I love the fireplace, is there a Priest Hole up there do you think?"

I'd never really given it any thought. The cottage was old enough and the fireplace certainly big enough. "I've never looked," I said. I also wasn't inclined to explore, the cottage was doing my head in as it was, I certainly didn't need any further quirks to deal with.

"I see you've started work on the garden." She nodded towards the patio doors. "Can I see? I miss having a garden in London, it's the one downside to living there."

That and the crime and the dirt and the constant noise and the masses of people pressing in on you all the time, I thought. But what I said was, "You could always get some plants for your courtyard, same as I did."

"I don't think one solitary Torbay Palm constitutes a garden." She smiled at me and opened the doors to step into the garden. I followed her. "It's really quite big out here," she said.

"Yes, apparently it's more than an acre."

"Really?" She ventured out of the cleared patch and started to head past the kitchen window, picking at the odd flower as she went. "You've got some unusual plants here."

I followed her and couldn't help staring at the patch of wall that ought to have a hole in it to match the one on the inside. After my experience with the kitchen doorway I'd been expecting this but it was still a bit of a shock. There was a definite raised area to the rendering but that was all.

"Yes," I said. "I need to get a book on plants. And birds, I get a lot of birds."

She went round the corner of the cottage to the path between the wall and the log shed. As we went past where the doorway ought to be I wondered if she'd notice but she didn't seem to. Did that mean it wasn't there and I'd imagined it? Or did it mean it was there but she hadn't noticed? Which would be better for my sanity. I ran my hand over the wall.

"Ian?"

I suddenly realised she'd been talking at me. "Huh?" I managed.

"I'm going to have to go, I've a coach to catch. Are you sure you're alright?"

"Yes. Fine." I risked another glance at the wall. "Right as rain."

"Okay, if you say so. Now are you going to give me a lift to the coach stop or do I get another taxi?"

"Oh, of course. No problem. I'll just get my keys." I hurried back through the patio doors, picked up my car keys and locked the doors behind me. By the time I'd found Tania, she was already round the front.

"Where's your car gone, Ian?"

I stared at the drive in front of the cottage where I had left my car. Nothing. Yet it had been there when we'd returned from the pub not twenty minutes ago.

"I don't believe it," I said. "The nerve and in broad daylight too!"

"Oh dear. But you are insured, right?" Pragmatic and practical Tania as always. Never one to let a disaster disturb her equilibrium.

"That's not the point. Some thieving git has been here and had my car away whilst we were just there." I pointed at the cottage. "It can only have taken them a couple of minutes."

"You'd better call the police," she said. "And I'd better ring a taxi or I'm going to miss by coach."

"Oh hell!" I realised. "I'm sorry."

"It's not your fault, Ian." She pulled her phone out of her handbag and scrolled through the numbers. "As the Dalai Lama once said, 'Shit happens'." She pecked me on the cheek and headed off down the drive stabbing buttons on the phone as she went. "You take care now," she called back as she disappeared from view.

I pushed at the front door. It was locked. Of course, I'd come out the back doors. I headed back round the side of the cottage, getting momentarily distracted by the wall where the hole in the kitchen wall should be. I ran my hands over it. Would I have to do everything in the place twice? Two doors to create, two gardens to clear? I went back through the patio doors and locked them behind me. Time for a coffee.

I picked my way through the chaos in the kitchen and had a quick peep through the hole in the wall. Still a lawn in need of mowing and a stone wall.

It took me half an hour to finally get hold of a human being in a police emergency call centre in Mumbai. I tried to explain about my car and how important it was too me. I described it in detail including the scratch marks on the side from when I managed to get it stuck in my drive. I even gave a description of the contents of the glove box if that would help recognition later. They in turn gave me a crime number.

By the time I'd finished on the phone my adrenaline levels increased to such a point where 'going postal' seemed like a perfectly rational course of action.

Instead, I hefted the pickaxe and set about enlarging the hole until it resembled the shape of a door. When I'd finished

I stepped back panting to admire my handiwork. Not bad. Of course the shape had been there all along, all I'd had to do was knock out the bricks. I ventured to look through it. I had a clearer view of this new world. Without the high hedge and the sheds of my own cottage, this garden appeared much larger. A van drove up the lane and I slid my head back in. I wasn't brave enough to go any further through the hole. It only then dawned on me that perhaps I hadn't completely thought this through. I had a door sized hole in my wall but no door with which to fill it. I searched through the piles of packing materials I'd left in the spare bedroom and found a large plastic sheet. I found some tacks and nailed it across the opening. The semi opaque nature of the sheet diffused the view enough to allow me to kid myself there was nothing untoward on the other side. I rolled the small blue crystal in my hand.

I took a fresh coffee into the lounge and switched on the television. An Australian soap, Noel Edmonds and his sodding boxes, and a clutch of inane quiz shows. How I missed Virgin Cable. I'd have to arrange satellite. I glanced towards the patio doors. The late afternoon was beginning to smear the sky a deep red. It would be dark soon, I locked the patio doors and pulled the curtain. Giving a last glance in the direction of the doors I settled down to read some more of Schrodinger's Cat. I was asleep before I'd finished a page.

Chapter Eight

BREAKFAST THE FOLLOWING MORNING REPRESENTED a slight challenge. The task of preparing toast and coffee whilst picking my way through a building site and simultaneously avoiding looking at doors, windows or gaping holes proved problematic. I ended up with a slight dusty film on my coffee and crunchy bits in my butter.

I heard a knock on the front door and wondering what sort of nutcase I would encounter this time I opened it with a sense of caution.

PCSO Proudfoot stood just outside, his bulk blocking the sunlight. "Mr Faulkener?" he asked

"Yes," I replied. "You're Police Community Support Officer Proudfoot if I remember?"

He seemed slightly phased. "Ah yes," and handed me a card.

"I already have one," I said. "What can I do for you?"

"You reported a stolen car? A blue Ford Escort estate?"

"Oh, yes. I didn't really expect..."

"And where was it when you last saw it, sir?"

I squeezed past him to step outside. "Just there," I said, pointing at my car.

"So would I be right in saying that the motor vehicle you reported as being stolen would look something like this one?" he asked, following the line of my finger.

"Erm... I don't understand. It wasn't there yesterday? You can ask my agent, Tania Evans. She'll be in Cornwall with her sister. I can —"

"That won't be necessary, sir. You do know that insurance fraud is a very serious crime, don't you?"

"Insurance fraud? No, look, it had gone. Really."

"Well, I'll report it as a case of forgetfulness. Sometimes that happens. You know, a hard day and you can forget where you leave things."

I walked over to my car and patted the roof just to make sure it was actually there. "How could I forget where I'd left it? I mean my drive is hardly Gatwick Airport car park is it? Somebody stole it."

"And it looks they brought it back. I think we'd best leave it there, sir or I might have to charge you with wasting police time." He closed his notebook with an air of finality.

I was tempted to suggest his very existence was a waste of police time but resisted and just said, "Thank you, officer," then watched him amble out of my drive in that sauntering way that only beat officers seem to have.

After I'd double checked the car was still there I returned to the chaos in the kitchen. I needed to do something about this. I searched for a piece of paper on which to write a list. The only paper I could find was a letter from British Telecom mourning my absence and begging me to return. That would do, ignoring their pleas I turned it over and wrote; *Door and frame, Polyfilla, Thing to spread Polyfilla on with, Nails, screws...* I glanced around me, *Hoover, shovel and bin bags.*

The sound of flapping polythene caught my attention. I looked up just in time to see a shadowy figure through the sheet which covered the door space. I started back in my chair. A head poked round the sheet.

"Hello!" said the head. "Anybody in?"

My hand fumbled across the table feeling for something with which to protect myself. It settled on a tin of baked beans I'd left there after clearing out the cupboard. Great, so as long as I wasn't about to be attacked by anything more deadly than a packet of biscuits I should be okay.

The face and body pushed through the polythene. I relaxed slightly when I saw that it was a tall woman wearing a tweed jacket and skirt with matching hat. She wasn't carrying any biscuits. She jumped slightly when she saw me. "Oh, sorry. Didn't realise anybody was here."

"And you are?" I asked as I stood up, ensuring I kept the chair between us.

"Mrs Stainswick. You know, from the bakery. Or perhaps you don't. Nice to see the door open again." She ran her hand around the freshly exposed brickwork. "You're new here?"

"Yes," I said. "Couple of weeks. Excuse me, who...? What bakery?"

"Sorry, have to dash. Can I use the lounge door?" She headed towards the lounge without waiting for an answer.

"Hang on," I said as I followed her through from the kitchen. "Why do you have to go through here?"

She stopped briefly with her hand on the patio door handle. "Why, that's where it leads!" She gave a disarming smile, slipped through the doors and disappeared out of sight around the corner. I went back to the kitchen and peered through the open gap in the wall. It was the sheer normality of the view which I found most disturbing. I pulled the plastic closed again.

I cleared some of the mess in the kitchen and pushed a pile of rubble through the new door. That would keep for now. I made myself another coffee and sat down to finish my list for the DIY centre. When I was happy I'd thought of everything I picked up my keys and headed for the front door. Just as I was about to open it I heard a noise from the kitchen. I quietly retraced my steps and peered round the corner of the dining room from where I could see through to the kitchen. I came face to face with a small balding man in his sixties.

He froze. "Ah!" he said. "Whoops." He turned and scuttled back through the polythene sheet leaving me stalled in the dining room.

"I really am going to have to close that door," I said to myself, eventually breaking my catatonic moment.

I locked the front door behind me although I wasn't quite sure why as there was a gaping hole in the kitchen. Or was there? Not from this side anyway, so locking the door made some sort of sense I supposed. Disappearing doors, Ley lines, multiplying cats. Either I was on a fast track back to The Ealing Special Unit or there was something very odd here. Cat in the box stuff, best not to look too closely. My hand reached into my pocket and settled around the crystal. I felt slightly calmer immediately.

B&Q had most of the things on my list with the exception of the bin bags so I headed off into the centre of Glastonbury to find a bin bag shop. I parked in The Abbey car park and set off up the hill. I found the bin bags in a small convenience store, along with a packet of chocolate biscuits, a bag of onion rings and a strange pie called a Higgidy. Never wise to go into a food shop when hungry.

My twelve o'clock trigger drew me into a nearby cafe that offered a selection of local vegetarian food and more importantly, ale brewed from the water of the Chalice Well here in Glastonbury. As a confirmed carnivore I found the menu slightly intimidating. Avoiding the obvious charms of lentil fritters in tomato and garlic or the homely quirkiness of roasted tofu in peanut sauce, I settled for a schnitzel burger and hand cut chips. And a large glass of Glastonbury beer. Too many meals in the Camelot had hardened my pallet, and probably large sections of my liver as well, so I was taken by surprise at how delicious the burger tasted, and the chips really were hand cut with just the right level of crispiness. The Chalice Well Ale went down way too easily and a replacement appeared on my table that I didn't remember ordering. I looked up as it arrived and straight into the eyes of the woman from New Dawn. She smiled at me and the fine lines around her eyes each laid a path to the sparkle that glinted from the striking blue of her irises.

"I noticed you were empty." She nodded towards the glass and sat down opposite me, placing her own beer glass on the table.

"Thank you," I said.

"The Chalice Well is a particularly nice beer but be careful, it's got a bit of a kick."

A waitress placed a bowl of soup in front of her, it looked like tomato.

"I could probably do with a kick," I said.

"Still having trouble with your windows?" She broke pieces of bread roll into her soup.

"Yes, windows. And doors. It seems to be the doors which are causing me most trouble at the moment." I finished my lunch and pushed the plate to one side. That had to be the tastiest meal I'd eaten in months. "I'm sorry, I never did catch your name, I'm Ian, but you knew that already."

She held out her hand for me, "Serafina, but my friends call me Saphie."

I held her hand briefly, "Pleased to make your acquaintance, Saphie," I said and kissed the back of her hand in mock humility.

She smiled and returned her hand to the job of soup eating. "How's your schnitzel burger? They're famous for that."

"Wonderful, I can see why," I said. "Is this your lunch break? Only I was going to pop in after eating here, do you have any books on hidden doors?"

"Not that I can remember." She pushed her empty bowl to one side and supped deep on her beer. "What is it you need to know?"

"I found this door. It sort of... That is, from the other side it's not..." I lifted my beer and supped at it slowly to hide my confusion. "It had been blocked off and I opened it but then..." I caught her staring at me. "I'm not crazy," I continued. "I've got a certificate that says so. Would you like to see it?"

"The certificate or the door?" That smile again. Why did she make me feel so flustered all the time? After all she sells crystals and magic potions and I see disappearing trees. Our respective levels of craziness should be roughly equal. Not including the cats of course.

"Well, I haven't actually got either with me at the moment," I said. "Although I do have a door in the back of the car you're welcome to look at if you like. But it's not the door that goes to other places. That one's still in the cottage."

"I see," she said. I was sure she didn't.

"You probably get all sorts of people in your shop with lots of strange ideas."

"What? In Glastonbury? Never!" She finished her beer. "I've got to get back. If you want to come up I'll see if I've got anything that might help. That is, if you can perhaps open up a bit more about exactly what it is you are looking for." She stood and picked up her multi coloured handbag. "I don't bite. Unless invited." She turned and left, that faint scent of rose hung briefly in the air again.

After a short period of procrastination and a little bit of time wasting I plucked up the courage to follow her into her shop. She was serving an American woman who wanted a guidebook to the secret labyrinths of Stonehenge. Despite Saphie's protestations that no such thing existed the American persisted. She explained loudly how she had attended this seminar in California by a woman who had been held in the labyrinths by aliens whilst undergoing what appeared to be a rather thorough gynaecological examination. I had to admire Saphie's control as she guided the woman gently out of the door and pointed her in the direction of the Avalon Information Centre.

"This place can be a bit of a nutter magnet," she said. "I had the reincarnation of Tutankhamen in here the other day wanting to buy a sword with which to sacrifice a virgin."

"Did you sell her one?"

"No, I don't do weapons. But there are dozens of shops that do in Glastonbury. Although I expect it won't be as easy trying to find a virgin."

I picked up a wooden staff that had a crystal set in the head. "You said you might be able to help. A book or something, you know about doors?"

"Yes, but you also said you were going to give me more of a clue as to your problem?"

"You'll think it's weird." I glanced around the shop taking in the array of weirdness piled high on each shelf. "Or maybe not."

"Doors," she said. "You were going to tell me about your doors."

I put the staff down bumping a china fairy off the shelf. I caught it midair as it tumbled towards the floor. I placed it carefully back on the shelf. "I used to be a ninja," I muttered.

"Your doors?"

"Hmm, yes, okay. You see, I have a door that only goes one way. From inside it goes out but from outside... it's not there. And then the oak tree is there if I look out of the window but not there when I go to find it. That's not to mention the magpie. And the cats, did I tell you about the cats? I've lost count of the cats." I stopped talking and waited for her to call the police.

"I knew there was something odd about Flora's cottage from the occasional comments she'd make. Nothing obvious but I remember she once let slip something about a person being from 'The Other Place'.

"You don't think I'm mad then?" The sense of relief rushed through my body like an especially good single malt.

"Not at all. Mind you, this is Glastonbury so everything's relative I suppose. Look, it's Sunday tomorrow and I'm not open, why don't I come over and have a look at your doors?" She repositioned the china fairy an inch to the left on the shelf. "I might even help you count your cats."

I gave her directions to Tinker's Cottage and headed home, wondering which of us was the crazier.

* * * * *

As I walked up the path I immediately noticed the front door was ajar. I was sure I remembered locking it. Thoughts of goblins were quickly replaced by mad Spanish woman paranoia and then the more rational perhaps it's Wayne resurfaced. Either way, just to be safe, I picked up an ornamental gnome and hefted it in my hand. It felt reassuringly heavy albeit somewhat ridiculous. 'Stand still or I'll let the gnome loose!' didn't really have the sort of threat value I was hoping for but it in the absence of a shotgun it would have to do.

I pushed open the front door with my foot and raised the gnome above my head. I'd seen them do this on Ultimate Force, although not with a gnome. "Anybody there?" I called. Silence. I crept in with my best ninja creeping and went from room to room. No Wayne, mad Spanish women or thankfully goblins. Maybe I had forgotten to lock it. I didn't really believe that, but I was prepared to put my head in the sands of self delusion for the time being.

I returned the gnome to his position by the fishpond and unloaded the car. Fixing a door frame is perhaps not quite as easy as the label 'Easy Fix Door Kit' would have one believe. For a start, the assumption of the Easy Fix people is that your hole is straight, which mine wasn't. And then there's this whole business of trying not to look out through the doorway as one is fixing it into place. In the end, with the help of a dust sheet nailed to the outside and copious amounts of Pollyfilla, I had a passable resemblance to a functioning door. I opened and closed it a few times and felt quite pleased with the result. I'd left the dustsheet nailed to the outside so as to obscure the slightly disturbing view each time I opened it. Anticat seemed pleased with my new door and demanded to be let in and out several times so as to test its agreeability to cats. I needed to fix a cat door in it or I could be doing this for the rest of my life. At one point I was sure she came in twice to only to go out once.

I swept up the debris and dumped it in a sack outside the door. It felt good to have a back door even though I had no idea where it went. As I sat at the table with a coffee I glanced at the Luis Royo picture that hung over the window hole. Was I brave enough to risk another look through there? I decided not. A tapping on my new door startled me. I froze and stared at the door until the tapping repeated. I stood and pressed my ear to the door. "Who's there?" I called. This could be the start of a bad knock knock joke.

"George. George Bergoglio." The voice sounded slightly frail and croaky as though it belonged to somebody elderly who'd spent a lifetime on forty a day. There was a strong London accent with a slight overlay of something else.

I opened the door a fraction and peered out. All I could see of course was the dust sheet. "I don't know any Georges," I said as I risked pulling the dust sheet to one side. Despite his age, I put him about seventy, he stood tall and straight just a few inches shorter than me, I guessed about five seven. A thick shock of white hair protruded from under a blue baseball cap. He wore a red check shirt over which a pair of braces held his jeans in place.

He held his hand out. "George," he said. "Although everyone calls me Boggy."

I took his hand without thinking. "Erm, pleased to meet you, George... Boggy."

"Glad to see the door's back. We missed it. Where's Flora?" He walked into the kitchen as he spoke. His gait was slow and deliberate, probably the result of arthritis.

"She died," I said. "Or rather presumed so. Went missing ten years ago."

"Oh, I am sorry," he said, sounding like he meant it. "You in charge now then?"

"Well, I live here now. I've just—"

"Got to dash," he interrupted. "Can I go through the lounge door?" He didn't wait for an answer and headed off through the dining room and to the lounge. I followed him wondering if I should stop him but couldn't really think of a valid reason why I should. I let him out, closed the patio doors behind him and went back to the kitchen.

I zapped my Higgidy pie in the microwave, opened a beer and settled down in the lounge in front of an old Carry On movie. The pie was remarkably tasty although I still had absolutely no idea what went into a Higgidy. The beer did its job and within half an hour I was losing the battle of the eyelids.

Something jerked me awake. A noise? I pushed the tendrils of sleep to one side and did my best attempt at alert. A knocking noise came from the kitchen. I waited for a while and it repeated, slightly more insistently. I stumbled to my feet and glanced at the clock on my way to the kitchen. Nine thirty, somebody was going to regret this. The knocking came again just as I entered the kitchen. I picked up the shovel and weighed it in my hand. It certainly felt more effective than a garden gnome.

I turned the key and yanked open the door. "What is it now?" I shouted as I poked the shovel at the dust sheet, flicking it to one side. A small boy smiled at me. He looked to be about ten, his toothy grin confused by a brace that looked slightly too large for him. He wore jeans and a white shirt with a red tie.

"Hello," he said. "Please may I come through, mister?"

Nine thirty seemed a bit late for a child this age to be out and about, although never having had children I didn't really know what the norm was. As I stood back to let him in and immediately another figure came into view through the dustsheet. Then two more. The mother, a large woman in a floral dress said, "Say thank you to the nice man, Tommy"

"Thank you," Tommy obliged.

"We didn't believe it when they said the door was back," the father said. He was shorter and significantly smaller than his wife. He held the hand of his daughter, a pretty girl in a denim dress. "Are we there yet?" the girl asked, looking up at her father.

"No, darling. Bit of a way yet." The man turned to me, "The garden?"

"Garden?" I repeated.

"Yes, we need to go through the garden."

"But you've just come..." I tailed off, pointing through the door. "Didn't you see the garden out there?"

"Not that garden." He sounded offended. "The back garden of course. We've just come from there." He nodded towards the door.

"The garden? You mean the back garden? It's through there." I pointed towards the lounge.

"Thank you," the mother said. "Say thank you to the nice man." She poked each child in turn.

"Thank you, mister." The children said in perfect unison.

"Come along now." The father picked up a large blue suitcase I'd somehow completely failed to notice and ushered his family through to the lounge. I followed and in a sort of daze, unlocked the patio doors and let them through.

"Say goodbye to the nice man," said the mother as she stopped in the doorway.

"Goodbye, mister," the children said and then they were gone, heading off into the dark.

I closed and locked the door behind them, pulled the curtains and collapsed in a confused pile onto the sofa. Somehow, in the moment between closing the door and sitting down, another beer had found its way into my hand. I drank gratefully then still in a state of bewilderment I made for bed.

Chapter Nine

I GAVE THE KITCHEN A quick tidy in preparation for Saphie's visit, for some reason I felt slightly elated by the thought. Probably I was just grateful that somebody seemed to believe me, especially as I wasn't sure I believed myself most of the time. My breakfast of cornflakes and coffee was interrupted twice by visitors at the kitchen door. Once by an elderly lady with a wheelie shopping basket and then again by a business type in a suit and carrying a small suitcase. They were both very polite and requested exit by the front door. I was beginning to formulate theory about this door business but it all seemed little more crazy each time I thought about it, so I persisted with my plan of not thinking about it and just answering the door.

Saphie arrived just after ten. She wore low cut jeans that tucked into a pair of calf high brown leather boots. A tight white T shirt accented her lightly tanned skin and stopped three inches short of her waistband. This was the first time I'd seen her with her hair loose, in the shop it was always tied up. It fell across her shoulders in a light brown tumble threaded with sun streaks. She handed me a brown paper bag as I let her in.

"Housewarming present," she said.

"Oh, thank you." I peeped into the bag as I led the way into the kitchen. It looked like a pile of dried herbs. "Is this... only I don't—"

"Well, you'll be the only one within thirty miles that doesn't," she said. "Anyway don't panic, I'm not trying to corrupt you, it's only sage."

"Sage. What an unusual gift." I picked up the kettle. "Tea?" I asked.

"Just burn a bit of it in each room. Sends the nasties away. And yes to the tea, thank you."

I filled the kettle and gathered a pair of mugs. "Would you rather have Witchblade or Souvenir from Rome?"

"Oh, let's go with Witchblade. I always had a thing for her."

I tried to see if I could read what she meant by that. But her smile gave nothing away. "What do you mean by 'Nasties'?" I asked.

"Just things that shouldn't be here, misplaced souls."

"Oh great. Something else to worry about." I finished making the tea and put the mugs on the table. "There's sugar in the Dalek."

"No thanks. It's a nice place," she said, casting her eyes around the kitchen. "I see you've got a Rayburn. They're great, I always wanted one of those."

"I shouldn't bother. They don't cook pizza, or bacon."

"So, what seems to be the trouble with your doors?"

I felt slightly reluctant to confront the issue of the doors again. I'd been enjoying her company and I was going to look like a fool now when she saw that there was nothing untoward with my doors and I'd imagined it all. As it happened the situation unravelled without my help. A knocking on the kitchen door caught us both by surprise. Saphie gave a little start.

"That'll be the door," I said.

I opened it slowly, and pulled the dustsheet to one side. Saphie stood and moved slightly back from the door as if expecting the hounds of hell to burst through. Of course she might have been right for all I knew. But fortunately, this time no hounds only a small woman who looked to be in her seventies. She clutched a blue handbag. There was something strangely familiar about her.

"Would you mind awfully if I just popped through?" she asked.

"The front door or the patio?" I held the door open for her to come in.

"Oh, the front door I think, Dearie."

Two versions of Possicat took the opportunity of the open door and slipped in, threading themselves through the woman's feet. I showed her through and opened the front door to let her out. Saphie followed but stayed just a little back. "There you go," I said.

"You're very kind." She gave a little wave and shuffled off down the path.

I closed the door and turned to Saphie. "More tea?"

She sank into the kitchen chair and pointed towards the kitchen door. "Was that...?"

"It certainly looked like her," I said, as I refilled the kettle. "But I doubt it was. Somebody would have missed her by now."

"This is the door you're having problems with I assume?"

"And the patio ones in the lounge but mostly this one."

"Why? I mean where did she come from?" Saphie stood and pressed her hand against my new door as if feeling for a heartbeat.

"I haven't the faintest idea."

She pressed the handle down and I felt a spike of panic when I heard the click of the latch.

"And why did she want to walk through the house?" Saphie opened the door a few inches and peered through.

I froze, steaming kettle poised above the Witchblade mug. What she saw now would determine what was in the box. Had the world really become disjointed or had I lost the plot completely this time? Either way was disturbing. She pulled the dustsheet to one side and I stopped breathing.

"It doesn't make sense," she said.

I couldn't speak. Why hadn't she been shocked at what she saw. Did that mean it was me? Then I realised she hadn't been round the outside of the cottage so she wouldn't know if something was wrong anyway.

She pulled the dustsheet further away and stepped through. "Nice garden."

The kettle slipped from my grip and I jumped back just in time to avoid most of the boiling water as it cascaded out of the fallen kettle and ran over the edge of the worktop. "Damn!" I yelled as I jerked out of my catatonia.

Saphie scurried over to me. "Are you alright, Ian?" She grabbed a tea towel and mopped at the water.

"You saw it?" I said. "The garden, you saw it?"

"Of course I did. What did you expect me to see? The hanging gardens of Babylon?" she teased.

"No, but maybe my log shed. Have a look at this." I beckoned her to follow me as I headed for the front door.

I led her round to the side of the cottage. We stopped by the missing door. "There," I said, pointing to the area of wall that should contain a nice new Easy Fit door.

"What? I don't understand. What am I supposed to be looking at?"

I pointed at the log sheds. "You were just looking at this from the other side. Only the sheds weren't here then. Just the garden. But the door was there." I pointed at the wall. "But only on the other side. You see?"

She looked from me to the wall then back at the log sheds. At first her expression told of sympathy for the lunatic that stood in front of her. Then she gazed around again and a new expression slid into view. Confusion, disbelief.

"The door? Where the hell's the door? It should be here."

We returned to the kitchen and Saphie opened and closed the door repeatedly.

"I'm not mad am I," I said. "You saw it. You saw the garden?"

"Garden, yes. There's a garden. Where did it go?"

"I don't know. I was hoping you could tell me. You sold me the book."

She closed the door and patted it as though it were a naughty child. "Book? What book?" She sat down but without taking her eyes from the door.

I passed her a fresh tea and sat opposite her at the table. "Schrodinger's Cat."

"Oh yes. I've never read it but I saw a programme on the telly with Brian Cox explaining it. I thought you might find it interesting with your... your, err... door issues." She pulled a small brown bottle from her bag and measured a few drops into her tea. "From what I can make out, every time something happens where there's more than one possible outcome, the universe divides so that both things happen."

"So I gather but what about the garden?"

"Tinker's Cottage is on the intersection of several major ley lines. Have you got the other book handy?"

I went into the lounge to retrieve and she followed me.

"Is that the real garden?" she said, nodding towards the patio doors.

"Yes. Maybe. I'm not sure anymore, but I think so."

We sat on the sofa and I handed her 'Ley Lines and Earth Forces'. Possicat and Anticat played hunting games behind the sofa. There was a sudden affronted meow and Possicat leapt on to the back of the sofa, making us both start.

"I see you like cats," Saphie said. "Never trust anybody who doesn't like cats, my old gran always used to say. How many have you got?"

"Hard to tell, I haven't counted today."

She gave me a sideways look and returned to the book, thumbing through until she found a map of South West England.

"Here," she said. She moved closer to me to show me the page she had open. Her leg pressed against mine and I felt her warmth. "Saint Michael's, the most important, runs right through here. And two others," she stabbed at the page, "including one that cuts right through Stonehenge, cross over just here."

"I'm still not sure I understand?"

"This is a very powerful place in the lines of Earth Forces. Maybe the conjunction has created links through the different universes." She looked right into my eyes as if trying to read how I was taking this.

I sat for a moment trying to understand what she was saying. A couple of times I thought I had a handle on it and my mouth made some practise movements ready to speak before the understanding dribbled away again and I remained silent. Eventually, all I could to say was, "I suppose I should block the door off again."

She touched my arm. "Why would you want to do that? This is amazing!"

"You don't have to live with it. Gardens that aren't there, oak trees that were there but aren't now and let's not forget the magpie. And the cats of course. Did I tell you about the cats?" I stared out of the patio doors at the area of garden I'd cleared with the chainsaw. "I also seem to have to do all the gardening twice. Here, watch this."

I picked up a standard lamp and carried it out of the patio doors and planted it in the middle of the area I'd cleared a couple of days ago. "Now, have a look through here." I led the way to the kitchen. "There!" I said pointing at the kitchen window.

"What am I supposed to be seeing?" she asked. "Wait... there's no lamp? Where did it go?"

"That's a different place again."

"Different to the patio doors one you mean?"

"Yes." I recalled the problem I'd had with the magpies, "And probably different to the one outside the front door."

"But that looks the same." She returned her gaze to the window. "The window here and the patio doors view. It looks the same."

"I know. That's what's confusing, but if you want to see something really different, take a look at this." I unhooked the Luis Royo picture that covered the new hole in the wall.

"Have a look through there." I pushed the chair underneath the hole so she could stand on it to see through. She climbed on the chair and peered through the gap. "What can you see?" I asked. I was still having doubts about my own sanity and sought confirmation that she could see the view I had seen earlier.

"Trees! I see trees. It's a wood. How can that be?" She turned to look through the other window and wobbled slightly on the chair.

I felt partly relived that it wasn't my sanity at fault. I remember in my teens I'd once had a T shirt that proclaimed in big psychedelic letters, 'Do not adjust your brain, reality is at fault.' I wondered what I'd done with that.

"So," Saphie said then paused in thought. "So, your cottage is sitting on the conjunction of what, three... four different realities?"

"I don't know. I lost track."

"Where do they go?" She climbed down from the chair and I held her hand to steady her.

"I haven't the faintest idea. I've not looked."

"Aren't you curious?"

"I haven't got to curious yet. So far I've just been pretending it's not there. When I've done with that, I'll probably move on to hoping it will all go away then I'm expecting a major session of alcohol abuse before arriving at curious sometime in the next millennium."

"But this is incredible. We have to find out where these go."

"Some things are better left alone. Didn't you ever see the movie 'The Bermuda Triangle'? They never found their way back you know. I think I've already mislaid a handy man and quite possibly a literary agent." I hadn't wanted to face up to that possibility before but it did seem somewhat inescapable once one thought about it.

"But you've been out in the garden, you spent half a day there clearing it and you still came back okay."

I tried to work that through. "But I didn't go very far. Only as far as the cable would reach. So I was still sort of connected. Who knows what would happen if I went any further, probably —"

A faint knocking from the lounge and a "Yoo-hoo!" stopped my paranoia mid flow. We both caught our breath and listened. The "yoo-hoo" repeated followed by a slightly more persistent knock.

"Wait here," I said and headed through to the lounge, trusty shovel in hand.

A tall slim man waved through the glass when he saw me. He wore thick rimmed glasses, a small moustache and a grey tank top. As he looked fairly harmless I left the shovel against the sofa and opened the doors.

"We heard the place was open again," he said as he stepped inside. "Do you mind if I use the front door?"

"Be my guest." I turned to let him past and noticed Saphie standing behind me.

"Where did you come from?" she asked the man.

"Through there of course," he said, pointing at the doors then headed for the front door. I went ahead of him and opened the door to let him out.

I returned to the lounge to find Saphie poring over the book on ley lines. Anticat was helping by walking to and fro across the book.

"You see," she said, pushing the cat to one side and

pointing at a map overlaid with a complicated diagram of swirls and triangles. "There's a series of vortices on some of the leys, bit like acupuncture points, and there seems to be cluster around here."

"Yes, but how do I stop it?" I stood at the doors and stared out at the garden.

"I don't think you can, anymore than you can stop gravity. It's an earth force."

"You hungry?" I asked. "I've got some pizzas in the freezer but that oven thing doesn't really cook anything. Just sort of annoys them."

"What the Rayburn? Fantastic things for cooking on, but you need to keep them going. You can't just turn them on like a gas oven. Do you want me to show you?"

"Er... yes. Thank you, that would be great."

Saphie led the way into the kitchen. "Where's your coal?"

"Ah, I might be a bit short on coal."

"Wood? These things will burn pretty much anything."

"No, I used all that up at the last attempt with a pizza." It had been a long time since I'd entertained and clearly I hadn't thought this through. "Let's say we call cooking 'Plan B' and we go to the pub for a pasty?"

* * * * *

"Long time since I've been here," Saphie said as we arrived at the bar. "Must be ten years. Wasn't it called something else?"

"The King's Head, I believe. Food is a bit of a random affair here so I apologise now."

"Don't worry, I spent three years in Nepal you won't

believe some of the things I've eaten." She raised one eyebrow and smiled.

Arthur appeared behind the bar and started pouring my pint without waiting to be asked. "What can I get you, my dear?" he asked Saphie as he pushed my pint towards me.

Saphie glanced at my drink. "I'll have one of those as well," she said.

"We've got a barbecue special on today, if you're interested," Arthur said.

"Sounds good," I said. "What's in it?"

"Sausages mostly. We were going to do pork loin slices, spare ribs and pork chops but the pig escaped."

"Mostly sausages then?"

"And fried onions of course. You can't very well have a barbecue without fried onions."

"Of course." I glanced at Saphie. She shrugged assent and I turned back to Arthur. "Okay, we'll have two barbecue specials then."

"Excellent," he said, carefully writing the order on his pad. "Do you want fried onions with that?"

"I think so."

"And bread?"

I glanced at Saphie again and she nodded. "Yes please. Bread with the barbecue special."

"How many slices?"

We settled down at a table near the fireplace as my favourite table by the window was occupied by man who looked oddly familiar. I stared for a moment then nudged Saphie. "I know it can't be, but doesn't he look like David Beckham?"

Saphie risked a glance. "I see what you mean. But I'm sure Beckham doesn't smoke roll ups!"

I hadn't noticed the tobacco tin next to his pint of what appeared to be Guinness. "Maybe the recession even affects football heroes?"

Arthur arrived with our barbecue specials, four sausages, fried onions and a few slices of white bread on a plate. More of a dismantled sausage sandwich than barbecue I felt.

"You missed all the fun here earlier," Arthur said. "Right old kerfuffle. Pair of queens going at it hammer and tongs in the car park. Never seen the like before."

"Queens?" I asked. "You mean transvestites?"

"No, I mean queens. As in 'Long to reign over us' type queens. Pink handbags at dawn." He headed off back to the bar.

"That's odd," said Saphie. "I thought that woman looked like her." She manipulated a sausage with her knife and fork and dropped it between two slices of bread.

"But where did the other one come from?" I speared a sausage on my fork and bit into the end. It was surprisingly tasty.

Arthur reappeared and asked if we had everything we needed. I assured we did.

"I'm slowly turning this place into a 'Gastro Pub'," he said proudly. "A 'Destination Pub'. I saw that on Dragon's Den. Or was it Ramsey's F Word?"

"I'm sure you'll do really well," I said. "What's happening around here? Is there a Lookalike Fair or something going? Britain's Got Talent?"

"What do you mean," he asked.

"Well, so far today we've had The Queen and David Beckham over there and a couple of days ago Stephen Fry turned up in my garden."

"Probably to do with the festival. It's usually to do with the festival anytime anything odd happens around here." He gathered some empty glasses and headed back to the bar.

"The festival's not for another month," Saphie said. "And you didn't tell me about Stephen Fry?"

"It wasn't actually him, I don't think so anyway. His nose was straight. But it is all a bit odd."

She finished her barbecue special and wiped her fingers on a paper napkin. "Do you usually eat here?"

"Mostly. I keep trying to cook, but one can only achieve a certain limited repertoire with a microwave and toaster. Although I haven't quite got as low as microwaved toast yet."

"You need to get that Rayburn working. There's a petrol station up the road, that will be open today and they're bound to have coal. Let's pop up there after here and I'll show you how it works."

"That would be very kind of you."

"Don't mention it. After all, you did treat me to a slap up lunch!"

"Yes, sorry about that. But on the plus side you did get to meet David Beckham."

As Saphie had predicted, the garage did indeed sell coal. We also picked up some kindling and firelighters. When we returned to the cottage, I noticed that once more the front door was open. Saphie looked surprised as I picked up my usual weapon of choice.

"It's a Siamese fighting gnome," I explained. "You really don't want to get on the wrong side of these guys."

"I can believe it," she said. "That fishing rod of his looks quite lethal."

She waited outside whilst I did my Special Forces search

of each room. I found him in the small front room I'd designated as my library, an optimistic label for sure but I did need somewhere to store my huge collection of paperbacks and graphic novels. He was short and very thin, wearing what looked like green fatigues with an orange circle about the size of a saucer on the breast.

"Where's the cellar?" he demanded.

"I don't have a cellar. And why are you in my library?" I held the gnome over my head and shook it in what I hoped was a threatening manner.

The man stopped and looked around the room. "Library?" he said, disbelievingly.

"What's wrong with it?"

"Well it's hardly a library is it? I mean, it's more a pile of paperbacks in a cupboard."

"I'll have you know a library is a collection of books wherever they are and it's... Why am I discussing my library with a burglar? I should be calling the police." I shook the gnome again but it was getting heavy and I would need to decide whether to hit him with it or put it down before I dropped it on my head.

"I'm not a burglar! I'm Eric Three Four Nine."

"Three Four Nine?" I heard Saphie say from behind me.

I turned to face her. "I thought you were waiting outside?" How am I supposed to do my alpha male protecting stuff if she was going to follow me in to the danger zone? Then I noticed she carried the pick axe handle and I glanced up at my gnome still held in an increasingly wobbly arm above my head.

"What's wrong with Three Four Nine?" Eric asked. "It's a perfectly proper assignment."

"It sounds more like a Hotmail address," I said, turning back to my intruder.

"I'm not here to be insulted."

"Oh, good, at least that's something on which we are all agreed then. Now if you'll just go back to where you came from."

"The cellar! I'm telling you I came from the cellar."

Despite his agitation he didn't appear dangerous so I settled the gnome on a bookshelf alongside my first edition copy of The Hobbit. "I think you must be in the wrong house. I don't have a cellar."

"But you have, it's there!" He pointed to the end wall of the library. "Just there."

I stared at my rows of pine shelves that supported my endless rows of neatly alphabetised books. "You came through there? Through my bookshelves?"

"Not just now of course. That's ridiculous. Four years ago and there was a door there then. Just now I came through the kitchen door but originally I came from the cellar."

"Well obviously you can't go back that way. Even if there was a cellar there at one time there isn't now and I'm not about to beat any more holes in walls. I've enough trouble with the ones I've got."

"But you have to let me, I left Katrina Two one eight there."

"Katrina Two one...?"

"My wife. I left my wife there. I have to get her now."

Over the last few days I had begun to almost come to terms with the way the world was turning inside out in front of me, but this was just lunacy. I told him so. "This is lunacy," I said. "If you left your wife in my cellar four years ago you're probably a bit late." I had a strong feeling I should be calling the police about now.

"Why would you do something like that?" Saphie asked. "What sort of monster locks his wife in his cellar for four years?"

"My cellar," I corrected. "He locked her up in my cellar."

"I didn't lock her up in the cellar." He sounded affronted. "She's through your cellar on the other side. I had to leave her behind, but now I've come back for her." He started removing books from my shelves and dumping them on the floor.

"If you don't go now I'm going to call the police." I stepped to one side to give him room to leave.

He hesitated as if testing my resolve. My resolve remained positive but I couldn't vouch for the response of Glastonbury Police, that's even supposing it wasn't early closing day. I hoped he wouldn't test either. He paused for a moment and then marched out of the library and through the front door. I closed it behind him.

"Well, that was all very strange." I looked at Saphie. She set the pickaxe handle in the corner and I wondered how she'd removed it from the head so quickly.

"I'm guessing there's yet another universe through there somewhere," she said.

"If there is, it can stay there. I'm not making any more holes."

* * * * *

We unloaded the car and Saphie showed me how to set up the Rayburn properly. It seems these beasts have to be kept going all the time. No much good for a spur of the moment snack.

"You'll need to get a bigger order of coal," she said. "But this'll keep you going for a few days."

The green beast glowed in the corner of the kitchen. "So how many days do I have to wait before I can chuck a pizza in?"

"Oh, I'd give it a week or two just to be sure." Saphie gave me the green eyed twinkly smile that I was beginning to find increasingly seductive. "I need to get back. I've left the dog locked up all day, he'll be frantic."

"There's nobody there to walk him for you?"

"I live alone if that's what you were asking. But I also need to sort out some stock out for the shop tomorrow."

"You're going to leave me alone with that thing?" I nodded in the direction of the Rayburn.

"You'll be alright. Just feed it regularly and try not to make any sudden movements."

"I'll be careful. I have a story to finish anyway."

"You should explore these doorways. You never know what they'll lead."

"That actually seems like a very good reason not to."

After Saphie had gone I settled down at my desk and opened the laptop. I stared at the screen for forty five minutes and gave up, I had a long bath and risked my last pizza to the clutches of the Rayburn. It cooked surprisingly quickly with just the right amount of crispiness. I felt the beginnings of a beautiful relationship.

Chapter Ten

THE NEXT MORNING I MADE myself a fried breakfast on the Rayburn. Saphie had shown me how to set it so it stayed in all night and the kitchen was lovely and warm when I'd got up. The cats had also noticed this new facet to the kitchen and three Possicats had arranged themselves in a perfect equilateral triangle in front of it. One Anticat sat on the table giving them a slightly sinister green eyed stare. Obviously a territorial thing going on here. The trio on the floor had refused to budge and I found myself picking my way through them as I fried my bacon and eggs.

As I ate, I felt a slight sense of elation. It might have been the thought that I could finally cook something or more likely the realisation that I wasn't actually having a return of bewilderment issues. Thinking about the implications of the doors and windows still scrambled my head though so I continued to not think about it as best as I could. But at least another person had confirmed that it was really happening. I thought about Saphie. She was an odd character, for somebody that made a living selling potions and magic crystals she seemed incredibly well grounded. I found myself wondering if she might come out again next Sunday. I stared at the door as I recalled her attempts to enthuse me with a sense of curiosity for what lay out there.

Of course I had been halfway round the house, I remembered. On the first day, I'd repeatedly tried to put bird food on the bird table. That had involved going out the front and round the back. And hadn't I gone all the way round when I'd attempted to open the shutters? I couldn't remember now. Perhaps it wasn't so dangerous?

I refilled my coffee cup and went to the front door. I paused for a moment then opened it and stepped out. The world looked perfectly normal, no shimmering pools like on Stargate when they plop through dimensions as though hopping on a bus. I'd take a walk round the house. I started round the side and then had a thought. What if I moved to a different universe without realising? The ones from the kitchen window and patio doors looked identical. I could end up in the wrong one and not know. I went back to the front door and placed my coffee cup on the doorstep. Now, if I went round and it wasn't there I'd know I'd come back to the wrong place.

I set off round the left side of the cottage and through the narrow walkway between the cottage and the garage. I peeped around the corner and looked at the garden. Overgrown and just as it had been when I'd arrived, with no sign of my afternoon spent out there with the chainsaw. I panicked and hurried back to the front door. The coffee cup was where I'd left it and I steadied my breathing. Of course it would still be overgrown, the garden I'd cleared had been the one out of the patio doors. I ventured back around and this time walked along the back wall. As I passed the patio doors I peeped in. Of course, I remembered, the mad Spanish woman. She'd been in that room not my lounge. A different universe again. I felt a moment of panic and resisted the temptation to scurry back. The lounge looked similar but there was a different coffee table and sofa. There were also quite a few trinkets scattered around. On the sideboard sat three framed photographs. I squinted against the reflected sunlight and could just make out a picture of a boy playing with a dog. That picture looked vaguely familiar. Where did I know that from? I suddenly felt like a voyeur and continued around the cottage. As I passed the wall where the kitchen door should be I ran my hand over the wall. All solid. I carried on round the corner back to the front door and with great relief I saw the coffee cup still where I'd left it. I picked it up and hurried back into the kitchen and sat at the table, limbs shaking slightly. I'd done it! I looked round the kitchen to reassure myself I'd arrived back in the same place. Three cats by the Rayburn, recently used frying pan and toast crumbs on the worktop. Yes, this was my world.

I tried to think through the permutations of which opening led where and felt a slight sense of confused panic creeping up on me so switched on the radio. The BBC were discussing the economy once more and apparently we are all doomed. Some expert propounded his theory of global economic collapse brought about by China cornering the world's honey supplies or something. Better learn to speak Chinese then. That should take my mind off the doors. My mind went back to the doors. Saphie had seemed excited by the possibilities out there and couldn't seem to understand my reluctance to explore. Perhaps I should. I risked a peep out of the kitchen door, half expecting a queue of people to be waiting outside. No people, just the same view of the untidy lawn and low stone wall. But that was still too far from what I should be seeing and I closed the door again.

The patio doors led to a world that looked pretty much identical to the one I inhabited so perhaps if I was going to explore, that would be the one to try. At least then I would have the comfort of the familiar. And besides, I'd already spent an afternoon out there without coming to any harm. I went to the lounge and pushed open the patio doors in my moment of bravado. My bravado evaporated as I ventured outside and by the time I rounded the corner of the cottage I'd already moved from bravado through caution and was now firmly in panic. I peeped around the front corner of the cottage and started as I noticed my car had vanished. Of course it had, it was in my own universe I reasoned. Apart from the missing car, everything else appeared normal.

Missing car? A sense of unease started somewhere near my stomach and spread around my insides like a particularly cold ice cream. The last time my car had gone missing was when I'd been seeing Tania off. I tried to think through what had happened that day. We'd left the cottage via the patio doors, just as I'd done now. That would explain why the car wasn't there both times. However, that also meant that Tania had gone off unknowingly into this world. I'd had a vague notion earlier that something like that might have happened but up until now I'd chosen to ignore the possibility. Whoops.

I hurried back inside and paced around the cottage. What would happen? Maybe everything just joined up again down the lane or something? Or perhaps the differences between these two universes were so slight she'd never notice them? After all, the only difference as far as I could see was one had my car in it and the other had a cleared back garden. No big deal. Perhaps I was the only thing different and everything else was the same.

That was alright then. Nothing to worry about. Tania was with her sister in Cornwall and all was right with the world.

I grabbed my keys and headed out of the front door, jumped in the car and terrorised the lanes between Trembly and Glastonbury.

* * * * *

"But you see," I said to Saphie, "the only difference is the little bit of garden and my car."

Saphie took a ten pound note from a pretty young woman in jeans and denim jacket and rang it through the till. "Thank you," she said, handing the woman her change and box of incense cones. She turned to me as the woman left. "What are you talking about?"

"Tania, my agent. I think she might have accidently wandered into a different universe."

"Yes, so I gathered. And you're hoping she won't notice?"

"Well, that's not really what I meant. I just—"

"Sorry, Ian. I'll be with you in a minute." She turned to serve a couple of hippy types who had just placed a selection of crystals on the counter.

"Are you sure that's all?" she asked them.

"What do you mean?" asked the man.

Saphie pulled a small brown bottle from a stand behind her and dropped it into the bag with the crystals. "Take two drops of this each night before sleep. It will stop the dreams."

The man looked horrified. "How... I mean... What makes you say that?"

His companion tugged his sleeve. “Come on, Ewan. I told you she knows stuff.” She paid for the crystals but as with me, Saphie refused payment for the bottle. They left the shop with Ewan shaking his head in confusion.

“Rather an interesting business model,” I asked her when the shop was empty once more. “Do you ever actually sell any of that stuff?”

“One must never sell healing or it is robbed of its power.” She tidied the counter. “On the other hand it’s perfectly in order to sell it to those who don’t need it. American tourists generally. Mostly all they need is a diet.”

I remembered the estate agent telling me about the American tourist who’d gone missing. “But you think Tania will be alright then? If it’s all much the same I mean.”

She made an entry in her Day Book then closed it and faced me. “If you’re convinced that the world is the same then I’m sure she’s okay.” Her eyes challenged me.

“I see. So I suppose I should go look. I mean... just to check?”

“That would seem to be the best plan.”

I searched her eyes for signs of sarcasm. “I don’t suppose—”

“No, I can’t afford to shut up shop just yet. Go on, you’ll enjoy it. It will be an adventure.”

“Did I ever mention my allergy to adventure? It’s like peanuts only worse.”

“I’ll drop round later. You can tell me how it went.”

There was the trap. Right there. Sprung with such finesse I hadn’t seen it coming. If I didn’t explore she would have no reason to come round.

“I’ll get a pizza in,” I said.

* * * * *

I sat in the lounge staring through the patio doors. A perfectly ordinary day in a perfectly ordinary village. I wondered if there was another me out there somewhere. What would happen if we met? Would we explode in an antimatter annihilation? What if I met a different version of myself, a Scottish version or something. Could I have been born as a female in a different universe? That opened up a conundrum. If I met a married female version of myself and we had an affair, would that be adultery or incest?

I realised I was mentally burbling and closed the lid on that particular corner of my insanity. I would go out through there and go for a pint in the Camelot. That would be my reward for outstanding bravery.

I hesitated slightly when I reached the drive and saw no car there and then again as I walked down the drive to see the hedge pushing in from both sides. It showed no evidence of my afternoon of chainsawing a few days ago. The walk to the pub was pretty much as any other. Apart from the bakery next to the general stores. In my universe this was just a modernised terraced cottage, probably owned by a Londoner as a weekend retreat. Here it had a loaf shaped sign hanging from a beam; 'Stainswick's Bakery', it said.

The pub was quiet for a lunchtime. Just two men in overalls sat at the bar.

"Ah, mister Faulkener, sir," one of the men said as I approached the bar. "I've been trying to find you but you never answer your door."

"Wayne?"

"Yes, sir. I fixed your door. Don't tell me you've gone and got the Al Zymers too!"

"Al Zymers?" I looked at the other man who was the absolute double, right down to the overalls. "Oh, I see, Alzheimer's. Sorry," I said, slightly confused. "I've been in most of the time. I'd been wondering what had happened to you." I looked from one to the other. The only difference I could determine was that Wayne had three days worth of beard whilst the other man was clean shaven.

"Not to worry," he said. "As you're around now I'll pop round direckley and finish off. You ain't seen my van have you? Some bugger seems to have nicked it. Or maybe I just forgot where I left it. That's been happening a lot lately."

"It's still in the lane outside my cottage. At least it was yesterday."

"See, I told you it wouldn't be far away," said the other man. "You just forgot where you parked it, you silly sod."

Still confused I looked back at Wayne and asked, "I'm sorry, who is this?" I pointed to the second man.

"That's my brother Wayne," Wayne said. "Same name like me. Funny that, ain't it?"

"Yes," I said. Not thinking it was funny at all. Strange yes, and quite probably downright disturbing. But at least that answered one fear. They hadn't gone bang in an antimatter explosion.

Wayne number two held his hand out. "Nice to meet you, sir," he said. "I'm Wayne.

I shook his hand. "Hello, Wayne."

Just then Arthur appeared behind the bar. "What can I get you, sir?" he asked.

"A pint of my usual please, Arthur."

"Arthur?" he said. "Nobody here called Arthur. Sorry, what's your usual?"

"Of course," I said and pointed to the Old Grumbler pump. "I'll have a pint of that one please."

"Coming right up, sir." He pulled the pump with the care of a master engineer. "You met my boys then?"

"Yes," I said.

"This is mister Faulkener, dad," said Wayne number one. "Like I told you. The fellow down Flora's old place. I did his door for him."

"Oh, right," said the barman whose name I no longer knew. "I remember you told me that. Doors it was, yes." He paused momentarily to let the head settle on the beer.

"You got your Alcohol Indemnity Card?" he asked me as he finished pouring the beer.

"Um, er... no, sorry."

"You'll have to sign a temporary one then," he said pulling a form from under the counter and handing it to me.

I started to read it. 'I the undersigned party of the first instance being desirous to engage in the purchase of alcohol for possible consumption do hereby...' it went on for several incomprehensible paragraphs. I finally gleaned the intent of the document was a waiver absolving the landlord from all responsibility regarding my actions after having consumed alcohol provided by him. Including, but not limited to, having sex with totally unsuitable partners it seems. I signed the form and gave it back to him.

He placed the beer on the bar and pushed to towards me. "There you go," he said.

I suddenly recalled Arthur telling me that when he'd changed the pub name to the Camelot the locals took to calling him Arthur although that wasn't his name. Albert, that was it. He'd been Albert.

"Thank you, Albert," I said.

Albert looked quizzical as if he should recognise me now I knew his name. "That'll be four euros twenty," he said.

"Four euros twenty," I repeated, patting my pockets as if that would magically conjure euros out of nowhere. I pulled a ten pound note out of my pocket and placed it on the bar. "Sorry, I've only got this. Is this any good?"

Albert looked at the note. "That's the third one of those I've seen this week! Somebody found a secret stash or something? Like I said to the lady, you'll need to take it to the bank to change it. They stopped being legal over ten years ago."

"Oh, sorry." I had a quick think and remembered I had a pile of euros left over from my last holiday. They were in a drawer somewhere. "If you can hang on, I'll just pop home and get the money." I headed to the door, just as I slipped out I realised Albert had followed me out.

"Hang on," he said. "Did you say you knew that man in there? The one that looks like my Wayne?"

"Yes," I said, confusion growing.

"Only I think he's a bit of a nutter." Albert looked over his shoulder as if in fear of being overheard. "He turned up here the other day saying as how he was my boy Wayne."

"I don't understand," I said. "I thought they were brothers?"

"Wayne and me just played along with it. Felt sorry for him. But he's been hanging around for a few days now and we're worried in case he's one of those stalkers."

Light dawned. "I see. Yes I've met him before, he's a sort

of odd job man. Harmless, but I think he's... I think he's sort of lost."

"Do you think you can get him to move on?" Albert almost pleaded. "No need to pay for your drink. Have another if you like."

It was a persuasive move on Albert's part and I followed him back into the bar. The Old Grumbler went down smoothly and another appeared seamlessly in its place.

"I tell you what, Wayne," I said to my Wayne. "If you come back with me now you can pick your bits up straight away."

Wayne hesitated then "You still got my drill? Only I was wondering where that had gone."

Wayne and I finished our drinks and headed back to Tinker's Cottage. I led the way round to the patio doors and into the lounge. Wayne tested the lock on the door.

"That seems alright. If it gives you any trouble you just call me," he said.

I collected his drill and a couple of other tools he'd left behind then guided him out of the front door. If I'd got this right, he was going to be very confused when he found himself back where he belonged. Hopefully he'd put it down to another case of the Al Zymers.

After he'd gone I sat at the kitchen table. My body tingled as the adrenaline settled and I thought through the events of the last couple of hours. The important thing was to make sure I went in and out through the same door. A crashing noise from the library snagged my attention. I picked up the pick axe that still lay on the kitchen floor and cautiously followed the noise. I pushed the library door quietly and saw a figure with his back to, he was dragging my books off the shelves and dumping them on the floor.

“What are you doing?” I yelled. The man jumped then turned to face me, a copy of The Colour of Magic still in his hand. It was Eric Three Four Nine.

“I have to get my wife,” he said.

“How did you get in?

“The door was open. I did knock.”

“Your wife is not in my bookshelf or in some imaginary cellar.” I waved the pickaxe towards the door, it was heavy and unwieldy. “Out!” I shouted, trying my best to look frightening.

He succumbed to my fierce face and slipped out through the front door. I closed it shut after him and tugged at it to make sure it was firm. I was going to have to invest in some serious ironmongery for these doors.

I returned my attention to the doors and decided that if I was to avoid accidently disappearing into the wrong place I would need to keep track of what goes where. I could do a map. I’m a fantasy writer, maps are our mainstay. But first I would label each doorway. I decided to call my universe number one and go from there. I soon had Post It notes on each door and window. The front door said ‘1’ and the patio doors ‘2’ and so on with each reality I’d noticed. I finished with the landing window which I labelled ‘6’ and placed the Post It notes back on the desk, wondering as I did so if how many more I’d find. I looked out of the window at the oak tree that sat defiantly in the middle of the field in Universe Six. There was something about that tree that drew me. I’d have to find a way of getting there. I had a ladder in the garage, if I put that up I could climb out of the window and explore. I was feeling pleased with my new found sense of adventure so no point in wasting it.

I dragged the ladder out of the garage and propped it up against the back wall just under the landing window then went back inside and upstairs again. I swung the window open and climbed on the desk to clamber out of the window. I stalled as I looked out. No ladder. Idiot, I scolded myself. Of course it wouldn't be there, the ladder was in Universe One, out of the front door and I was looking at Universe Six. Okay, I would need to put the ladder out of the window from here if I wanted to use it there.

I brought the ladder into the house, destroying one vase of flowers and a light fitting on the way. In its collapsed state I should just about be able to manoeuvre the ladder across the desk and through the window.

Everything went fine until I found myself kneeling on the desk, hanging on to the top of the ladder that now dangled outside and trying to unclip the catch that would let it extend to the ground. I nearly had my fingers on the catch when I lost my grip and the ladder crashed to the ground outside. It was only when I went back outside to retrieve it to try again that I realised for the second time the level of my stupidity. No ladder. Damn! The ladder was now in the garden of Universe Six and with no way of retrieving it. I would need to be more careful with my things in future. I now had a selection of universes in which to lose my possessions.

I heard a knock on the door and prepared myself for the next stage of lunacy as I went to open it. I was pleasantly surprised to find Saphie there.

"Oh," I said, looking at my watch. "I didn't realise it was that time."

"I told you I'd come over after I closed."

We went through to the kitchen and I put a kettle on the

Rayburn. “See,” I said. “Getting the hang of this thing. Tea?”

“Thank you.” Saphie opened and shut the kitchen door a couple of times. “I still can’t quite get my head round this. What’s this sticky note for?

“Oh, that, I needed a way of remembering what door goes where. Post It notes seemed like a sensible quick fix until I can get round to drawing a map.”

“So, how did your adventuring go?”

I gave her the highlights of my brief sojourn into Universe ‘2’.

“Euros?” she said when I’d finished. “That’s interesting. So in that universe we join the euro. I wonder how that worked out? Now, what about your agent, Tania?”

“Oh, yes. She’s okay.” I poured the tea into the Witchblade mug for her. “I think. Probably.”

“You haven’t the faintest idea, have you?”

A knocking at the kitchen door rescued me. “I’ll just get that,” I said and tentatively opened it.

“Hi!” said Richard Branson.

I stepped back in surprise and he walked in. “Look who it is,” I said to Saphie.

“It’s... It is you, isn’t it?”

“That depends on who you think I am,” Richard Branson said.

“You’re Richard Branson?” Saphie said.

“That’s good. Then Richard Branson it is then. I take it I’m famous?”

We reassured him he was famous and he asked to be let out of the front door.

After he’d gone we finished our tea and chatted about doors, leylines and alternate universes.

"So, that makes one David Beckham, one Stephen Fry, a pair of queens and an assortment of nobodies." I counted on my fingers.

"Why do they want to come through to the other universes?" Saphie asked.

"I haven't the faintest idea, but it does seem odd that most of them are famous."

"Let's go explore!" Saphie's eyes sparkled with adventure. "I'd like to see the place where they use euros."

"Oh, I don't know," I stalled. "It's not that great. Much the same really. And we might get stuck or something, like on Stargate Atlantis. They went through a wormhole and couldn't get back. Million light years or something. We shouldn't really mess with these things."

"I'll buy you a drink in the King's Head?"

Saphie had learnt my buttons very quickly and pressed them astutely. "I'll fetch the euros I had left over from holiday," I said.

Chapter Eleven

FOR AN EARLY MONDAY EVENING, The Kings Head was already busier than I'd ever seen it as The Camelot. Albert recognised me and pulled a pint of Old Grumbler as I approached the bar. As the froth settled he turned to Saphie. "What'll it be, my dear?"

"Just a glass of tonic with a slice of lemon, please." She obviously noticed my expression. "I'm driving. I don't drink anything at all when I drive."

I admired her discipline. I also admired her figure which showed as a slight silhouette through the white cheesecloth dress she wore.

"That'll be five euros twenty five," Albert said as he rang the drinks through the till.

I pulled my holiday money from my pocket and put a ten euro note on the bar. Albert picked it up and studied it.

"You got anything else? Only I'm not sure these are still legal."

"What?" I'd only brought them back from Spain a couple of months ago. I picked through my handful of notes. "How about this?" I put a twenty down.

Albert looked at it with the same disdain he'd shown the

first. “Where’d you get these? You raided your grandmother’s piggybank?”

“What’s wrong with them?”

“They ain’t got the president’s head on them, that’s what. Thought all the old ones had been pulled out of circulation.”

“The president?”

“President Blair. Where’ve you been? Outer Mongolia?”

“President Blair?” I felt stupid just repeating his words but it was all my mouth would do.

He opened the till and pulled out a ten euro note. “There,” he said as he placed it next to mine. “All notes are supposed to have the President of Europe on them now.”

I stopped myself before I repeated ‘President of Europe’ and picked up the note he’d put down. It did indeed show the face of the President of Europe. President Blair. President Cherie Blair, first president and Primus of Greater Europe.

“Oh,” I said

“Hell, I suppose I can take them,” Albert took the notes off the counter then gave me my change. “What can they do? Send me on another awareness course?”

We carried our drinks over to a table near the fireplace.

“That’s a thing, isn’t it?” Saphie said as we sat down. “President Cherie Blair. Who’d have thought?”

I glanced around the pub. It all seemed much the same as my world. A couple of middle aged women supped their tea and at the next table three men in their twenties were locked in animated conversation. A flat screen television hung from the wall showing muted news footage of a storm somewhere that had palm trees. Or more correctly, judging by the video, used to have palm trees.

"You see," I said. "All normal, nothing to see here. And I'm sure Tania's perfectly alright."

"So you are worried about Tania then?"

"That's not what I said."

"Yes you did. You said you were sure she's alright. People only ever say that when they're worrying about somebody."

"Well, it's not easy getting an agent these days. One should try to hang on to them. She'll be at her sister's in Cornwall by now anyway." I finished the beer, it didn't seem to have worked so I headed to the bar for a replacement. I returned to the table hoping Saphie had forgotten about Tania. She hadn't.

"But what if she hasn't got a sister in Cornwall?" Saphie continued as if she hadn't even noticed my trip to the bar.

"What? Of course she's got a sister in Cornwall. That's what she said. Why would she tell me she was going to visit her sister in Cornwall if she hasn't got one? That doesn't make any sense."

"I mean in this universe. Universe Two, as your sticky note calls it. She might not have a sister here, then what's she going to do?"

"I'm sure she's perfectly alright."

Saphie realised I'd assigned Tania to the 'Don't Look Too Closely' box for the time being and picked the menu from its holder. "Seems quite nice food if you're peckish?"

We studied the menu together. It offered a more normal pub selection than that of The Camelot. No attempts at Arthur's Speciality Menus, just a good selection of burgers, pizzas, pies a couple of roasts and fish and chips.

"I think I'll have the fish and chips," I said. "What do you fancy?"

She gave me that odd look with which I was becoming familiar, even if I didn't understand it. "I'm going for a vege burger with salad I think."

I took the menu to the bar and waited a moment while Albert served a young man who looked remarkably like Robbie Williams. After the man left the bar Albert turned to me.

"Do you know who he is? Only he kept asking me to guess who he was. Hadn't the faintest idea. Very strange."

"Looked a bit like Robbie Williams." I noticed Albert's blank expression and continued, "The singer? Let Me Entertain You?"

"Who's that then? Is he on the television?"

I decided to avoid what could be a difficult explanation and settled for, "I think he was once."

Albert noticed me clutching the menu. "You wanting to order?"

"Yes, can I have—"

"Hang on, need to get you to sign a food request waiver. I'm guessing you haven't got your Edibles Indemnity Cards?"

"Er, no. Sorry." I patted my pockets to indicate I really should have my Edibles Indemnity Card but that I had simply forgotten it this time.

He placed a clipboard on the counter. "Both to sign here... here..." He turned the page. "And here."

I took the form back to Saphie and we attempted to decipher the legalese that smothered two sheets of perfectly innocent A4.

'The party of the first part hereby warrants they are free from allergies including but not restricted to nuts, milk, cheese...' the list of potential allergens seemed to include every food type known and a few I'd never even heard of, let alone contemplated putting anywhere near my mouth. The next page dealt with ensuring we understood that food was often served hot and that due care is to be exercised when either eating it, touching it or just spilling it all over ourselves. I skipped to the final page that absolved the purveyor of the foodstuffs from all responsibility of any weight gained either directly or indirectly as a result of coming into contact with said purveyor's aforementioned foodstuffs.

Feeling my life seeping away, I signed the form, turned it to Saphie for her signature and returned to the bar to place the order.

When I came back to the table Saphie was busy chatting with a middle aged woman at the next table. I strained to hear what they were saying but the general hubbub made it impossible. Eventually Saphie turned back to me.

"What was all that about?" I asked.

"I was finding out a bit more about this place."

"You can't do that! They'll think we're escaped lunatics or something. We need to be low key."

"You worry too much." She reached across the table and gave my hand a little squeeze. "Did you know the Queen has moved to Germany?"

"Can't say I blame her. All these forms would be enough to drive anyone to move out." I didn't know what to do with my hand. Should I squeeze back? Or should I just leave it there for a moment? But for how long?

The problem was solved when Albert arrived and told us our meals were ready for collection at the counter. "Sorry, but the person who's insured to carry plates to tables is on Paternity Leave at the moment."

I went to the bar and collected the plates, along with two sets of plastic cutlery. I struggled with the blunt plastic knife for a while then resorted to fingers. The fish was delicious but fell to pieces each time I picked it up. I wished I'd settled for the burger as Saphie seemed to be much more in control of her meal than was I.

After we'd finished, my sense of adventure had exhausted itself and I persuaded Saphie to abandon any further explorations in favour of a warm fire in a familiar world. We stopped off at the general stores to buy kindling, observing the warning label which announced that under some circumstances kindling was likely to be inflammable. I also bought some bread, which might contain wheat, some milk which almost certainly contained dairy products and a packet of peanuts oddly devoid of any warning labels.

Saphie fired up the Rayburn which I had let die earlier in the day whilst chasing ladders through three separate universes. As soon as it was underway three cats, all Possicats, appeared from nowhere and arranged themselves in such a manner that it was impossible to get within six feet of the Rayburn. I found a bottle of Vino Blanco I'd forgotten about, another souvenir of my holiday, picked up two glasses and headed into the lounge. Saphie already had the lounge fire underway and I idly wondered if she'd ever been a Girl Guide, given her skills for fire starting. I had to forcibly stop myself thinking about her in a Girl Guide's uniform. The flames from the fire danced in the huge fireplace and threw a golden haze over her white dress, the silhouette of her body showing clearly through the now almost transparent material. I poured two glasses of wine and placed hers on the small oak coffee table in front of the sofa.

"Thanks," she said and sat next to me, not quite touching

but close enough that I could feel the warmth of her. "I thought I said I never drink when I'm driving?"

"Oh, sorry. I forgot. Would you prefer a tea or..." I mentally searched my supply of non alcoholic drinks and came up empty. "Or a tea?"

"This will be fine." She took a sip of the wine and gave me a smile that for some reason made me stop breathing for several seconds.

"I can sleep on the sofa," I said, gallantly. "Or I could always phone for a taxi if—"

She placed two fingers over my lips effectively terminating my adolescent babbling. "Shush," she said. "I'm sure we'll work something out."

We chatted into the evening, consuming the last of my supplies of Spanish wine. She explained more about the ley lines and how our ancestors had been unconsciously drawn to arrange all their important monuments along them. She made it a lot clearer than the book had done.

"You see, humans have always been drawn to places of mystical significance. Historians will try to tell you that that the monuments came first then the people were drawn there, but in actual fact it's the other way round. Iron age man recognised certain points where the earth forces were strong and built there." She twisted in her seat to face me and took a sip of wine, her other hand settled on my leg, perhaps in emphasis for her theories? "I mean, why else would they build Stonehenge where it is? Two hundred miles from where the stone was quarried?"

"I thought it was because of the river," I tried to recall a programme I'd seen on The History Channel. "Or the sunrise points there."

"Idiot," she said and patted my leg. "The sunrise gets everywhere, if you hadn't noticed."

"Not really," I said. "Me and the sunrise don't exactly have a strong working relationship."

She laughed and sat back on the sofa, her hand slipped off my leg leaving a noticeable cold patch. "The crystals deep within the earth create strong electromagnetic fields that find resonance in the magnetic field that surrounds each human. We can't help it. We have to go to these places."

"But that doesn't explain the doors."

"They're just a manifestation of what happens when too many of these forces congregate in the same place. Space-time gets all twisted up at these points. The same thing happened inside the pyramids." She finished her wine and gave a slightly disappointed frown.

I got up to put another log on the fire and as I returned to the sofa I noticed she'd shifted her position slightly making it impossible for me to sit down without coming into physical contact. I slid next to her feeling the firmness of her thigh press against mine as I wriggled into the space she'd left me.

"What are you so tense about, Ian?"

"Tense? What do you mean?"

"Your Crown Chakra is disturbed."

"Uh?" Not one of my most coherent expressions of confusion and certainly not from one who claims to be a writer.

"I can see it in your aura." She twisted to face me, her thigh sliding across the top of mine. Her dress had ridden up showing a glimpse of said thigh. She opened her open hands and made a circular sweeping movement over my head. "It shows tension and inner pain."

"That'll be the doors. I'm not good with doors that don't behave in the way to which one has become accustomed."

"It's older than that." Her face took a concerned expression and her hands settled each side of my head. "There is deep damage here." She held her hands in place, only just making contact with my head. Her face seemed to lose focus and the firelight brought an ethereal glow to her skin.

"I can... I don't... I..." My words stopped forming as I felt a heat coming from her hands. A slight tingling like a thousand tiny needles ran across my scalp. I wanted to push her away but at the same time her hands felt oddly like home. All the time she remained silent, her eyes only just open.

I felt her give a little shudder and she broke contact, her eyes opening wide. "Oh," she said. "You certainly have made a mess of that." Her hands fell into mine and she squeezed.

"Must have been the cheap wine," I said. "Sorry, but it was all I had."

"One day you'll have to deal with it." She slid her hands up to the side of my face and we locked eyes. My own hands found themselves reaching around her and pulling her close. The feel of her firm breasts brushed my chest just moments before our lips made contact and I sank towards her.

We spent the night together and made love twice with a kind of warm passion I couldn't ever remember feeling with another woman. The following morning she rushed off to open the shop leaving me staggering around the kitchen in a pre-caffeine fug.

As I sat at the kitchen table with my second coffee and toast I wondered about the universe we'd visited last night. The small differences actually made it feel in many ways quite alien. I thought about what Saphie had said about my aura and was that real or just New Age fluff and waffle? I certainly felt more relaxed this morning, but that might just be because we'd had a night of glorious sex. Even when the inevitable knock came at the kitchen door I didn't jump, I just opened it with a mild curiosity as to what I'd find this time.

"Hello," said a smartly dressed man in his mid thirties. I was sure I should recognise him but couldn't quite place.

"Good morning," I greeted with a level of cheerfulness that surprised me. "Front door?"

"Please, that would be most kind."

I led him through the cottage and he departed with a wave and a smile. I returned to the kitchen and peered through the back door. This world was a long way from my own. The outside entirely different. So different that up until now I'd felt a sense of panic each time I'd opened the door. But this morning I was only sensing curiosity. I stepped through the door, quite expecting to be overcome by the familiar wave of panic. My heart did beat a bit faster and my breathing fell shallow but I had no overwhelming urge to run screaming back into the house. I padded across the unkempt lawn and it was only when a felt my feet becoming wet that I realised I was still in my dressing gown and the morning dew from the long grass was turning my Marks and Spencer's slippers into a sodden mess. I stopped at the bottom of the garden next to the low stone wall that stood where there should be a large hedge.

The lane looked much the same except it was wider and there appeared to be a bus shelter about fifty metres away. I wonder if The Kings Head existed here. What would Trembly be like in this universe? I decided to investigate.

After a shower and another coffee I dressed in jeans, sweatshirt and trainers and headed out of the kitchen door, over the wall and into the lane. I paused in the lane and glanced back at the cottage with a moment of concern that I might never find my way back. Don't be daft, I told myself. As long as I go back through the same door from which I left all would be fine. The danger was in forgetting which door I'd left from and returning through a different one. I didn't even want to attempt thinking through the complexities of that scenario.

As I passed the bus shelter I noticed the stop was designated as 'Tinker's Cottage'. That was certainly odd. Most bus stops I knew were named after the road or a landmark rather than the name of a dwelling. As I walked through the main road into Trembly I noticed the houses seemed much more brightly decorated than the ones in my Universe. My Trembly had been designated as a Conservation Village and as such the houses were restricted to maintaining the feel of the original buildings. Stone walls, slate roofs and sash windows were the order. Here each house was different. Many had been painted or faced in modern brickwork. One even had timber cladding all across the front. Windows were mostly modern and double glazed and the front doors were all colours and styles.

The building which in my world had been the small general store, here was a large supermarket spread across what had once been a row of three stone cottages. I ventured inside. I needed to see what went for currency here before any more difficult moments. The prices on each item were in familiar sterling but each with a rider saying 'All Currencies Accepted'. I picked up a packet of biscuits and took them to the tills. As I waited behind an elderly woman paying for a basket of cat food I noticed the display behind the counter.

The usual cigarettes and tobacco lined the shelves but there were also packets of more exotic smoking materials. Moroccan Gold, Jamaican Skunk and a host of other offerings from the cannabis producers of the world.

The woman finished paying for her cat food and I placed the biscuits on the counter.

"What currency would you like to use today?" asked a bored looking teenage girl in a white T-shirt that clearly showed her dislike of underwear.

"Sterling please," I said and placed a ten pound note on the counter.

She picked it up and glanced at it briefly before ringing it through the till and handing me my change. I thanked her and left the shop studying the handful of coins I'd been given. The coins were different to the ones with which I was familiar but the queen's head was in evidence on most of them. There seemed to be more cars in the village than I was used to, and they all had what seemed to be personalised number plates. Some fairly normal but several slightly quirky and one on a four-by-four parked outside the butchers which was downright obscene. I headed towards the pub. I reasoned that as it was the place with which I was most familiar I would see the differences more clearly.

The Kings Head, as it was still known here, announced its presence with a huge neon sign all across the front facade. I was immediately hit by the wall of smoke that confirmed that pubs here were not subject to the non smoking regulations of my world. I could already feel the onset of chronic bronchitis by the time I reached the bar.

"I'll have a pint of Old Grumbler," I asked Albert or Arthur.

"Coming right up, mate," he said as he poured the beer. "What currency do you want to pay with?"

"Euros please," I said and handed over a twenty euro note.

He gave me my change in sterling without a second glance at the note I'd given him. I found a table by the window and supped on my beer. It was as good as the others from the previous two universes. A surprising constant in the multiverse. It was still relatively early so I was the only occupant of the pub. People drifted by outside in much the same manner I was used to. Two small boys kicked a ball down the pavement, bouncing it off the odd parked car as they went. I decided this world wasn't that far removed from my own and certainly less scary than I'd originally thought.

Two young women arrived, picked up a pint of beer each and sat at the table next to me. They looked to be in their early twenties and both dressed in skimpy tops and skirts that seemed way too short for this time of day.

One of them caught me looking at them, she smiled. "You here for Tinker's Cottage?"

"Yes... I mean no. I mean what's that?" Smooth as usual, Ian.

"Tinker's Cottage? Didn't you know it's open again? It's all over Wikidoors."

"I hadn't noticed. Perhaps I need to have a look?" I wasn't sure I was making the slightest bit of sense but it seemed the only thing I could come up with.

She returned her attention to her friend and they exchanged a few whispered words before they both erupted into giggles. Clearly I'd said something very stupid. I finished my beer and headed home. I remembered to go back through the kitchen door and closed it firmly behind me. I collapsed onto the chair and I suddenly realised my heart was racing. I scanned the kitchen to be sure it was the one to which I belonged. All seemed okay. I was just feeling pleased with myself when I heard a crashing sound from the other end of the cottage. Not feeling quite as brave as I had done earlier, I picked up a carving knife and went in search of the sound.

Eric Three Four Nine stood in the library, pickaxe in hand.

"What are you doing here?" I yelled. A totally redundant question as even an idiot could see what he was doing here. My precious book collection was scattered all over the floor and covered in the dust created by the huge hole that now existed in the end wall.

"I have to get my wife. I promised her."

"But look what you've done to my books."

"I'm sorry, but I didn't have time to be tidy. I thought you might come back at any moment." He took a couple of steps towards me, the pickaxe still swung from his hand.

"And you can put that down." I waved my knife towards him.

He dropped the pickaxe to the floor and raised his hands in supplication. "Can't you just let me finish and go through? I promise I'll clean up. You'll never know I was here."

"This will take a team of builders a week to put right." I thought about Wayne. "Or possibly a month."

"I can do it. My secondary designation is that of maintenance. It's what I do."

"Your secondary what?" For the first time I saw a truly desperate man in front of me. His eyes a mixture of fear and determination. I softened slightly. "I don't understand. What exactly happened with your wife?"

"I escaped but I had to leave her behind. Only one could

go, I didn't want to leave her but she made me go." He looked close to tears.

I put the knife on one of the remaining shelves and said, "Come on, I'll put the kettle on and you can take it more slowly."

Eric Three Four Nine followed me into the kitchen. I motioned him to sit and he carefully positioned the chair so it was across the table from mine. I saw a small frightened man and wondered why I'd been worried about him. "Tea or coffee? I asked. "Or maybe something stronger. I have beer?"

"I don't drink stimulants or alcohol. None of us do. It's not allowed."

"That only leaves tap water then I'm afraid. My selection of soft drinks is somewhat limited."

"Water's fine," Eric said.

I poured a glass of water for Eric and made tea for myself. It took a bit of coaxing to get him to tell me what had happened but once he started, a story worthy of one of my plot lines spilled from him. His world was one where it seemed people were selected to be organ donors for the rich and powerful. He wasn't sure of how it all worked; he just knew that he and millions of others were kept fed and looked after very well until one day someone would just disappear. Sometimes they would return with scars from surgery, but often they were never seen again.

I was horrified. He continued to explain that many years ago somebody had found a way out through the cellar of a small cottage that somehow led into a different world. He told how some sympathetic guardians would, for a fee, help the odd person through. He and his wife had raised the necessary fee for one escapee and she insisted that he go as he was best placed to earn some money on the other side and come back for her. He'd agreed but shortly after his escape the access door back had been sealed and he had no way of returning. Until that is, I turned up and took a pickaxe to the kitchen doorway.

"Okay," I said. "If what you say is true, I'll help." Where had that come from? Had I been taken over by the spirit of The Falconer?

"You will?" Tears glistened in his eyes.

"What do you need?" I asked, regretting the words even as they left my lips.

"About three hundred credits, a way back though the cellar and somewhere to stay while I'm waiting for her to be brought out."

"Three hundred credits? What's that?"

"On my side it's about enough to buy a television."

"But how can you get credits here? We have pounds."

"When the door was open people would trade pounds for credits. A busy black market ran through the doors. Probably will again if the doors stay open."

I agreed to fund him the three hundred pounds which he guessed would be a straight swap for credits and for his part he agreed to make a tidy job of reopening the cellar door. It also looked like I was going to have a lodger for a while. I set him up in the spare room and found a towel and some bedding.

That evening Saphie came round again and I reintroduced her to Eric Three Four Nine, explaining the problem of his wife. She was as horrified as I, and offered to help in any way she could. Eric had already made a good start on the doorway. A neat hole now exposed a set of wooden steps descending into the darkness. He told me there was another bricked up doorway at the bottom of the steps and there would be one more across the other side of the cellar. Somebody had really wanted this lot closed.

We all adjourned to The Camelot for supper. As soon as we stepped inside the pub I had a moment of panic, fearing I'd slipped universes accidently. Gold, green, and black bunting draped around the ceiling and reggae music filled the air. Arthur stood behind the bar; he wore a garish Hawaiian shirt and a plastic lei around his neck.

"Aloha," he said as we approached the bar.

"Aloha," I returned. "What's all this about?"

"We're having a Caribbean evening, would you like to see the menu?"

The prospect of Arthur's Caribbean menu filled me with both curiosity and a slight sense of dread. "Yes please," I managed.

He placed three menus on the bar and took our orders for drinks. I noticed with a slight degree of disappointment that Saphie ordered a glass of tonic water.

"That's certainly a varied menu tonight, Arthur," I commented as my eyes took in the selection on the A4 sheet; Cajun Chicken, Chilli Con Carne, Rice and Peas, Barbecued Prawns and Doner Kebabs.

"Well, these days you have to do something a bit different if you're going to keep your clientele." Arthur placed the drinks in front of us.

"This is certainly different. How did you come up with this selection?" I sipped at my Grumbler.

"I just asked Jamaica Billy, the Rasta, he works in the scrap yard on the Wells road. You know, Metal Mickey's? I simply asked him what his favourite foods were. Genius huh?"

"Yes, genius." We placed our orders and found a table. The place was surprisingly busy. I noticed in one corner a sort of a stage had been set up. More of a pallet with an amplifier on one end in reality.

At Saphie's prompting, Eric opened up a bit more about his world.

"It's not all that bad," he said when Saphie had expressed shock at the concept of people being kept to be donors. "We have a good life. We're well looked after and we don't have to worry about bills or food or any of that stuff. And many people are never used anyway."

Our meals arrived and as usual Arthur's enthusiastic menu turned out to be really quite good. I'd opted for the barbecued prawns with rice and peas while both Saphie and Eric had gone for the Cajun Chicken.

"I went out of the kitchen door today," I announced as I mopped grease from my fingers. "It's very different."

"When are you going to go find Tania?" asked Saphie.

"Oh, that."

"Yes, that. You need to find her. You can't just leave her wandering around a strange world with no clue how it happened or any idea how to get back."

"I'll need to arrange some money first, I haven't got enough holiday euros for that. And I'll need a car, I won't be able to get mine through the patio doors." That should give me a couple of days breathing space.

"I'll be able to get you some currency," Eric offered. "Once I can get through to the other side it will be an easy job to change your notes into anything you like."

“That’s the plan then,” said Saphie. “You help Eric with the doors and he’ll change the money, then you can go find Tania.”

A tall black man with long dreadlocks wobbled onto the pallet and picked up the microphone. “Hiya y’all. You guys chillin’?” He pressed a button on the amplifier and the metronomic thump of a huge base beat vibrated our table. “I got some bad tracks for you dudes with some wicked grooves, man. Yo muthus gonna rip it up.”

“What’s happening?” asked Eric, his eyes wide.

“I think it’s time to go,” I suggested.

We finished our drinks and headed through the door with the sounds of a hybrid reggae rap following us as we went.

Saphie left for home almost soon as we arrived back at the cottage. I poured myself a nightcap and introduced Eric to the delights of Newsnight.

“So, what have you been doing for the last four years?”

“In what your sticky note calls Universe Five. Outside the kitchen door.”

“I went there today,” I said, feeling quite pleased with myself.

“I know, you told me.”

“What’s it like, living there?”

“Hell,” he said. “Absolute hell. It’s all so chaotic. No order. Everybody seems to do whatever they like.”

“Why did you stay there?”

He looked at me with a slightly quizzical expression. “Because somebody sealed up the door and trapped me there!”

“Oh, sorry. But that wasn’t me. I’ve only just come here. I’m the person that opened it again.” I emptied my gin glass and contemplated going for a refill.

"I tried to work to gather some money and just hoped that one day the door would open again. But it's impossible to save money there, everything's so expensive."

He was beginning to look forlorn again. "Anyway, we'll get to work on the cellar doors tomorrow and you can go find Katrina." He seemed to brighten a bit so I left him with the television and headed for bed.

Chapter Twelve

WORK ON THE CELLAR DOORS went well. Eric kept up a furious pace and by the time I returned from B&Q with a set of three doors he already had the openings at the top and bottom of the newly exposed steps squared off and ready. I insisted on the doors being in place and lockable before I would let him venture to the other end of the cellar to create the exit. I'd made that mistake before with the kitchen door and I had no desire for a random stream of characters from his world coming up the steps to my library. They all sounded way too odd for my liking.

Once the doors were fixed we rigged up a light on an extension lead. The cellar was huge. It seemed to run the full length of the cottage although only about a quarter the depth. The far end wall, which would be about under the dining room, contained a lumpy brickwork section the same shape and size as a doorway.

"There it is," Eric said.

"Why can't somebody on the other side just punch a new hole through?" I asked.

"It doesn't work. It was tried many times with your kitchen door. It winds up just going through the kitchen wall in that universe. For some reason the doorways can only be created from this side."

I ran my hand over the brickwork. "I need another sticky note." I counted on my fingers. "This one is eight."

Eric gave me a strange look. "I'll start on this one then?" He picked up the pickaxe and swung it at the wall.

I went upstairs and made us both a sandwich. He reappeared shortly after and announced he was through, now it just needed tidying up. As we sat and ate I realised it was gone one o'clock and I hadn't had my midday beer yet. I pulled a couple of cans of Budweiser from the cupboard and put them on the table.

"Have a try," I said and slid one towards him then opened the other for myself. "The rules don't apply here."

He picked up the can and studied it. "Not today," he said and slid it back towards me.

We ate in silence then both set to work on the doorframe with one of us keeping watch on the stairs leading to his world. He tried to convince me that nobody from the other side would notice yet but it pays to be paranoid I've learned.

Eventually we had a series of three lockable doors, one at each end of the cellar and the other at the top of the steps in the library. I didn't exactly feel safe, given what he'd told me about his world, but I could live with it until he'd retrieved his wife and I could brick them up again.

"When do you want to go through?" I asked him.

"Now," he said.

By the time I'd found him the money he had changed back into the green fatigues with the orange circle he'd been wearing when I'd first caught him trying to find the cellar door. I gave him the money and wished him luck then saw him through the doors, locking each one securely. He had keys to each one so he could come back when he was ready.

Suddenly the cottage felt empty, even the cats seemed to have disappeared. I contemplated going up to The Camelot then decided I couldn't be bothered and settled for a packet of biscuits in front of the afternoon movie on Channel Four. There was nothing I could do about finding Tania until Eric returned with some currency I could use to get around in Universe Two. If he returned. I just had to wait.

I glanced out through the patio doors into that other world and wondered how she was getting on. It was then I recalled looking through these doors from the other side. The Spanish cleaning woman I'd frightened half to death. I smiled at the thought then froze.

The picture! The second time I'd looked through those doors from outside I'd seen a picture that seemed familiar. A boy playing with a dog, a black and white Labrador. Of course I remembered that picture, it was me aged five! This didn't make sense. I replayed the encounter with the mad Spanish woman and things started to come together. What was it she'd said about Aunt Flora? "Senora Flora lives here. Not you."

I tried to dismiss the explanation that was staring me in the face and thrashed about for a more rational conclusion. The obvious explanation stopped staring me in the face and took to beating me round the head. What was it Holmes used to say? 'When you've eliminated the impossible, whatever remains, no matter how improbable, must be the answer. But what if the impossible solution really is the only answer? What then?

Time to look into another box, Ian.

I left the house through the front door and headed round the side between the wall and the garage. I came to the garden that I hadn't yet cleared and the patio doors through which I'd seen the Spanish woman and the picture. This universe I'd mentally labelled as Universe Seven. Only mentally, as the physical act of sticking a Post It note on the outside of a door had proved problematical as it kept falling off. I peered through the doors. There was the picture of me and... what was the dog's name? Sam, that was it. The lounge looked so different to my version I wondered why I hadn't noticed it first time. Trinkets and ornaments adorned most surfaces and glass cabinet filled with chinaware stood against the far wall.

The room was however, devoid of people. What had I expected? It had been a stupid idea. I pushed at the door to see if it would open. It was locked. Should I knock? As it happened, I didn't need to. Obviously having heard someone at the door, the woman had come to investigate. She was small and slightly stooped, her hair white and tied into a bun. Just the way I remembered her. She froze when she saw me at the doors and we stared at each other for what seemed like minutes. Eventually she seemed to regain her powers of movement and opened the door.

"Aunt Flora?" I said. "It is you isn't it? But how?"

"Hello, Ian. My, you've grown! Come along inside, dear. You'll catch your death of cold standing out there."

I followed her into the lounge. "I thought you were... well, actually we all thought you were..."

"Rumours of my demise, as Oscar Wilde once said. I've just put the kettle on and I've got some nice treacle tart put by. I know how much you like that."

I stood in the centre of the lounge, Aunt Flora's lounge,

not mine, and looked around. Many of the ornaments I'd remembered from my childhood were here. The china peasant girl, the small brass lattice bell with a ruby coloured clapper. "What happened?" I asked.

"It's a bit of a tale and that's for sure," she said. "Why don't you just sit yourself down and I'll fetch the tea. Oh, by the way, your birdseed's on the sideboard."

I settled into an overstuffed armchair and glanced at the sideboard. A packet of birdseed sat on top of it. Of course, I'd left it in here when I'd first seen the Spanish cleaner. I'd thought she'd stolen it. Next to the birdseed stood a silver framed photograph of my aunt with someone who appeared to be Roger Moore.

She returned with a silver tray and fine Wedgewood service and placed them on the small table. "There we are," she said. "Shall I be mother?"

"Is that...?" I said, pointing at the picture.

"Yes, dear. That's Roger. My husband. Now, tell me how you've been getting on." She started pouring the tea. "I heard you had a nasty turn?"

I related the story of how Tania and I had come to split up and my breakdown. She made suitably sympathetic noises.

"But what about you?" I asked. "How come you're still... still... well, you know, here." I suddenly felt slightly angry that we'd all been deceived.

"I just wanted to retire, dear. I'd been here for a very long time and when young Roger came along, well, who could resist?"

"Retire? Retire from what? I thought you had already retired."

"Oh no, dear. Gatekeepers don't usually retire. It's

supposed to be a lifetime commitment. A bit like vicars, I suppose."

"What do you mean, Gatekeeper?" I juggled teacup on delicate saucer whilst trying for a slice of treacle tart. Aunt Flora's homemade treacle tart.

"The doors! All those doors. The coming and going, it all gets a bit much after a while. Especially when that blessed Wikidoors business started up. That was the final straw."

Wikidoors? I remembered those young women in The Kings Head in Universe Five talking about that. "What's Wikidoors?" I asked.

"Wikidoors? An abomination, that's what Wikidoors was. Everybody has a right to be famous with no consideration for rest of us and Dopples getting everywhere they shouldn't." Her hands started shaking and she grabbed the arms of the chair to control them.

"Dopples?"

"Dopples, Doppelgangers, people who look like other folks but aren't. In this door, out that one. Another piece of treacle tart?"

"Oh, yes, thank you."

"So when Roger Moore turned up one day, he just whisked me off my feet. Well, he would, wouldn't he? I mean, what girl could resist those eyes? Anyway, he helped me seal up the doors and windows and we retired here where none of the buggers can find me."

"I'm sorry, I'm still not understanding this business about dopples?"

She gave me the look I remembered only too well from childhood. The one that says, 'Have I really got explain about not eating the purple berries again?'

"Dopples, my dear. Dopples are what you get when you have infinite universes. Give an infinite number of idiots an infinite number of universes to play in and sooner or later one of them will turn up as president of America."

"Or of Europe," I said.

"What? Oh, yes. I see."

She went on to explain about the doors. Some of which I had already managed to deduce with help from Saphie and Eric, but much was new. The universe was made up of infinite parallel universes and Tinker's cottage sat on a point where the many of these actually broke through. The anomaly had always existed in our universe, but only ours. The cottage had been built on the site of an earlier stables and before that, who knew. But a building of some sort had always existed there to control the accesses. In many of these universes, alternate versions of individuals existed and people would drift around to find out what their dopples were doing in alternate universes. Aunt Flora, it seems, had been the Gatekeeper. Her job had been to keep some sort of order and prevent potential troublemakers.

"But what is it with all the famous people, or at least their... what do you call them? Dopples?" I asked.

"I blame Andy Warhol," Aunt Flora said. "Everybody was going to be famous for fifteen minutes. All of a sudden we have this whole fame business going on and it's not enough anymore to discover that your other self is a butcher in an alternate world, people want to find their rich and famous version."

"But surely Tinker's Cottage only links to a few universes at best. After all, there's only a very small number of doors or windows?"

"Go in one door, out another, in through a window, out through the first door and all of sudden you're four steps away from where you started. Keep that up for ten minutes and the potential universes already numbers in the thousands. The permutations are truly infinite."

I struggled with the image of this grey haired, elderly woman opposite me as she poured tea and spoke of cosmic infinities. My Aunt Flora, cosmic gatekeeper.

"But until Wikidoors came along it was all fairly random," she continued. "It could take centuries to find a rich or famous version of yourself."

"What is this Wikidoors?" I asked.

"There used to be a door from the kitchen that led to a version of Britain run by anarchists. Anything goes, quite disgraceful. Did you know they even held general elections via television game shows?"

It struck me that wasn't that far removed from what we had. It also struck me that perhaps I ought to own up to reopening the kitchen door. Instead, I just opted for, "Dreadful!" and hid my eyes in my teacup.

"Some computer whizz geeky person sent some beetly creepy things through the universes. Like these search pages on your computer?"

"Spiders? You mean search engine spiders?" I suggested.

"Yes, that's the ones. He sent these spiders out that crawled the universes and compiled a massive list of who was where. Called it Wikidoors. Now you could just look on the internet and see where all your dopples were and how to find them. Dreadful mess!"

"So everybody wants to meet their successful selves? Why's that so bad?"

“Not just meet, dear. Replace.”

I supped at my tea as I tried to think through the implications of her statement. People hunting down rich and famous versions of themselves to take their place. Instant fame and fortune. Beats trying to audition with Simon Cowell I supposed.

“Did that happen a lot?” I asked, wondering if I should try to warn Stephen Fry.

“Well, we never worried too much about the Elvis Presleys or the Freddy Mercurys, most of them just ended up working in bars anyway. It’s the Osama Binladens that are a bit more problematical. We lost a George Bush once. Gas station worker from Idaho. Oddly elusive for a High School dropout with an IQ below his hat size.”

“What happened to him?”

“Lost him completely. He’s still out there somewhere.”

“I think I might know where he is,” I said.

“American presidents were always a problem though. Don’t know why. Most of them ended up just getting shot anyway. The crunch finally came with The Amazing Blair, a magic act who specialised in mesmerising a whole audience into believing he was the second messiah who was going to rid the world of tyrants and bring peace to the Middle East. Funny when you think about it.”

I checked my watch, it was gone six. “I need to get back; I have a friend coming round.” I hoped at least.

Aunt Flora replaced her plate on the tray and dabbed at the corners of her mouth with a serviette. “Well, now you know where I live, pop round anytime. You must meet Roger. He’s such a lovely boy.”

I left through the patio doors and returned to my world.

* * * * *

Saphie arrived just after seven and I made us both supper. At least Sainsbury's made us supper of French stick, instant salad and a selection of cheeses in a plastic box.

Afterwards we decided to take advantage of the late May evening and go for a walk. We headed up into the woods behind the village. A path led us through both ancient woods and modern fir plantations. It was nice not to see any obvious signs of which universe we were in. No anomalies or surprises. Woods were a timeless and placeless constant. A bit like Old Grumbler.

"So," Saphie said, trying to get to grips with what I'd told her about Aunt Flora. "She just sealed up the troublesome doors and left?"

"That's pretty much it. Roger Moore's dopple turned up one day, it was all hearts and flowers and so she decided to retire. They had to go somewhere where Roger wasn't known so they just moved in through the patio doors."

"Roger Moore?" Saphie mused. "Do you think Johnny Depp's out there somewhere?" She gave me a mischievous grin.

We sat for a while in a small meadow where the woods opened up over a view of the levels with Glastonbury Tor in the distance. Everything looked so normal. I'd brought a bottle of wine with me and we shared it as the sun cast its final embers across the sky. As the evening began to cool the warmth from her body drew me like a moth to the flame and we fell into each other's embrace.

Chapter Thirteen

SAPHIE STAYED OVERNIGHT AND THE following morning we were interrupted during our toast and coffee by a knock on the front door. I answered it with my usual trepidation to find Aunt Flora on the doorstep.

"Good morning, dear. Just thought I'd pop by to see how you're settling in. It's so nice we're going to be neighbours."

I invited her through to the kitchen and introduced her to Saphie.

"You probably don't remember me," Saphie said. "I run The New Dawn in town."

"Oh yes, dear," Flora said. "Of course I do. Lovely shop. I often used to... What have you done?" Her voice turned to shock and I realised she'd just noticed the new door.

"Ah," I said. "I meant to mention that."

"But they'll be all over the place again," she said. She turned to Saphie. "They get everywhere you know."

"So Ian told me," said Saphie.

"They're a menace, especially the religious ones. We lost a barely literate bible thumping, bear shooting teenage girl from Alaska once. Apparently she managed to switch places with an American politico on the rise. Dreadful mess, dreadful. Not going to tell you where she ended up. You'd never believe it."

"I just might," I said.

"You have to close it up again before anything terrible happens."

"There's only a few people gone through," I said and gave her a quick run down of those I could remember.

She didn't seem concerned about Stephen Fry, David Beckham or even The Queen. It was the little elderly man who concerned her most.

"What did you say his name was?"

"Bergoglio I think," I said. "George Bergoglio. He said everybody called him Boggy."

She went very still. "Where did he go?"

I tried to remember the encounter. "Out through the patio doors in the lounge," I said. "Why? Who is he?"

"George Bergoglio didn't ring any bells? Jorge Bergoglio? Pope Francis?"

"The Pope?" I heard Saphie say.

"Ah, that Jorge Bergoglio," I said

"Yes," said Aunt Flora. "That Jorge Bergoglio. Only in the universe from which he came, he's a retired market trader from Clapham."

"Well that's not too bad is it?" I asked.

"No, except that in his world he's a Spiritist. He's been trying to slip through that door for years."

"A Spiritualist?"

"A Spiritist," said Saphie. "It's a major, and very old, religion in Brazil. I've got some books on it in the shop. Brazil, of course, that's where his family come from. Anyway, Spiritists believe in God but also reincarnation and spirits floating about doing... spirit stuff."

"Oh," I said. "I can see why that might be a problem."

"Can you imagine the trouble that would cause if he manages to get in The Vatican? We'd have hippies running the church." Aunt Flora said.

"Dan Brown would have a field day," suggested Saphie.

I glared at her. "Not helping, Saphie."

She grinned back at me.

"You have to find him," Aunt Flora said.

"I have to find him?" I was incredulous. "Why me? I'm not the one that just wandered off. Aren't their rules about this sort of thing? Aren't there Timelords or something to stop this stuff going on?"

"You might be getting this confused with Doctor Who," Saphie said,

I gave her another of my best glares. Not easy when staring into those eyes. "Still not helping, Saphie."

"I sealed up the doors before I left," said Aunt Flora. "You reopened them."

"Not all of them. But what about the American tourists who stayed here then disappeared? That wasn't my fault."

"Oh piff-poff" she said. "Don't be such a fusspot. What does it matter if the odd American tourist disappears? It's not as if there's a shortage of them. But a Pope is a different matter. You can't go around mislaying Popes. Especially not Spiritist ones."

"But I've got a literary agent to find," I pleaded. "Haven't I, Saphie?"

"I'm not getting involved," she said. "I've a shop to open." She gathered up her small rucksack that seconded as a handbag, pecked me on the cheek and left me with a "Talk later."

I stared at Aunt Flora in silence. She had always been quite strict and although I had a great deal of affection for her, I had always found her slightly intimidating. As I did now.

"Well, I can't go until Eric comes back with some money," I said eventually, realising immediately that was probably a mistake. Maybe she wouldn't pick up on it.

"Eric?" she said. "Tell me about Eric."

* * * * *

Saphie phoned at lunchtime to let me know she wouldn't be able to come over that evening. I felt more of a sense of disappointment than I was entirely comfortable with. I spent the afternoon trawling the internet for information about Pope Francis and gathering some photographs. Trying to find pictures of him without his Pope uniform on was not easy. Excluding, that is, the ones that were obviously the work of perverts with hooky copies of Photoshop and way too much time on their hands.

That evening I gathered the last of my holiday euros together and left the house through the patio doors. I headed first for the King's Head where I ordered a pint of Old Grumbler and showed Albert the pictures of Tania and George Bergoglio.

"I remember her," he said. "She was in here a few days ago. Had some of that old money like you did."

"Do you know where she went?"

"Got quite agitated she did. Said she had to go to Cornwall to see her sister. I think she went to Glastonbury to see if she could change some money."

I hawked the pictures around the village. The woman

behind the counter in the general stores remembered Tania. She'd been sympathetic to her and changed some of her old sterling into euros.

"Don't expect the banks'll honour it though," she said. "You know what they're like. Ever since they were all taken over by the Bundesbank it's like trying to deal with a flock of sheep with OCD."

Nobody had seen George. I guessed he might be a bit more prepared than Tania and may well have currency already or at least something to trade. He might be harder to find.

I headed home and decided that I would brave Universe Two's version of Glastonbury tomorrow to see if I could pick a lead on either of them.

* * * * *

In the morning there was still no sign of Eric returning and I was beginning to wonder if he'd done a runner with my money. I left through the patio doors and headed to the King's Head. A bit early for a drink, even for me but I needed information so I steeled myself to the task. Sacrifices sometimes need to be made. I chatted with Albert and explained my problem with a missing ex girlfriend.

"She's suffering from depression and I'm worried. I think she's gone into town only my car's off the road at the moment."

Albert kindly offered to lend me his van for the morning and I set off to Glastonbury in the hope of finding some sort of trail on George and Tania before I'd exhausted the last of my euros. As soon as I left Trembly I noticed the cameras. Speed cameras I'd grown used to, but here there were cameras watching every junction or pedestrian crossing. There were even cameras that watched other cameras. I wasn't sure whether that meant some cameras were not to be trusted or if it was simply protection against vandalism. Each camera had a little sign attached that read, 'Keeping an eye on your safety.'

As I approached Glastonbury I noticed a proliferation of road signs appearing. Some told me to ensure I kept my distance from other road users while others told me mind the cyclists or the pedestrians or the turning lorries. Traffic lights sprouted from every junction making my drive through the outskirts of the town feel like wading through treacle. I finally found myself in a convoluted one-way system that spat me out back on the road to Trembly. I gave up and parked in a side road on a green line. I hadn't the faintest idea what that signified but it seemed less serious than parking on red ones, yellow ones or even the strange purple wriggly ones.

Even the pavements came with their share of signs though. Apparently the council took no responsibility for tripping on raised paving stones or slipping on leaves. Crossing roads can be hazardous, road signs contain flashing lights and passing traffic can be loud and may cause hearing damage. At one point I came across two workmen working in a 'Person Hole' in the pavement and had to wait until the 'Hole Attendant' escorted a group of us past in convoy. It took me back to my primary school days of 'The Crocodile' and I found myself tempted to hold hands with the person next to me. .

I eventually found my way to the bank at the bottom of the hill. In my universe it had been Lloyds, but here it was something called Banque de Europe (UK) PLC. I stepped inside and made my way through the metal detector, having first had to leave my shoes and belt with a seven foot security guard. I joined the snaking queue that coiled round the hall and wasted the next half hour of my life holding up my jeans and shuffling forwards six inches each time I heard, "Teller number sixteen, please." It was always teller number sixteen as there was only one window open.

My turn came to cross the hallowed white line and stand in front of the bullet proof glass and tiny speaker that crackled at me unintelligibly.

"I'm trying to locate a man who might have been in here," I shouted at the little microphone.

"Do you have an IPC7615?" the speaker asked.

"No, sorry. Only he might be lost and—"

"You need an IPC7615 before we can release information pertaining to individuals who may or may not have entered these premises."

"But he might be lost," I repeated then immediately felt a pair of concrete hands clasp around my shoulders.

"You need to leave now, sir," the security guard said as he guided me to the door.

I found myself standing outside the bank in my socks and still holding up my jeans. I contemplated going back in to retrieve my belt and shoes but thought better of it.

I shuffled up the street to the next bank that also seemed to be a branch of Banque de Europe (UK) PLC. So much for open market economies. Fearing this time I might lose both my socks and trousers if I attempted going in I gave up the idea of trying to trace George or Tania by the banks and wandered aimlessly up the High Street. Many of the shops I remembered from my Glastonbury had vanished. Gone were the Wiccan Treasure Store, the Crystal Gazer and Mysts of

Avylyon only to be replaced by faceless insurance brokers and Ezee-Money Payday Loans. Only one shop stubbornly and incongruously remained. I stepped cautiously through the entrance of New Dawn and froze. Inside it was exactly the same as the one in my Glastonbury. Was this was another doorway? I stepped back outside then in again.

"Hello, Ian," a voice came from the back. "I've been expecting you."

Saphie appeared from behind a shelf of Gothic greetings cards.

"What? How? I don't understand." Not my most intelligent greeting for sure.

"I just knew you'd be coming. It's the crystal."

I reached into my pocket and my hand found the small blue stone. I withdrew it and stared at it as it sat in the palm of my hand. Glowing.

"But how can you be…? You're in the other Glastonbury?"

She looked puzzled. "What other Glastonbury?"

"The one with you in it," I said then immediately realized that wasn't very helpful. "Through the patio doors. Where it's Lloyds bank and not Banque Europe or whatever." I stalled for a moment then added, "Where you gave me this." I held out the crystal.

"I gave you that? That doesn't sound like me."

"You said it belonged to me already and that you'd been looking after it."

"Ah, that sounds more like me."

I gazed around the shop. The layout was the same however there were a few differences. Different pictures on the walls, a lack of the more erotic ones certainly and a plethora of official looking notices behind the counter. I strained my eyes to see. They seemed mostly concerned with health and safety warnings regarding the efficacy of herbal remedies.

"So, how does this work?" I asked.

"Sorry?" she said. "How does what work?"

"This," I waved my hand around the shop. "And you, being here and there at the same time?"

Saphie squinted her eyes in obvious puzzlement. "I'm not sure I know what you mean. I don't know of any other place and I certainly haven't seen a Lloyds Bank for fifteen years." She paused as if in mid thought, then, "And patio doors really aren't my thing."

"But you knew about the crystal. And my name." I was more confused now than since I had first tried to get a handle on the magpies.

"I get feelings, sort of messages, they come from my inner self. We all have an inner self, if only we will open our soul and listen. I have a book on it somewhere" She thumbed a nearby rack and pulled a slim volume from the shelf and gave it to me. "That'll give you a start."

"Thank you," I studied the cover. 'The Eyelids of Perception. A Manual for the Soul.'

"That will be ten euros fifty. Anything else you'd like?"

"Erm… no, thank you."

"I've got some nice hessian rope sandals." She nodded towards my feet.

"Oh, yes. I suppose they might be useful. Do you have anything in a size eleven?"

She smiled that same smile I had come to know so well. "One size only. The Initoban Indians haven't quite grasped European sizing conventions yet."

I slipped them on my feet. They felt quite comfortable. "I don't suppose you've got a belt have you?"

"Might not be quite your style but it will do the job." She selected the least ornate belt from a nearby rack. It consisted of braided leather thongs with beads and feathers.

"Thanks." I slipped it through the loops on my jeans and tied it together.

"Very fetching." Saphie ran the numbers through the till. "Thirty-three euros seventy altogether then."

I dragged the last of my holiday euros out and placed them on the counter. A ten, a twenty and a few odd coins. "Sorry, that's all I have."

She picked up the twenty and studied it. "These are old. Don't get out much?"

"Something like that. Can I pay the rest next time?"

"Don't worry." She pushed my crumpled notes back towards me and folded my hands around them. "I have a feeling there's more between you and I than I understand at the moment."

I felt the familiar warmth in her hands and longed to pull her close. But this wasn't my Saphie. Not quite.

"Thank you, I'll pop in next time." I wondered if Eric had my money yet. "Tomorrow, with a bit of luck."

"We're intertwined somewhere so I'm sure my thirty-three euros seventy is safe." Her eyes caught mine and something sparked between us. Confused, I said goodbye and headed back up the high street in the hope of finding some trace of Tania or George.

Although Glastonbury appeared to have been homogenised there were still traces of the counter culture that made the town feel so different from any other in England. I wandered up to the top of The Tor in the vague hope that high ground would somehow reveal some answers. Oddly enough, that is exactly what happened.

* * * * *

A group of people stood around the tower and I moved closer to see what was happening. I pushed my way through and saw that the focus of attention was a man in a white cloak and holding a large wooden staff. For a moment my senses jumped as I thought it might be George. But the man was too tall and about thirty years younger. He was holding court with his improvised and enraptured audience.

"I'm telling you, he's been there for the last three days."

"How can you be sure it's him?" A man in jeans and a blue sweatshirt asked. "Isn't he still in Rome?"

"I'm only telling you what I saw. As clear as I stand here, Pope Francis." The man made the sign of the cross across his chest in a weak attempt at the Catholic sign.

"What's he doing here?" somebody else asked.

"I don't know. How would I know? All I'm saying is that he's been there, kneeling by King Arthur's grave."

I pushed forward a bit. "What time was he there? I asked.

The man in the cloak looked at me and paused. He tipped his head to one side is if in concentration. I felt as if he realized I didn't quite belong here. "Dawn," he said eventually. "Just as the sun tips the Tor."

I thanked the man and made way down the Tor. George, what are you up to? It surely can't be any good whatever it is.

I found my way back to Albert's van. It was still parked on its green line. I'd half wondered if The Green Police or some such might have towed it away for transgressing an obscure European rule on green lines. But no, just a flyer on the windscreen that thanked me for being a Green and Considerate citizen.

I returned the van to Albert with many thanks and headed home. Whilst remembering to go in through the patio doors I wondered for a moment what I'd find if I entered through the front door. Would that be Nine?

* * * * *

That evening Saphie came over and we adjourned to The Camelot for supper. Arthur had decided that his international theme nights were the way forward so had headed for Germany and tonight, despite being mid June, was Oktoberfest. Not being a country widely regarded for its cuisine the menu consisted primarily of sausages in rolls with various sauces. Although there was a plentiful supply of sauerkraut and chips. A German flag hung behind the bar and oompah music drifted around the room. Arthur greeted us with "Guten Morgen, Vat does sie vant?" He wore lederhosen and a Hitler moustache.

For a moment I was rendered incapable of either speech or movement as I took in the full horror of the scene. It was only when I heard Saphie struggling to suppress fits of giggles that the spell broke.

"Beer?"

"Ah Gut! Ve have lots of ze special beers tonight as zis is bierkeller nacht!" He swept his arms across the bar. He had indeed outdone himself with the choice. A host of Bavarian ales jostled for my attention and demanded sampling. I chose a Dortmunder and Saphie a Rothaus, because she liked the cute picture on the bottle.

After placing our orders for food we settled at my favourite table by the window.

"Still no sign of Eric then?" Saphie asked.

"No, I'm worried he's disappeared with my money."

"I wouldn't think so. He seems very straight." Saphie took a sip of her Rothaus. "Ooh, that's nice. I could grow to like this one."

"Be careful, that's quite strong."

"Worried I might let my inhibitions slip and let you take advantage?" She smiled coyly across the top of the glass.

"I had a weird experience today," I said.

"Okay, so my charms are fading already?"

"Sorry." I reached for her hand. "Bit preoccupied. Let's talk about your charms and inhibitions, or lack thereof."

She withdrew her hand in mock affront. "No. Lost your chance. Tell me about your weird experience."

I took a sip of my beer. "I met your dopple today. Only I'm not sure it was a dopple."

"It?"

"Sorry, she… you. You were you as well as your dopple. Both. If that makes sense."

"Perfectly!" She took a sip of beer and smiled.

Arthur brought our food, a hamburger with sauerkraut for Saphie and a currywurst with chips for me. The sauce was delicious. I went on to explain what had happened and she became increasingly interested.

"I've always felt a sort of connection with other souls, entities. I just didn't realise they might be alternate versions of me! What fun. Was she cute?"

"Er…" I wasn't sure how to answer that. It felt a bit like a trap. "How could she not be?" I looked into her eyes, they were full of mischief.

"Fancy a threesome?" she asked.

She caught me mid-sip and my laugh exploded Dortmunder over the table. I mopped at it with a paper napkin.

Arthur returned with two more beers that I hadn't remembered ordering. He placed a Tucher in front of Saphie and a Bockbier in front of me. "With the compliments of the gent at the bar," he said.

I glanced over to see who our benefactor was. The unmistakable figure of Eric in his green overalls with the orange circle stood at the bar. He looked somewhat like a trustee from Guantanamo Bay. He picked up his own drink and plate and carried them over to us and sat down.

I held up my beer towards him. "Thanks." I realized that the beer I held was not the one Arthur had placed in front of me. I looked at Saphie.

"What?" she said with a slightly guilty expression then looked at the bottle in her own hand. "Oh, this. Hmm, I preferred the picture on this one. Look, it's two people sitting on a goat. How cool is that!"

"Very cool." I squinted at the bottle. 12% ABV. I glanced at Eric who just shrugged.

"How did it go?" I asked him.

He reached into a plastic Tesco bag he'd been carrying and dumped a pile of euros on the table in front of me. Notes of all denominations fluttered on the table and threatened to blow away. I gathered them up. Tens, twenties, fifties even some hundreds and each one displaying the smiling face of Supreme President Cherie Blair.

I turned to Saphie. “All set then. Looks like I’m off through the looking glass tomorrow.”

We finished our meals and headed back. Much to my disappointment, Saphie collapsed into slumber as soon as she hit the futon. Eric and I chatted for a while about his exploits in Universe Eight. He told me he’d paid over the money to ensure the safe passage of Katrina and that he was going back in the morning to meet with the intermediary who would take him to her. I wished him luck and set about helping a dozing Saphie up the stairs and into bed. I lay there for a while wondering what tomorrow would bring. I had funds now and a clear lead on George but still no sign of Tania. I would probably have to make my way down to Cornwall to her sister’s and with luck, I might find her there.

Chapter Fourteen

MY ALARM CLOCK BUZZED ME into life at four a.m. I reached for the off button as quickly as possible to avoid disturbing Saphie. The buzzing silenced, I glanced at Saphie. I needn't have worried she was still in the arms of German beers. I stumbled downstairs. This was an ungodly hour but if I wanted to catch George I needed to be in Glastonbury around sunrise. I had a quick shower, several cups of coffee and abandoned a piece of toast after one mouthful. The human body is not designed to digest food at this time in the morning. I dragged my bicycle out of the garage and pushed it through the house and out of the patio doors.

I wobbled up the lane following the puddle of totally ineffectual light dumped in front of me by the high tech LED headlamp. I'd never ridden in the dark. Although bicycles were the only sensible means of transport in London of course it never gets dark there so there'd been no need to test out the lighting system before.

I actually reached Glastonbury in shorter time than when I'd taken Albert's van. Not having to navigate complex one-way systems or wait at traffic lights makes life simpler and these obstacles are merely voluntary to the cyclist. We understand this in London. I chained my bike to the railings outside the Abbey and ventured into the ruins. The approaching sun smudged reds and oranges above the Tor and cast long shadows from the Abbey ruins. I closed my mind to the creatures that lived in the shadows and wove my way to the knave where King Arthur's grave lay.

The figure knelt by the side of the grave. He was dressed in a white cloak, similar to the one the man on the Tor had been wearing. He held his hands clasped together in obvious prayer. I heard a movement slightly behind me and turned ready to fight the goblins. An elderly woman shuffled out of the shadows of the remains of the southern knave wall.

As she approached my position she asked me, "Is it him? Is it really him? His Holiness?"

"No," I said. "It's just an old man who looks a bit like him."

I moved closer. I could hear his low mumbles, it certainly sounded like prayers. "George?" I called softly. The mumbles stopped but the man didn't move. A Spiritist Pope dressed as a druid in the ruins of an English abbey praying to the grave of King Arthur. This was wrong on so many levels. "George," I called again.

I heard a voice behind me and turned. It was a small woman with a child in tow. "Be quiet," she said. "Let him pray."

"What? It's not him you know," I tried to explain but she wasn't listening. She fell to her knees pulling the child with her and started to pray.

A few more people had started to gather. If I didn't do something soon this was going to get out of hand and the police would likely turn up any minute. And whatever papers they were going to ask me for I was sure my library card wouldn't go very far. I moved forward and knelt beside George. He turned to look at me.

"Ah, the Gatekeeper," he said.

"What are you doing here, George?"

"Why, I'm tending the wounds of the past." He sounded slightly incredulous as if I should have realised.

I touched his shoulder. "Come on. We've got to go. The police will be here soon."

"I welcome them. That militia of the unjust. It is time we returned to the true path." He shrugged his shoulder free of my hand.

"Leave him alone," I heard someone call from the growing crowd.

I needed to take action. I grabbed his upper arm firmly and pulled him to his feet. A slightly awestruck murmuring washed over the assembly. "You've got to come with me." He felt frail under my grip as I guided him to a gap in the rear wall. I glanced over my shoulder and saw the people starting to move forward. All thoughts of goblins left my mind now as I fled the abbey grounds, if I wasn't quick this was going to be a good old fashioned lynching.

"Hey, he's kidnapping the Pope," I heard from behind me.

"Come on, George. We've got to get out of here." I dragged him half running, half stumbling across the gardens and fallen stones and into the bottom of the high street. A quick look behind me gave encouragement to my feet and I was now virtually pulling George up the hill of the High Street. We ducked into an alley, cut round the back of a car park and doubled back on the opposite side of the road from the Abbey. I risked a glance and saw about a dozen people heading up the High Street. All that was missing were the pitch forks and burning torches. George was wheezing badly so we slid into a narrow street and I helped him out of his robes and bundled them into a nearby wheelie bin. He tried to protest but he couldn't catch enough breath to speak. I led him down the street and we found an early morning café. We went inside and I ordered a couple of coffees.

"What on earth do you think you were doing?" I asked when we were sat down. "You trying to start another inquisition?"

"It's my purpose. My raison d'etre if you like." The vision of Pope Francis sat opposite me drinking coffee in a Greasy Spoon in Glastonbury and expounding pop philosophy was not doing any good for my state of mind. I closed my eyes hard and wiped my hands across my face before looking again. No, he was still there.

"I've got to take you back, you know that, don't you."

"Why is that?" He transferred some of the coffee into the saucer and slurped noisily at it.

"Because you're... You're..." I struggled to remember what Aunt Flora had said. "You're upsetting the timeline or something. I don't know. This is all bonkers to me anyway."

"I'll only run away again."

I pondered that for a moment. "Then I suppose I'll have to take you with me where I can keep an eye on you." Oh joy. What could be more wonderful than dragging a kidnapped Pope around Cherie Blair World in search of a misplaced literary agent?

"Where are we going?"

"Cornwall."

"Oh lovely. I've never been there."

* * * * *

It was nearly eight, so I hoped Glastonbury Car Hire would be open by now. It was. I approached the counter and the woman behind it greeted me with a smile.

"I'd like to hire a car for a couple of days please." I said.

We discussed models, although the total stock seemed to consist of either Renault or Citroen and I chose a cheap run around which in my world would have been a Clio only here it was a Martin.

"I need your license and your Driver's Personal Injury Waiver," she said.

Ah, I hadn't thought this one through. I patted my pockets as if that would magically make them appear. "I don't seem to…"

"Here, put it in my name." George placed a small pile of documents on the counter. The woman gathered them up and took them to a scanner on the desk behind her.

"Thanks," I muttered.

"Need to plan these things, my boy." He gave a self satisfied grin.

She returned with George's documents and placed them on the counter along with another pile of paper.

"That's all in order, mister Bergoglio. Here's the contract, your insurance, your temporary owner's form, our Faults Disclaimer, Your Roadworthiness Statement your…" The list went on and the pile of paper grew.

George gathered the papers together and they all fitted neatly in a medium sized box file the woman kindly provided. We were shown to the car by an attendant who laboriously pointed out the safety features of the vehicle, including airbags, foot brake, handbrake, seatbelts, toughened glass and a host of other trivia that just washed over me. The attendant then drove the car out of the compound and left us to it. As soon as I was sure we were not being observed, I climbed into the driver's seat and we set off. George grumbled that he should be driving as it was his license at stake but I ignored him.

* * * * *

Being early, the traffic was light and even allowing for two circuits of the one-way system and slowing down for each of the numerous speed cameras we made the motorway in good time and headed south for Cornwall.

"I was surprised they would hire a car to you," I said as I nudged the little Renault into the outside lane.

"Not allowed to discriminate on age here. Used to come here sometimes just so I could hire a fast car and have fun. Of course, that was before you closed the bloody door," he added, sulkily.

"It wasn't me. I didn't close the door. I opened it!"

"All gatekeepers. You're all…"

I glanced over to see why he'd stopped speaking in what appeared to be mid-grumble. He'd fallen asleep.

* * * * *

I settled into the drive and even started enjoying the scenery. Much was the same but the differences were striking. Speed limits changed seemingly randomly, signs warned of high winds, low flying aircraft, uneven surfaces and slippery when wet. The central barrier seemed to be plastic as opposed to the metal with which I was familiar.

"You need to pull over."

"You're awake then," I said.

"You've got to stop. I need a piss."

I glanced at my passenger. The Pope was struggling into wakefulness and fidgeting. "I can't stop, it's a motorway."

"You have to."

"Can't you hold on? There's some services coming up."

"Well put your foot down, there's a good lad."

"Yes, your Holiness."

We pulled into what I remembered as Taunton Deane Services but which were now labelled Eurostop Rest Park UKM5/25. I stopped as close to the toilets as I could and George scuttled over to them with remarkable agility for an eight-five year old pontiff. I waited for what seemed like ages and he eventually returned carrying a pair of cardboard cups.

"Bought us something to drink," he said and passed me a large mug with what looked for all the world like Coke but said Le Cola on the carton.

"Thanks." I stared at the murky, fizzing liquid.

"Keeps you awake," George said. "What you need on a long journey."

I placed the drink in the cup-holder and noted the warning sign on the holder telling me it is inadvisable to drink hot liquids in a moving vehicle. We set out once more southwards and I settled into the outside lane once more.

"So what's with the robes and King Arthur's grave?" I asked.

"He's the link. Arthur, The Druid Merlin, Glastonbury

Abbey, you see? It all points to me!" He drank his cola down and threw the cup into the back seat.

"No, I'm not sure I understand."

"In my world religion is dead. All that matters is the individual but in this one it's the State. I'm the only one who can reunite the spiritual cohesion of the universe."

"You? The spiritual welfare of the Multiverse is resting on the shoulders of a retired market trader from Clapham?" I looked at him. He was asleep again.

I drove on and wondered quite how I was going to find Tania. I just had to hope that her sister lived at the same address in this world. Or that she even had a sister here. Tania would have been totally bewildered when she found herself here. It must have seemed like a bad dream. But she was resourceful and would no doubt deal with the bureaucrats better than I could. She could be quite scary at times. I drove on and enjoyed watching this new world go by. The trucks were much bigger than the ones in my world and had access to all three lanes, which made for some interesting driving experiences at times. Especially as most of them seemed to be of East European origin. I checked my watch; we were making quite good time and would probably be in St Just by lunch time.

"You're gonna have to stop. I need a piss."

Or maybe not.

Chapter Fifteen

BY THE TIME WE REACHED Penzance, I felt I had visited every services on the M5 and A30. The roads had been familiar enough for me to recognise until we approached Penzance then it appeared as though a concrete swathe had been carved through the heart of the town. It certainly made for easier driving through the town but probably did little to enhance the lifestyle of the residents. The road north took us between continuous fields of poly-tunnel greenhouses, they looked like they were growing tomatoes. I parked in the square in the centre of St Just. Cape Road was a narrow street within a short walk of the village square. In fact, everywhere in St Just is a narrow street within a short walk of the village square. I hesitated to leave George alone in the car but he was fast asleep again so I decided to risk it.

Number twenty eight Cape Road was a tiny terraced cottage made of Cornish stone. Tania's sister Emma, had left the cut and thrust of Recruitment in the City and opted for the quiet life here some ten years ago. Of course, that had been in my world, not Cherie Blair World. I wondered if there could be enough similarities to cause the same thing to happen here. It was a long shot but it was the only lead I had. I knocked on the door and waited. No answer. I knocked again but there was still no answer. I checked my watch. It was just gone four so there was a chance she'd be out at work. I could try again later. Whatever happened, I would need to spend the night here so I headed back to the square.

The car was empty of course. George had obviously woken up and decided it was time he was on his way to who knows where again. I contemplated looking for him but he really could be anywhere. I had more pressing matters than scouring the countryside for an errant Pope, Tania had to take priority.

For such a small town the traveller is presented with a bewildering choice of places to stay. I chose The Smuggler's Haunt simply because I liked the name. The owner seemed somewhat surprised that I'd arrived without luggage and even more reluctant when I failed to produce my necessary Citizenship ID card. However, a quick exchange of the folding stuff reassured him and I was shown to my room. Some things are universal. Or should that be multiuniversal? The room was small but comfortable. A television sat in the corner, a kettle on the sideboard, a small armchair and a table lamp by the bed. Each carried little labels testifying they had recently been checked for electrical safety and fully complied with Energy Efficiency Directive 423001 part seven. A little instruction booklet told me how to switch on the table lamp in 35 different languages with dire warnings that this unit was not to be operated whilst under the influence of alcohol, narcotics, excess caffeine or whilst sitting in the bath.

Once settled, I headed over to the village store and stocked up on some essential toiletries and a bottle of gin then headed back down Cape Road to try number twenty eight again. Still no answer so I went back to the pub and ordered a pint of the local ale, after signing the necessary disclaimers of course. The menu looked basic but wholesome. I settled for a homemade potato soup and local crab salad. My attention was directed to a notice which informed me that homemade meant made within the walls of this establishment or other property owned by the proprietors and that local was defined as within waters not exceeding seven miles from the point of purchase. I also had to read and sign a disclaimer that I understood potato soup might contain ingredients that might not necessarily be defined as have origins in potatoes and that soup is hot.

When the meal eventually arrived though it was delicious and I sat at the window and watched the world go by. In many ways this village was similar to Trembly though more obviously geared to the tourist. After I'd finished I tried number twenty eight once more with no luck then settled down in my room. The only programme of any interest on the television was a comedy about an Iranian family living in Kensington. It seems they had won their version of the National Lottery and chosen Kensington as their dream location. Everybody loved everybody else and the show was a masterpiece in multiculturalist propaganda. It was also a masterpiece in boredom and I was asleep in the armchair within twenty minutes. I woke briefly at around midnight, showered in a lukewarm drizzle then settled into the softest mattress I'd ever experienced. It seemed to eat me up as I lay in it.

I awoke in the morning with a backache that the excuse for a tepid shower did little to alleviate. After dressing hurriedly I headed for twenty eight Cape Road, hoping to catch Tania's sister before she left for work. The door was answered by a large unshaven man wearing a tattered thick blue pullover and tracksuit bottoms. He filled the little doorway and blinked into the sunlight. This clearly wasn't Tania's sister.

"Er, hello. Sorry to disturb you, only I'm looking for a friend who I thought might live here?"

He gave unintelligible grunt. I had the feeling I'd just woken him.

"Emma Shapwick?"

"What is it, dear?" a voice called from inside the cottage.

"Fella 'ere lookin' for someone. You'd best talk to 'im." The man shuffled back into the darkness of the small corridor behind the front door.

A moment later a small woman appeared, she was dressed solely in a large white T-shirt. "Excuse Brian. He's not long been in," she said.

"I'm looking for Emma Shapwick," I said. "I think she used to live here?"

"Now, there's a thing now. There was a nice young lady round here asking the same thing. Not three days ago!"

My spirits lifted. "Do you know Emma Shapwick?"

"I'll tell it to you like I told it to her. There's no Emmas in this village. Shapwicks or not, they're ain't none."

"Oh," I said.

"Mind you, like I said to the lady, pretty young thing she was, she your friend? Like I said to her, there was an Emma Trevarick lived here not more'n ten year ago."

"Trevarick?"

"Only she came down from London too. Like your lady friend. You from London? You look like you're from London. Long time now mind. Only I got to thinking she might have been Shapwick afore she married young Lee. Lovely couple, Emma and Lee. Do you know Lee? And all those boys!"

I brightened again. "Where do they live?"

"Oh, they moved out. Bright girl that one. She saw the writing she did. Got out before the Fish Treaties killed everything stone dead."

"Got out?"

"Left the country. Just wish my Brian had been nearly so smart." She turned to face into the cottage. "Wouldn't be in 'alf the mess we're in now, you silly old sod."

A mumble reverberated out of the depths of the dark hallway.

"Never shift 'im from 'ere anyways," she continued. "Three generations in the churchyard and more to follow directly if'n the fishin' don't pick up soon."

"Abroad?" This was getting more and more complicated. I couldn't chase Tania round the world. "Where abroad?"

"The Islands, of course. You're as daft as 'im." She nodded her head into the house. "Where most of the fisherman with any brains went."

"Islands?"

"Scilly Islands. Soon as they went and declared independence Lee was off, along with 'alf the village."

I thanked the woman and headed back to the Smuggler's Haunt for breakfast. I needed to understand a bit more of what happened in this world but it did seem there was a good chance this world's version of Emma had moved to the Scilly Islands. Which probably meant Tania would have followed.

* * * * *

Breakfast at the Smuggler's was a meal designed to set one up for the day. Bacon, sausages, eggs, fried bread, mushrooms and a pile of beans so big that it ran off the edge of the plate as soon as I touched anything. I gave it my best attempt but in the end it defeated me and I pushed the half empty plate to one side.

"Never grow up to be a big strong lad if you don't eat all your breakfast up, you know." Mary, the owner, chef and general everything said as she cleared my plate away.

I patted my stomach. "Sorry." I smiled.

"Doing anything nice today? The weatherman says it'll be nice. Not that I believe 'em of course."

"I'm trying to find an old friend of mine. Think she might have moved to the Islands so I thought I'd go over there."

"The Island, huh. You'll need to book."

"Book?"

"The flight. Goes from the airport just down the road but they get booked up."

I thanked Mary, had another coffee then headed for the airport.

* * * * *

Land's End Airport consisted of a large field with a few buildings clustered at one end. I parked my car in the fenced car park and went into the booking hall. Security cameras bristled from every corner and guards in ominous black uniforms patrolled constantly. I was beginning to get the hang of this world so I patiently waited at the painted white line in front of the booking desk until called. Although I was the only person there the woman behind the security screen still managed to keep me waiting for ten minutes whilst she attended to obviously more pressing concerns. Eventually she called me forwards.

"I'd like to book a flight to St Marys please," I said.

"Just the one way?"

"Yes." I figured I'd sort out the flight back when necessary as I didn't know how long I'd be there.

She checked her computer screen. "First available seat is tomorrow at eleven twenty."

"Thank you. That's fine." I paid in cash and collected the pile of paper that I was now beginning to expect with every transaction in this world.

I returned to The Smuggler's Haunt and settled down in the bar and ordered a glass of Duvel. Mary brought it to my table and noted the pile of papers I had in front of me.

"Booked your ticket then," she said as she placed the frothing glass on a beer mat in front of me.

"Just trying to sort out how all this works." I pulled random pieces from the pile. Immigration forms, health statements, nationality status report plus the usual injury waiver forms and liability acceptance document.

"Got to keep Brussels happy," she said.

"But at least they make good beer." I picked up the Duvel and sipped gratefully.

"Just as long as you don't forget your passport or the buggers won't let you back in!" She gave a chuckle and wandered off.

Passport? I hadn't even considered the fact that I might need a passport. Although now it seemed obvious. If the Scilly Islands were an independent country it would be essential. Damnit! I scanned through the papers trying to find the relevant section. It took me fifteen minutes but eventually I located the bit I needed. Document IOS373B section 8 carried a list of requirements for both inbound and outbound passengers. Oddly enough a passport wasn't required to exit The United Kingdom, only to return. It seemed the Islanders weren't overly concerned with who went in and out of their country but of course the UK had very tight rules. That's what Mary had meant, once I'd left I couldn't get back in without a passport. That could prove problematical.

I toyed with the idea of giving up and heading home. If Tania was on the Isles then she was probably safe and I seemed to have lost the Pope again anyway. I thought of explaining that to Aunt Flora or Saphie and realised I would have to go on and attempt to bring at least one of them back. I asked Mary if there was anywhere I could get internet access as I wanted to research a bit more of the Isles before I got there. I thought it might save me some time. But apparently one has to register for internet access and then wait for three days for the Security Services Report before it is granted.

"It's all to do with these terrorists and baby dealers," she told me. "All for our own good they say. More to do with their bloomin' taxes shouldn't wonder."

I gave up and took a wander around the village, browsing in a few of the art and craft shops. After a stroll down to the Cape for a look at the Atlantic I headed back feeling suitably braced by the north winds and just about ready for supper. George was sat in the lounge bar of The Smuggler's when I entered.

"Oh, there you are," he said. "Wondering where you'd got to."

"Me? You disappeared on me!"

"Only went up on the moors to realign my chakras. They get all tilted when I spend too long cooped up. Like in a car or something. You found your girlfriend yet?"

"Realign your chakras? And she's not my girlfriend."

"Did you know the druids used to do human sacrifices just up there?" He waved his arm in a vague westerly direction. "They got stones, just like Stonehenge. Only smaller."

I settled into an overstuffed armchair near the fireplace. "I've got to go to The Scilly Isles tomorrow. Seems like Tania might be there."

"Nice place, the Scilly Isles. Had a girlfriend from there once. Ruby, that was her name, Ruby. Eyes like rubies too." He chuckled.

"Can I trust you to stay here?"

"Where would I go?"

"Oh, I don't know. I rather thought you might have a trip to Rome in mind at some point."

"Why would I do that? They've already got a Pope there. Now, if he was to fall of his perch, that'd be a different matter. That might create an opening for an enterprising individual with a bit of religious charisma!" He gave me a mischievous grin that would have had Machiavelli watching his back.

* * * * *

I spent the rest of the evening poring over maps and guidebooks of St Marys which I'd found in the bar. I hadn't really the first idea how to go about finding Tania once I'd got there and reading the books gave little in the way of clues apart from the fact that most of the population seemed centred around Hugh Town. One book, The History of The Scillys made for interesting reading though. It gave a detailed history of the islands right through ages up until the point of their secession from Europe in 2002 when it started to reveal its bias. It talked of the traitorous fishermen who deserted their heritage in favour of personal gain by emigrating there. The diatribe continued accusing the Islanders of stealing British territorial waters for their own fishing fleet and even providing a potential ingress point for terrorists to the mainland. I closed the book and looked at the back cover. 'Printed By The European Office For Information.' Goebbels would have been so proud.

Chapter Sixteen

THE PAPERWORK REGARDING THE FLIGHT had warned me to be in the departure lounge at least two hours before the flight time so I set off early in the morning. The journey to Lands End Airport only took a few minutes and I parked my car in the Long Term car park where sixty five cameras were busy keeping an eye on my safety. Although, just in case I might think for a moment the cameras would actually serve some useful purpose, a large notice informed me the airport took no responsibility for loss, accident, death or any other misfortune that may befall either my person or property.

The Check In desk was surprisingly efficient, perhaps due to the fact that I appeared to be the only passenger, and I followed the signs through to the departure lounge. For an airport that boasted only one flight a day, of less than twenty minute duration, the departure lounge was cavernous. An array of shops lined one side and food franchises on the other. It appeared I could buy a new laptop, designer perfume and a pair of socks then have a three course meal, or if feeling a little more frugal, I could settle for a paperback and a burger. I also appeared to be the only occupant of this particular corner of shopping hell. A big carved marble sign over the entrance doors announced ‘Redevelopment Funded by the Greater European Union’.

I settled down with a Starbucks coffee at one of a dozen empty tables. A departure board announced flight 2015A to St Marys would be departing at 11:20 and the departure gate would be announced in approximately one hour. It was the only flight listed on the board. And from what I could see, there only appeared to be one departure gate, Gate G, for some inconceivable reason.

I waited for ninety minutes and then the board changed to declare ‘Flight 2015A Delayed.’

A little while later an announcement came over the PA system, “Celtic International Airlines regrets to inform passengers on flight 2015A that this flight will be delayed by approximately fifty minutes. This is due to a baggage handlers dispute at Le Blair Airport, Paris. We would like to apologise for any inconvenience caused.”

The early morning finally caught up with me and I slid into a doze in one of the airport lounge chairs only to be dragged into wakefulness later by the squawking PA telling me it was “Last call for passengers on Flight 2015A boarding now at Gate G.” I picked up my bag and headed across the concourse to Gate G. I still appeared to be the only passenger.

Once through the gate, I noticed a little twin propeller driven aeroplane sitting on the grass runway. I stood at the barrier with my collection of paperwork in hand until safety barriers had been erected all around the aircraft and it was deemed safe for me to venture across the field to the waiting steps that had been erected.

A stewardess showed me to my designated seat, although I could probably have worked it out for myself as there were only eight seats and mine was number four. We sat there for a while until the captain spoke over the speakers. "Cabin Crew prepare plane for takeoff." The speakers were actually completely redundant as I could clearly hear him through the door not four feet away from me.

The stewardess began her safety drill as the plane taxied across the field. Welcome aboard this Otter Aircraft which is fitted with..."

The plane sped across the grass, gave a few little bumps and we were in the air.

"...As part of this journey crosses water..."

I gazed out of the window and saw the cliffs fall away and true to her word we were indeed over water.

"...There are two exits on this aircraft..." She waved her arms in the directions of the doors. "In the event of an emergency landing children should be..."

Wolf Rock Lighthouse drifted into view beneath us, waves crashing across the rocky base. At least some things don't change.

"...If you hear the words Brace - Brace you should adopt..."

The engines eased back as we started our slight descent towards the Scillys.

"...If you need to use the evacuation chute..."

Fishing boats littered the sea below, this must be the Free Fleet Mary had mentioned. They threaded their way between each other as some headed out and others returned with their catches.

"...Oxygen masks are not automatically dispensed on this model and you will need..."

The sandy beaches of St Marys appeared below us and a

couple of minutes later came the slight bump as the wheels touched the tarmac.

"In the event of an emergency, a post trauma counselling service..."

The little plane came to a halt within twenty feet of the arrivals hall. I knew it was the arrivals hall as a hand painted sign over a simple glass door told me so.

"...In the event of mid air turbulence the captain may at his discretion..."

I sat waiting patiently in my seat as she continued her pre-flight safety briefing which continued for another five minutes, by which time the doors were open, the steps attached and the pilot had gone off for his tea break.

Eventually I was thanked for choosing to fly Celtic International Airlines and was wished a safe onward journey. I exited the plane down the wobbly steps. There was nobody there to guide me and no red ribbons to stop me putting my head in the propellers. I made my way into the arrivals hall which consisted of a small cafe where disappointingly, nobody seemed in the slightest bit interested in my arrival.

* * * * *

I contemplated hiring a taxi into Hugh Town but as it was only about a mile and I'd been feeling stir crazy after my four hours trapped in Lands End Airport, walking seemed like a better idea. The road meandered between an odd mixture of whitewashed cottages and tall modern flats. It seemed the rapid influx of new residents following secession had created a building spree. Hugh Town merged with everything else and I found myself down by the small harbour where so many boats clustered within the sea walls one could barely make out any bits of water between them. I threaded my way carefully between the lobster pots and ropes that lay strewn across the edge of the docks, waiting to tip an unwary pedestrian into the water below.

My finely tuned instincts pulled me towards a building that if it wasn't a pub then it certainly should be. A huge carved ship's figurehead thrust out from the stone building and as I drew closer I saw a sign announcing 'The Frigate'. Feeling pleased with my unfailing navigation system I went inside. The smell of tobacco smoke hit me as I entered. The bar was filled with the sound of chattering and laughing. I checked my watch, four thirty, maybe all these people were fishermen just come in from the day. I weaved my way to the bar and surveyed the row of pumps.

A young woman in jeans and white blouse appeared behind the bar. "What can I get you, love?"

I pointed to the pump labelled 'St Mary's Thunder'. "I'll have a pint of that please."

She pulled skilfully at the pump and placed the pint glass in front of me. "A pound, please."

Her request threw me on two counts; Firstly I didn't have any sterling and secondly I don't remember paying a pound for a pint since I turned sixteen."

She noticed my obvious confusion, "Ah, you're from the mainland," she said.

"That obvious?"

"I'm afraid so!" She smiled. "Old Bob over there will change some of that foreign money you're probably carrying." She nodded towards a pair of weather-beaten individuals playing dominos in the corner.

I pulled a few euro notes from my wallet and headed over to the pair. “Bob?” I queried.

“Ooh ahr,” the nearest man said. He looked up at me. “You needing to swap some of that monopoly money for the Queens currency then?”

“Yes, thank you.” I held out the notes to him and he snatched them from my hand.

“What you got ‘ere then?” He counted them with the skill of a bank teller. “I’ll give you a hundred for ‘em, not a penny more.”

I didn’t know if it was good rate or not but guessed it was probably the only offer available. “Okay, thanks.”

The euro notes disappeared as if by magic and he laid a pile of sterling on the table. “Thank you for your custom.” He chuckled and returned to his game.

I handed over the money for the beer and took a sip. Delicious.

“You here on holiday?” the woman asked.

“Not really. I’m looking for somebody.”

“Not some sort of detective are you?” Her face flickered into instant suspicion.

“No, she’s my friend. I think she might have come here looking for her sister.”

She wandered off to serve somebody else and I headed for an empty table. The bar bustled. A constant change of customers as people came and went. When the opportunity arose I snatched a newly vacated table by the window and watched the little boats bobbing about. I suddenly realised I hadn’t eaten since breakfast and picked up the menu.

The barmaid materialised like magic. “Can I get you something to eat?”

"I was just thinking that," I said.

"We've got some fresh crab just come in. Could do you a nice salad with it if you like?"

I ordered the crab salad and another beer. It came to three pounds exactly. She brought the salad and drink to my table after a few minutes.

"So, what's this friend of yours look like? She pretty?"

"Er, yes. Shoulder length hair, with streaks. Slim. Her name's Tania."

The woman shook her head. "Not seen her. But we get hundreds in here a day." She turned to leave then paused. "You said she was looking for someone?"

"Yes, her sister. Emma Trevarick?"

The barmaid looked thoughtful. "Name rings a bell."

"Her husband is Lee, I think. He's a fisherman." I added hopefully.

"Lee Trevarick! Oh yes, everybody knows Lee. Runs the Leaky Sock."

"Leaky Sock?" I queried.

"That's the name of his boat. Long story. Usually moors it out there on the western wall." She pointed to where the sea wall curved around the harbour then glanced at the clock behind the bar. "Went out on the morning tide, probably back around seven shouldn't wonder." She went back to her duties.

The crab salad was the best I'd ever tasted and plenty of it. If Lee was not going to be in till around seven I was going to need a room for the night. I went over to the bar and asked the woman if she knew of any rooms to rent.

"We do them here, but we're all full," she said. "In fact, pretty much everywhere's nearly always full." She thought for a moment then rummaged in a drawer under the till. "You might try Mrs Miggins, she has a cottage out on Old Town Road. My Mike's just finished doing up her spare rooms so you might have a chance there."

I thanked her and headed off in the direction she'd indicated.

* * * * *

Toll Cottage overlooked a stretch of moor that led down to the sea. It was a white-washed two story building that nestled in a large beautifully kept garden. I ducked under the roses that overhung the door and tapped the brass troll's head knocker. Mrs Miggins answered the door. She was a small woman with a tight white perm that resembled a cauliflower. She wore a large apron that sported a map of the Scillys.

"Oh!" She looked surprised. "I was expecting the milkman. He always comes on Tuesdays."

"I was told you might have a room I could have for the night?" I asked.

"Oh my, there's a thing now. Well I suppose I have. Come in." She turned and disappeared into the slightly gloomy interior.

I followed her inside. It reminded me somewhat of Tinker's Cottage. I must remember to go out of the same door through which I entered. Just in case. She led the way up a twisty and slight wonky staircase and opened a door for me. The room was bright and airy in contrast to the rest of the cottage. It still smelled faintly of paint. A large window looked across the moor and the sea glinted in the late afternoon sun.

"It's lovely," I said. "How much is it?"

She thought for a moment then, “Ten pounds a night. Is that alright? I can do you a nice breakfast for another two pounds if you like?”

“It sounds perfect. And yes, breakfast would be great.”

“I’ll leave you to get settled in then. I’ll just go put the kettle on. You look like you could do with a nice cup of tea.” She disappeared down the windy staircase.

I sat on the bed and admired the view, it was truly stunning. From what I had seen so far, this island was a true mix of the old and new. Evidence of the sudden growth following secession was everywhere. Traditional cottages with huge extensions, modern flats nudging up against colonial houses and I’d even passed a field of what looked like log cabins. The island had clearly struggled to keep up with the influx of migrants. I unpacked my few meagre possessions and wound my way down the staircase.

Mrs Miggins lifted her kettle from a big green cooking machine in the corner and emptied it into a china teapot the shape of a cottage. I must get one of those.

“Cynthia told me doing up the rooms would be worthwhile,” she said as she poured the tea. “But I really didn’t think someone would turn up so quickly, I have to say. Sugar’s in the policeman if you take it.” She pointed to a china figurine on the table.

“How long have you lived here?” I asked.

“Not quite all my life.” She gave a grin that crinkled at the corner of her eyes.

“I suppose you’ve seen some changes?”

“When I was courting my Albert, that nice mister Harold Wilson used to come here for his holidays. Now they’re both in the churchyard down yonder.”

I glanced at my watch and finished my tea. "I have to go. Got to try to meet somebody."

"I'll leave the door on the latch for you when you get back." She gathered up the cups and clattered at the sink.

* * * * *

The boats in the harbour bobbed on the evening sea. I made my way round to where the woman in the bar had indicated The Leaky Sock would moor up. Scores of boats competed for space along the harbour walls and others linked together like the flotillas in Hong Kong harbour. Fishermen used each other's boats as stepping platforms to bring their catches ashore. The dockside was slippery with water and I had to watch my step, especially as it was also littered with ropes and boxes of still flapping fish. I did the full circuit of the harbour wall and no sign of The Leaky Sock so I gave up and asked a fisherman nearby if he knew of it.

"Lee? Oh he be twixt The Blue Mermaid and The Neptune's Folly. Down there, look see?" He pointed to a nestle of boats in the middle of the harbour. "The one with the net hung on the crosstree."

"What?"

"The Plymouth Hooker, over there."

"Huh?"

He looked at me like I was from the planet Zarg. "The cute little yellow boat next to the nice big blue one."

"Oh, I see. Thank you."

The thought of trying to hop across the decks of several bouncing fishing boats didn't fill me with excitement so I sat on a large metal cleat and watched for him to come ashore. I kept my eye on The Leaky Sock and noticed a tall man with a blue denim cap shifting plastic boxes onto the next boat. I guessed that was Lee and waited for him to get to the dock. The fishermen all seemed to work together tossing boxes towards each other in the general direction of the harbour side. Somehow they all piled up in separate piles. Eventually Lee made it ashore and as he tidied his pile of boxes together I went over to him.

"Hi, are you Lee Trevarick?" I asked.

The man looked at me through slightly narrowed eyes. "Depends whose askin' and what he wants."

"I'm looking for a friend of mine, Tania Shapwick?"

"Tania?" Lee said, suddenly interested. "What do you know about Tania?"

"She's a friend of mine from London and I think she may be..." I struggled for the words to explain to this fisherman the theory of quantum doorways without being dumped in the harbour. I settled for, "Lost. I think she's lost. And er, possibly disorientated."

"Disorientated is it?" Lee humped the boxes on to the back of a small cart. I thought I ought to help and picked one up. It was a lot heavier than it looked and the wet plastic started to slip through my hands. I brought my knee up under it to stop the whole lot falling on the floor. Lee picked it out of my hands as if it were empty and dumped it on the cart. "Best let me do that. Just spent all day dragging the little buggers out of the water, don't want you dumping them back in there again do we."

"Yes, there's obviously a knack."

"Not so sure about disorientated. Barking mad more'n like." He dumped the last of the boxes on the cart and started pulling it along the harbour wall. "Don't see her for years then turns up all posh like she's Lady Whatsit only she don't seem to know Tuesday from fried eggs anymore."

"So you know where she is?" I asked hopefully.

"She's sat in our spare room is where she is." He bounced the cart over some metal tracks in the road and I helpfully steadied the boxes for him. "Won't go out. Won't talk to anybody but Ems."

"Ems?"

"Emma, my missus. Says the world's gone wrong. There's only one thing wrong in that room and it ain't the world, that's for sure." He dragged the cart up behind a huge Nissan four wheel drive pickup and dropped the tailgate.

"Do you think I could see her?" I struggled to heft a box onto the bed of the pickup and Lee looked at me with a little smile and a slight nod that seemed to say well done.

"You can try." He swung the boxes from the cart to the truck with infuriating ease. "But doubt she'll talk to you."

We finished loading the truck and I climbed in the passenger seat. We bounced across the docks and headed out of town. Eventually we came to a row of about a dozen stone cottages overlooking the bay on the western side of the island. He pulled the truck to a stop at a garage behind one of the cottages.

"Come on in," he said as he jumped out of the cab.

He led the way in through a back door that seemed three sizes too small for him "Ems?" he called. "Got a visitor."

"Bit of warning might have been nice." Emma appeared from a doorway at the other end of the hallway. "Who is it this time, not another one of your drinking mates been thrown out?" She eyed me up and down.

"Says he's a mate of your daft sister."

"Tania?" She looked at me. "You know my sister?"

"Yes, I'm Ian Faulkener, from London."

"I don't remember you? She's never said anything about nobody called Ian? Come on through." She led the way into a small lounge and motioned for me to sit on the sofa. "How do you know her?"

"She's my agent. I write. Graphic novels, The Falconer?" I realised as I spoke none of that would make any sense.

"Agent? Tania is... was a Human Resources Outsourcing Liaison Officer for Walthamstow council."

I could see this was going to prove tricky. "There's sort of two Tanias," I began. "The Tania here is not the one you know."

"That much is for sure," Lee said.

"You're as daft as she is," Emma said. "She kept going on about there being two of this and that."

I tried to explain as best as I could about the cottage and the doors. Lee got up after a few minutes and announced he had fish to shift and this was all bollocks to him anyway. Emma listened and I could see her trying to make sense of it.

"Can I see her?" I asked.

"You might as well I suppose. You've both been playing with the pixies for far too long as best as I can make out anyway."

She led me upstairs and tapped gently on a white painted door. "Tania?" she called softly.

There was no response so Emma knocked again. "Tania? There's somebody here to see you."

After a moment I heard Tania's voice, "Who?"

"Says he knows you. Ian? From London?"

The door swung open and Tania appeared. She looked slightly dishevelled and somewhat wide-eyed. She stared at me. "Ian? Is that really you?" She flung her arms around me and started sobbing.

"I guess that's a yes, then," said Emma.

I just held her tight for a while until she pushed back. "What's happening?" she asked, her eyes scanning my face. "I thought I was going mad. Am I going mad?"

"No more than me," I said.

"Oh, good. That's reassuring then."

I laughed. "I tried to warn you about the doors."

"Doors?" Tania queried.

"Don't get him started on his doors," Emma said. "Had my head going round in circles he did. I'll make some tea." She disappeared downstairs.

"I don't understand," Tania said. "Everything sort of changed. It was all wrong. The more I tried to get to Emma's the worse it got."

I sat her on the bed and began my explanation. I knew she had trouble believing me but the evidence of her own experience won the case. Emma brought a tray of tea and chocolate digestives up and left them on the small table.

"And you just let me go!" Tania said, suddenly angry now.

"I didn't know. I thought I was having a bad day."

"A bad day! You open a doorway to another world, shove your ex through into oblivion and you call that a bad day!"

"I can see how you might take it that way." Therapy words, all those expensive sessions had to be useful for something.

She picked the pillow off the bed and swung it at my head.

"Don't try to weasel me. You're a category one, class A, self centred gitbag."

"A bit hard," I protested. "I think I was in denial."

"Like you were for most of our relationship." She turned to look and out of the windows and I saw her shoulders slump. Her rage abated.

I stroked her shoulder. "Sorry," I offered. "We can go home now though?"

"And how do we do that? I haven't got a passport in this ridiculous world." She turned to face me again.

"I haven't quite thought that one through yet, I'm sure that's not overly important though. They must have an embassy here I suppose."

"An embassy? Are you mad? Sorry, wrong question. Even if they do have an embassy here, have you tried to do anything related to any form of bureaucracy here?"

"We'll work it out. I'm sure Lee and Emma can help." I wrapped my arms round her shoulders and felt her sobbing gently.

* * * * *

That evening Emma cooked a fish pie and we sat round a large wooden table eating and drinking.

"Can somebody explain this money business?" I asked when we'd finished the meal. "Everything seems so cheap and mostly costs exact pounds?"

"It's because people don't have fixed prices," Emma said. "They charge what they feel's right at the time. And overheads here are minimal."

"But what about records, isn't that difficult? And tax?"

"There's no personal taxes here!" She sounded surprised I didn't know that. "And most people don't bother with records of any kind."

"No taxes? But what about things like schools and roads?"

"I'm beginning to believe you did come from another world," Emma said. "Thought everybody knew how it worked. The only tax here is the International Levy. A one percent charge on the turnover of any international company based here."

I was confused. I'd seen no sign of any international companies on my wanderings. "But that can't amount to very much? How many companies are based here?"

"At last count? Something like a hundred thousand. They come from all over Greater Europe to be based here. At a tax rate of one percent, who can blame them?" She saw my confusion and continued. "There's a huge office complex down near the Garrison. Most of these companies only need a phone line and accommodation address to validate their status here. Some have a desk with one employee, but most don't."

"So there's no need for taxes on individuals?" I was still trying to understand.

"Exactly. We have top schools, cutting edge hospital, big pensions. That's why everything is so cheap."

We sat drinking and chatting for a while then I said I needed to get back in case Mrs Miggins was waiting up.

"Lee will sort out the deals to get you both back to the mainland tomorrow. Drop by around ten, we should have something sorted by then."

"Deals?" I queried. "What deals? Can't we just take the plane back?"

"Tiny matter of a passport, in case you'd forgotten."

“Ah, yes. They’re hot on those then, are they?”

“Well,” Emma paused for thought. “I suppose only in the same way the Inquisition had a bit of a thing about crucifixes.”

I confessed I hadn’t really given that a lot of thought. I’d just assumed that as I was a British subject, I could turn up at the border and demand my inalienable rights to be allowed every support and whatever else it was the Queen had promised me in my passport. Of course I didn’t actually have a passport and come to think of it, I wasn’t even sure I had a Queen anymore in this universe. I probably needed to find that one out before I put my foot in it with some Republican Guard and found myself in The Tower.

I said my goodnights then wandered back to Mrs Miggins’ cottage, pondering all the way about the deals to be made. Visions of clandestine boats meeting under the full moon, swapping contraband and making deals. I didn’t realise then quite how close that would turn out to be.

Chapter Seventeen

I WATCHED THE SUN RISE spread its amber tentacles across the still waters of the bay as Mrs Miggins piled my breakfast plate high. I tackled the plate with determination but was finally beaten by the last slice of fried bread and a sausage. Mrs Miggins cleared my plate and refilled my coffee cup.

"I think I'm heading back today," I told her. "Can I settle up?" I leafed through my wallet.

She thought for a moment then said, "Well, let me see. We said ten for the room and two for breakfast but twelve pounds is such a messy number. Never did like twelve. How does ten pounds sound?"

"Ridiculously cheap. Are you sure?"

"I only do it as a hobby. Nice to meet new people. Yes, ten pounds is just enough."

I paid her the money then packed my few things and set out to walk back to Emma and Lee's house.

* * * * *

The sun warmed the island quickly so I took my time and enjoyed the countryside. For the most part it looked much like mainland southern England but the occasional palm tree and early summer flowers hinted at its almost tropical air.

Tania greeted me enthusiastically when I arrived. "Lee said he can set us up for a trip this evening. We could be home by tomorrow."

"Hopefully, just as long as the Pope is where I left him."

She opened her mouth to speak, hesitated then gave me a look that said she probably shouldn't ask and just said, "Okay. Whatever you think best."

She led me inside where Emma was busy preparing vegetables.

"Lee will be back around five and he said he'll take you out at eight. Another chap is going with you. Kevin something or other." She chopped at an onion with a sound like a machine gun. "Anyways, you'll need to get a load of stuff from the Smuggler's Shop in Hugh Town."

"Smuggler's Shop?" I remembered visiting Cornish seaside towns in the past, where Smuggler's shops were quite common. Usually mock Tudor buildings selling pirate's flags, pewter tankards and a plethora of other seafaring related souvenirs. I couldn't for the life of me see why I would need anything from one of those. Were we supposed to fly a pirate's flag or something?

Emma saw my confusion. "You'll need something to trade with the Others."

It must have been clear to Emma that I wasn't understanding the first thing about Smuggler's Shops or The Others because;

"The Smuggler's Shop sells stuff which is difficult to get in the Greater European Union," she continued. "You know, bananas, war films, fudge. You need to buy a load of it to pass on the Others, the fishermen from the mainland. It's your fee." She looked at me as though I were a child and she was trying to explain calculus. "Never mind, just go to The Smuggler's Shop and tell then what you're doing. They'll help."

"How do I find it?" I had visions of a hidden doorway and having to give a coded knock and ask for Bluebeard.

"It's in the High Street. Big sign above the door. Says Smuggler's Shop in big letters. You can't miss it."

"Doesn't that give the game away?"

She stopped her manic chopping and turned to face me, my eyes followed the knife as she stabbed it into the chopping board in apparent frustration. "You mainlanders really don't understand the world, do you. Why would they need to hide it? It does fantastic business. Everybody knows what they do. It's a bit like a ticket shop."

"Oh, I see." I wasn't entirely sure I did see but she closed her fingers around the knife handle and pulled it free in such a way as to give the impression the conversation was over and I was pushing my luck.

* * * * *

As predicted, The Smuggler's Shop was indeed conspicuous. A huge black and white sign over the shop window, a flag protruding into the street and as if that wasn't enough, a large bilboard on the pavement announced, 'All Your Smuggling Needs Here!'.

Tania led the way in and I followed. I'd half expected gloom and locked cupboards but I was greeted by bright lights and display cabinets that for the most part seemed perfectly ordinary, albeit somewhat eclectic. Rows of DVDs, books, jars of preserves, packets of sweets, fruit and of course a large selection of alcohol. I leafed through the rows of films on DVD trying to understand what made them contraband. There were a good number of John Wayne movies, quite few Clint Eastwood, almost every Carry On film and surprisingly what seemed like the full back catalogue of Judy Garland. There were box sets of TV series such as Only Fools and Horses, Are You Being Served and On The Buses. Book shelves were lined with Biggles, Enid Blyton and Grimm's Fairy Tales. I struggled to understand the logic behind the choices. I pulled a copy of Pride and Prejudice from the shelf.

"Ah, good choice!" A tall man with a pirate's hat on his head appeared alongside me. "Like gold dust since The Wicked Witch came to power."

"Wicked Witch?" I queried.

"The Evil Blair, The Brussel's Valkyrie. First thing she had banned was that. Then it was on to Morecombe and Wise, Tom and Jerry and now the poor buggers over there can't even get a decent cup of tea since she banned imports from India. Grow all their tea in France now, you know."

"I was told you could help," I whispered and glanced nervously around. "I need to get passage for both of us." I nodded towards Tania. "You know, to the mainland."

"You'll have to speak up, lad, bit thick in the ear since I was stood to close to the cannon in the Crimea."

I stared at him for a moment then he burst into laughter. "My little joke. But really, no need to whisper. No Revenue Men around these parts."

I still wasn't sure whether to take him seriously. "We need some stuff as a sort of ticket?"

"No problem," he said. "Two of you is it?"

"Yes."

"I'd go for a box of Goldfinger, that's always popular, a case of honey fudge, a few cartons of untipped cigarettes and I can do you a freezer box of cod fish cakes. They're going down particularly well at the moment since the silly sods sold their cod quotas to Iceland."

"Fudge?" I asked. "Why is fudge contraband?"

The pirate glanced at Tania. "Don't know much do he, your man?" he said then turned back to me. "Cornish Fudge. They forced the mainland to change the recipe for Cornish Fudge ten year back. Too much sugar they said. Caused hyper something or other. But we still do the proper stuff here like. Pomfrey's Cornish Fudge. Only not supposed to call it Cornish see, as they don't recognise the Scillys as part of Cornwell anymore. So we has to smuggle it over. Goes like Ussain Bolt with a rocket up 'is arse does that." He gave another chuckle.

"How much contraband do you think we need?" I asked.

"For the both of you? Usual rate is a chest each. Best take a small extra box just in case the mainlanders suddenly get all greedy like. Want me to put something together for you?"

"How much is it?"

"Let's say a tenner a chest? Give me a couple of hours and I'll have them ready for you. I'll even chuck in the small box."

* * * * *

We left the shop and headed along the main street. Retail smuggling, now there's a new one. We settled in The

Mermaid for coffee, it was a bit early for beer, even for me. The morning sunlight sparkled across the bay.

Our coffees arrived and I said to Tania, “Look, I really am sorry.”

She took a sip of her cappuccino, studiously avoiding eye contact. “For what exactly?”

“Erm, letting you go through that door? Screwing up our relationship?” I could see I was having little impact. “World War Two? Boris Johnson?” I offered.

She smiled at last. “I know you didn’t mean it. It was all just so frightening. At least you had a vague idea what was happening. I thought I’d gone completely mad.”

I opened my mouth to speak then she stared at me with killer eyes and pointed her frothy spoon menacingly. “Don’t say it!”

We chatted for a while. For the first time she opened up about her time after our breakup, how she’d met up with Aaron and they’d been having an on-off relationship ever since.

“He does something clever with aeroplanes,” she said.

“You mean a bit like the Red Arrows?”

“Idiot! No I mean he designs systems for them. Something to do with the thingies that make the whatsits stabilise if the inertial doohdah goes out of whack.”

“Oh, I see. I’d always wondered how that worked.”

“Oh hell, I’ve just remembered. We were supposed to go up to his parent’s farmhouse in the Cairngorms this weekend.”

“Well, with a bit of luck you’ll be able to ring him tomorrow and explain,” I said.

“Explain what exactly? Sorry I didn’t call but my ex

pushed me through an inter-dimensional wormhole and we had to smuggle copies of The Boy's Own Annual in order to get home?"

"There you go, I knew you'd find a way." I grinned. "Come on, we'd better go see if Captain Birdseye has loaded the treasure chests yet."

I paid the waitress on the way out and as I returned the change to my pocket my hand closed around the strange little crystal. I'd forgotten it was there. I pulled it out and stared at it. The glow had almost gone. Just a very faint shimmer seemed to transluce across its surface. I felt slightly deflated although I couldn't quite work out why.

* * * * *

The two chests awaited our return and as promised a small carton sat next to them. I was tempted to look inside and rummage a bit. As a boy I'd always enjoyed rummaging in my grandmother's chests in her attic. Generally they consisted of hats, shawls and countless copies of Woman's Own Magazines going back to before the war. Resisting the temptation to drag everything out all over the floor to see what we'd got, I paid the man and dragged the chests out onto the pavement. It wasn't long before the local bus polled up and took us to our door. St Mary's is a small island and the bus routes vary according to the passengers. A strange system but it seems to work well.

Once back in Lee and Emma's house Emma directed us through into the lounge.

"Kevin's there already," she said, with a slight smile.

Kevin sat on the sofa in the lounge. He was a small, skinny

man probably in his mid forties. There was nothing unusual about him, apart from the fact he was totally naked.

"Oh, sorry," I said and turned my head to look at the doorway through which I'd just entered. "I didn't realise... I'll come back when you're ready."

"You see," said Kevin, his voice rising in an attempt at indignation. "That's what I mean. Right there, that's the problem."

I had a feeling I'd either come in halfway through a conversation with an invisible man or I'd found another doorway, a very strange doorway. I couldn't decide which was the most disturbing. "Umm... I didn't mean... That is..." I continued to stare through the doorway, rather hoping that he was busy getting dressed behind me but doubting that was so. Emma came out of the kitchen and caught sight of me. "Ah, I see you've met Kevin."

"Yes, he's just... er... I was going to help you make some tea."

Emma bustled past me. "Oh, don't mind Kevin. He's a nudist. Sorry, should have warned you."

"I'm not a nudist," Kevin continued in his indignity. "I'm a naturist. Nudists are people who take their clothes off in public."

I risked a glance. No, he was still naked, or nude, or naturisty. "I see," I said. Truth be told I could see all too much but I tried to act nonchalant. Even as Kevin stood up from the sofa. I still managed nonchalant as he strode over towards me. However I think my nonchalance slipped slightly when took my hand and patted me on the back.

"That's alright," he said. "Common mistake. I apologise but I sometimes get a bit touchy."

I hoped the hand shake and the back patting was as touchy as he was going to get. "Took me by surprise a bit, that's all." I extricated myself from his handshake. "Don't tend to meet many nudist... I mean naked... naturists in Ealing."

Kevin looked puzzled. "This isn't Ealing?"

"I know but that's where I live. Lived. Now I live in Somerset but when I was in Ealing I didn't see many nudists. Naturists. Or in Somerset... Would you like a cup of tea? I was just going to help Emma make some." I looked to Emma and gave her the expression that I hoped said 'Help Me!'.

"Oh, don't worry, Ian. I can do it. You sit down and have a chat with Kevin. You're going to be stuck together for a while. Best you get to know each other." She turned and headed for the kitchen, a barely contained smirk on her face.

I sat on the chair at the furthest corner from the sofa. "So, you're heading back to the mainland then?"

"So it seems," he said. "It wasn't my plan. But things didn't really work out here. Not as I'd hoped."

"Kept taking his bloody clothes of in public." Lee came into the lounge and threw his lunch pack on the table. "A man should keep his clothes on in public. Apart from anything, most of the time it's too bloody cold for that sort of nonsense."

I wanted to agree with Lee but had a sudden recollection of my 'Interesting Day' in the Blue Water shopping centre a few years back. I settled for, "Each to their own, I suppose."

* * * * *

I left Kevin in the lounge and decided I could resist my curiosity no longer. I pulled everything from the chests and spread the contents across the floor. It was an Ali Baba's world of the politically incorrect, the slightly subversive and the downright peculiar. There were several copies of each of Jeremy Clarkson's books, obviously these were banned in Blairworld, as I'd taken to calling this universe. I could understand Mien Kampf being on the blacklist, although why anybody would even attempt to read it I can't imagine, but Noddy? Aspartame sweeteners, vitamin pills, Columbian coffee, Kinder Eggs, Absinthe, three-pin plugs, 100 watt light bulbs, factor 2 sun tan lotion, the pile grew bigger and stranger.

"I see Eddie's looked after you well."

I looked up at the sound of Lee's voice. He stood in the doorway, or rather he filled the doorway.

"This all seems very random," I said. "Are you sure this is what the others want?"

"Can't get enough of it, poor buggers."

"But what about this?" I held up a bar of whole nut chocolate. "Why on earth is whole nut chocolate banned?"

"It's got nuts in it." He looked at me with the same expression he'd used when I'd first tried to explain my doors to him.

"Well, that's self evident," I said. "The clue's on the wrapper. It says whole nut chocolate. But I don't understand. Are nuts banned?"

"No," he said with an air of exasperation. He dropped his lunchbox on the table and continued, "Nuts are alright, they're just not allowed to be in anything. Too much of that anaphylactic shock business going on there was. Some poor sod eats a pizza that's been near a peanut and off he goes like a champagne bottle in a tumble dryer. So they banned all nuts as ingredients to anything else."

"Even muesli?"

"Even muesli, whatever the hell that is."

"What about—"

"Everything," he interrupted.

We carefully replaced everything into the chests. Although I did keep out a copy of Billy Bunter Among The Cannibals. I remembered reading a copy of that I'd found in my grandmother's bookcase.

"What time are we off?" I asked.

He poured boiling water onto a teabag in a huge mug. "Well, we don't want to meet the others until dusk." He paused for thought, "So if we leave here around six, it'll take us a couple of hours to get to Black Buoy, the halfway point where we meet. Be dark by then."

I mulled over this information in a sort of silent terror. Two hours to the halfway point. That means four hours, in a fishing boat, in the dark.

"But it only took twenty minutes in the aeroplane?" I said

"Yes, but we've found stopping halfway to shift stuff from one aeroplane to another can be tricky. Which is why we do it by boats these days."

Chapter Eighteen

KEVIN WAS FULLY CLOTHED WHEN we met at the harbour side. I guessed Lee had probably insisted. "So," I said. "You mentioned things hadn't turned out the way you'd expected?"

"Yes, I'd rather hoped that the Islanders, given their renowned proclivity for liberalism and individual freedoms, might accept naturism in a slightly more accommodating way than the European Fascist dictators do."

"You've had troubles with your... err... lifestyle in England then?"

"England, France, Germany, even Sweden —"

"Isn't Sweden a bit..."

"Yes but that's not the point. It's to do with rights."

"Too many bloody rights, if you ask me." Lee said over his shoulder as he guided the little boat out of the harbour walls.

"The European Court of Human Rights says —"

"They say way to much most of the time," Lee interrupted. "And anyway, when they wrote their declaration of whatsits, they were probably more interested in torture and slavery than you taking all your kit off in the Anchor Tea Rooms. Right disturbed old Mrs Slipward, that did. Not been the same since, poor old dear."

"I didn't take my kit off in there," Kevin was back to his indignant best. "It was already off when I went in."

Lee pulled the throttle levers back as the boat left the harbour and the noise of the engine removed the chance of further conversation. Thankfully.

After awhile I grew used to noise of the engines and for the best part of the journey I sat and watched the sea roll by and chatted with Tania. The waves lifted the boat in a gentle movement which was actually quite pleasant once I'd got used to it. The smell of fish faded as the clear breeze took it to sea. Lee sat at the wheel drinking endless cups of tea and seemed to go into another world. I pulled my Billy Bunter book from my bag and started to read. After a while the evening drew in and the light made it difficult to the small comic print.

I tried angling the book under the running lights for a while until Lee said, "Nearly there." And the lights went out. After a few moments the engine noise abruptly cut off and all I could hear was the splashing of the waves on the bows and a strange whistling similar to something I'd once heard on a radio programme about sheep dogs.

A gentle bump indicated the meeting of two boats.

"Alright, Lee?" asked a muffled voice.

"Can't complain. Fish are runnin', the beer's good and the missus keeps the bed warm."

"What yer got for us then?"

"A trio of offlanders with no passports."

"Send 'em over."

I felt hands guiding me across the gunwales. The new boat

was significantly higher than Lee's and a degree of scrambling was required. Sounds to my right indicated Tania was being helped aboard by two men although I couldn't see anything in the almost total dark. I wondered how she was managing. A small giggle from Tania, a slight slapping sound and a hearty laugh from one of the men reassured me she was probably managing just fine. There was no sound from Kevin and I guessed the men had declined to help him. We were guided into comfortable seats in the back of the boat. They bid their farewells to each other and I heard the engines underneath me roar into life. This was no fishing boat. The boat lifted in the water as the engine noise increased and I felt wind on my face. The noise and the wind made it impossible to talk, or move, or think. After about thirty minutes the boat came to a stop and I felt a small bump. A torch shone a puddle of light on a concrete surface roughly level with the gunwales.

"There you go," said a voice from behind the torch. "Mind the step."

We scrambled onto the concrete and by the time we had straightened up the boat was turning away. The engines roared once more and a trail of fading phosphorescence was the only sign it had ever been there. I realised I'd never seen their faces or exchanged more than a couple of words.

"I wonder where we are?" I said to Tania.

"Buenos Aires if it's anything to do with you."

The moonlight cast a silver puddle across the small concrete pier onto which we had landed. I started edging forward, not entirely trusting my eyes and slid my feet to maintain contact. I felt Tania's hand slip into mine. I assumed for guidance but the familiarity stirred something. Our eyes acclimatised to the night and we stumbled up a steep gravel track that led to a car park. Beyond the car park small rows of cottages drew a stark line across the faint clouds. We ventured up the narrow road and I began to recognise our surroundings. This was Cape Cornwall, only a mile or so from St Just, a cup of tea and a warm bed.

I managed to persuade Kevin to keep his clothes on and once I'd found the right house, Mary gave him a room.

Once safely returned to the privacy of my own room, I made Tanis and I a cup of tea. Now I knew that is was not grown anywhere closer to India than Perpignan it explained the lack of taste and body. In fact, the lack of anything that resembled tea. Tania rinsed the cups and we settled for bed. Although we had been lovers once, we managed to nestle into the undersized bed without any actual bodily contact.

* * * * *

Morning sunlight burst through the flimsy curtains with no consideration for the hour. Tania's side of the bed was empty and splashing noises came from the shower. I put the kettle on and made us both coffee. I had sneaked a small bag of Blue Mountain from the chest. The rich taste set my system going and the day seemed slightly less challenging. Find the Pope, quick trip up the motorway, navigate the doors and everything's back to normal by teatime. How hard could that be? There was a knock on the door. I opened it.

"I've decided to back to Somerset with you," Kevin announced.

"Oh, you have, jolly good. And why is that?" The thought of being stuck in a car with Kevin and the Pope for several hours was not my idea of a good time.

"It's your doors. Emma told me about your doors."

"That was nice of her." I'd have to remember to say thank you to Emma for that. "And what is it about my doors you find so compelling?"

"Well, if as you say there are many different universes through them, then there ought to be one more suited to my needs."

"Several, I shouldn't wonder," I said. "But being as how there are so many combinations of door, finding the right one might prove tricky. Are you sure you wouldn't be better off here in Cornwall? Somewhere remote you practise your... err... lifestyle with a bit more privacy?"

"No. I've decided. I've had enough of this Totalitarian Uberstate that passes for democracy these days."

I'd convinced Kevin that staying fully clothed whilst in the hotel breakfast bar was probably a good idea. Mainly by the use of a threat that if he got us thrown out of the Smuggler's Haunt I was going to leave him behind. He reluctantly complied but I did notice he wasn't wearing socks. Clearly a protest vote.

As Mary cleared our breakfast plates I asked her if she'd seen George. Her answer caught me mid mouthful.

"He's gone where?" I spluttered toast crumbs at her.

She placed the silver teapot on the table and brushed her white top free of my breakfast debris. "Destiny," she repeated. "Said he had an appointment with destiny."

"What does that mean?" Tania looked at me.

"I haven't the faintest idea," I said. "I expect the silly old sod's finally lost the plot completely. Let's hope he hasn't bought a ticket for Rome."

"Rome?" Mary gathered up the empty breakfast plates.

"Rome? He never said nothin' about Rome. He did ask me how to find the Men-an-Tol though."

"They're standing stones aren't they? I've heard of that. Is it close by?" I asked. I was slightly worried as the last time George had mention standing stones I seemed to remember that the concept of human sacrifice had figured in there somewhere.

"Just up the road aways. Need your hiking boots though, got a few fields to cross. He's probably gone up there for the solstice nonsense shouldn't wonder. Usually get a bunch wierdos dancing around them stones at midday on the solstice we do. They need a job if you ask me."

Solstice? Of course, today was the summer solstice. What on earth did he mean by having an appointment with destiny? The Pope, the summer solstice and an ancient monument. What could possibly go wrong?

"Come on, Tania. We've got to hurry," I gulped down the last of my tea as I stood. "

"What? Where? I thought we were going straight back to London?" She looked distraught.

"Minor detour. Just got to stop the Pope opening the gates to hell. Shouldn't take long. Home before supper. Trust me."

Tania gave a little muttered grunting noise I thought best to ignore.

* * * * *

Mary was right about the boots. Midsummer's day in deepest Cornwall can be a soggy affair and today was no exception. "You'd think they'd have a miniature railway or at least a decent footpath," I grumbled. "How do they expect tourists up here when they can't even spare a bit of concrete."

"Perhaps they don't want tourists," Tania said as she marched on ahead of me like a Himalayan Sherpa being paid by the mile.

"I'm just saying. At least a sign or two wouldn't go amiss. How do we even know if we're going the right way?"

"Because I can see it up there. Look!" She pointed at yet another hill that inevitably involved yet another muddy field.

We followed what seemed to be little more than a goat track until I eventually heard the sound of distant voices and something resembling bells.

"There we are," Tania announced. "Just there, see?"

Another fence and two ditches later and we emerged onto a slight rise at the top of which a group of people gathered around a set of three stones each no bigger than an average Ikea wardrobe.

"Is that it?" I asked.

"What did you expect? The Great Pyramid of Giza?"

As we approached, the gathered masses, of which I guessed numbered at least twelve, fell silent and those who held bells held them still.

The Men-an-Tol consisted of three stones arranged in a line. The centre stone stood about two metres and wheel shaped with a central hole. The outermost stones were about the same height but simple standing stones. At each of the outer stones a figure seemed to be tied by rope. Each had a hood over their head. A white sheet was spread on the ground each side of the central stone. I had an uneasy feeling about all of this. The assembled figures all wore capes of either white or blue, I guessed there was a sort of hierarchy involved, but it made seeing their faces difficult.

"You can't come here. Not today, this is a private ceremony," a voice shouted from under a blue cape.

"I'm looking for a friend," I said. "George, are you there?"

"Ian?" came a voice from the figure tied to the eastern standing stone.

The horror of what we had clearly interrupted spread over me like a cold wind in January. They were going to sacrifice the Pope! I was not normally given to acts of impetuous bravery but I couldn't allow the Pope to be sacrificed in some pagan festival. Even if he was only a Dopple Pope. And a cantankerous old git. I ran over to him. The ropes were tight and I couldn't free them. A quick glance around and I noticed a knife laying on the sheet by the central stone. I grabbed it quickly and noticed a loud 'Ooh!" from the pagan hoodies. I tried to hold the knife in what I hoped was a threatening manner and shouted, "Stay back!" It seemed to do the trick as nobody moved. Back to the Pope and I started hacking at the ropes holding him.

"What the hell are you doing?" he shouted through his sack.

"Rescuing you."

"Well just sod off will you. You're going to ruin everything."

"It's alright, I can get us away." The ropes fell away under the sharp ceremonial blade.

"It's my time," he shouted. "Destiny!"

"Who's that at the other stone?" I asked as I pulled the sack off his head.

"Destiny!" he repeated.

"Tania," I yelled. "Take George, I'm going to free the other one." My adrenaline was running high as I moved with an eye on the pagan monsters and the knife held out in front of me. I cut the ropes holding the other victim and pulled at the sack. A mane of dark hair fell free and tumbled over the shoulders of a petite young woman dressed in a flimsy cotton dress.

"What's happening?" she asked. "Is it time?"

"It's alright," I said. "It's all over now. You're safe."

"Safe?"

"Come with us." I grabbed her arm and guided her through the menacing throng who had all fallen strangely quiet. They were probably in awe of my heroics. We caught up with Tania and the Pope then scurried down the goat track and across the fields. The Pope grumbled all the way saying I'd ruined his great day.

We all piled into the little Renault Martin and I locked the doors.

"We seem to have outrun them." I glanced all around and could see no sign of pursuing hordes. My adrenaline dump was fading and my hands had started to tremble. I held the steering wheel tight so it wouldn't show. This was the second time I'd had to rescue the Pope from religious lunatics and I hoped it would be the last time.

"You're an interfering twonk," the Pope informed me. He was obviously still in shock. "One chance! One chance and you come along and make dog's bollock of it."

My trembling subsided and I started the engine.

"Didn't you get my message? I told that silly old cow in the hotel to tell you,"

I eased the car into the lane. "She told me you'd gone to meet your destiny. If that's what you mean."

"A union with Destiny. I knew she'd screw it up, stupid old tart. A union with Destiny, that's what I told her."

""I don't see the difference. Meet your destiny or union with your destiny. All the same."

"Not my destiny, you idiot. This Destiny." I twisted in my seat and saw he was nodding towards the girl on the back seat with him. "This is Destiny."

I looked at the girl. "Hi," she said. "Pleased to meet you."

Tania squeaked from beside me and I turned back towards the road just in time to avoid a cyclist.

"You're Destiny?" I said to the rear view mirror.

"Yes," she said. "My parents were hippies and they conceived me whilst they —"

"He doesn't need to know all of that," interrupted George. "Couldn't you have left it just five minutes?"

"She's Destiny? And you two were going to..." I struggled for words. "You were about to... In front of all those people. At a religious shrine like that, you were going to... Oh for goodness sake, now there, that image is in my head it will haunt me for years. It doesn't bear thinking about." I swerved the car again. "And what is it with all these bloody cyclists?"

We drove back to St Just in silence. Or moderate silence since George continued to grumble from the back seat. I offered to take Destiny home but she informed me 'home' was a misconceived concept that created unnecessary ideologies which could never be fulfilled. So I dropped her just outside the village.

The church clock struck three which meant it was two in the afternoon, the bar should still be open and I needed a beer.

As my eyes adjusted to the gloom inside the Smuggler's

Haunt all seemed quiet and normal. With the exception of the naked man sat at the seat near the window.

"Kevin?" I said. "I thought we had an agreement?"

"Is he with you?" asked the barman, a man with an untidy white beard and unnaturally black eyebrows. "Only he can't sit there like that. Scaring off my regulars."

"You were gone so long," Kevin said.

"And that necessitated you taking your clothes off?"

"I don't know why you think clothes are so important anyway."

"Get dressed or I won't take you to Somerset. And who's this?" I asked noticing the man sat next to Kevin, thankfully fully clothed.

"This is Simon. He's an Overlord."

"Not actually a full Overlord," Simon corrected, his eyes gleamed behind his oversized horn rimmed glasses. "Just an Overlord second class. I need three more Death Hammers."

The beer had appeared in my hand with no thought from me. I stared at it briefly wondering how that had happened then decided not to question the gifts of a generous universe and sank it in one.

"Well," I said. "Lovely to meet you, Simon but we have to be off now. We have a motorway to catch."

"Simon's decided to come with us," Kevin announced.

"Oh, he has, has he? And just when did we decide that?"

Tania pressed another cold glass into my hands. Ah, so that's how it was happening.

"His skills are wasted in this world," Kevin explained. "He needs a universe that will appreciate him."

I was slightly scared to ask but I did anyway. "What skills?"

"Those of an Overlord of course," Kevin explained. "He's wasted here."

I glanced at Simon. He wore a T-shirt that announced 'Orcs Need Love Too.' "I have a feeling you're right," I said. "But it may have escaped your notice that there are already four of us and I have a car the size of a small Lego toy."

"We can all bundle up in the back," Kevin said. "It will be fun. A sort of a Road Trip."

I didn't want a Road Trip. I wanted to get back to my cottage and shut the doors against this lunacy. Whichever doors that would involve. "There's no room," I said, with what I hoped was an air of finality. "And will you put some fucking clothes on!"

Chapter Nineteen

TWO HOURS LATER WE WERE heading up the A30 as fast as the little Renault Martin would take us. Which wasn't very fast given there were five of us in a space designed for a small elderly woman with a shopping basket.

The Pope, Simon and naked Kevin squashed into the back seat whilst Tania sat beside me in the front. Simon had warmed to the company and continued to jabber endlessly about his tales of daring-do in the World Of Warcraft. It turned out he wasn't a real Overlord, just a mythical one in the online gaming world. But Simon was a geek with a mission. He was convinced that in one of the endless multiverses that inhabited Tinker's Cottage there would be a world where goblins ruled and Wizards smote dragons. A world better suited to his peculiar talents and skill set. One which would appreciate somebody who knew the correct spell to bring down a drawbridge when cornered by marauding orcs.

We made good time and all was looking well for a while. Until the brave little Renault Martin finally gave up its life for us at the top of Halden Hill just west of Exeter. A loud clunk and a mushroom cloud of black smoke signalled its unhappiness with the abuse to which it was being subjected and announced its final demise. We stood in a lay-by watching the death shudders of the little vehicle.

"I suppose we could always hitch-hike," said Tania.

"With a Pope, a Naturist and an Evil Overlord?" I said. "It's sounds like the beginning of a bad joke."

"I'm not an Evil Overlord," complained Simon. "Overlords aren't evil or good per se . They just are."

The little car gave another shudder and something heavy fell to the road underneath the engine. And as usual in my world, just when things seem to be deteriorating nicely, fate comes along with a twelve bore shotgun and empties both barrels at the remains of my optimism. A blue and white Traffic Incident Team vehicle pulled up behind us with a little whoop on its siren. Two policemen in green Eurocop uniforms jumped out and proceeded to cone off a large section of the dual carriageway. Warning signs were erected and a temporary speed limit introduced and enforced by a Mobile Camera Team. It all seemed a little over exuberant, especially as we were parked in a lay-by. When they had finished with their safety procedures the taller of the two Eurocops came over to us.

His pen poised expectantly over his clipboard. "Well, what's happening here?"

"It's broken." I pointed at the Martin.

"Ah, broken." He thumbed through several sheets on his clipboard then put a tick in a box. "And how long is it going to remain in this condition?"

"I haven't the faintest idea," I admitted. "It's broken."

"Hmm, you can't leave it here. That would constitute... umm." His pen ran down the little boxes looking for the appropriate category. "That would be... Littering."

"Littering?"

"Littering's not allowed in Devon. He pointed at a sign next to a rubbish bin. 'Don't Litter It, Bin It!' Whilst the Martin is not the largest of cars I was fairly sure I wasn't going to be able to deposit it in that little bin. Even if it wasn't already overflowing with what appeared to be the remains of a family of ten's Happy Meal Bucket.

"I'll be sure not to litter," I assured him.

"And why've you got no clothes?" He pointed his pen at Kevin. "You can't stand in a lay-by with no clothes on." He scanned the clipboard, becoming more agitated at the lack of appropriate box. He gave up, "Put your bloody clothes on or I'll arrest you for..." His eyes and pen scanned the pages. "For... possessing offensive images." Clearly the closest box he could find.

"I am not an offensive image," protested Kevin. "I have the right to express my —"

"Kevin!" Tania snapped. "Shut up." She turned to the Eurocop. "He's a nudist."

"Naturist! I'm a naturist."

The officer glanced towards his colleague who was directing traffic around the cones. Clearly no help forthcoming from that direction. "Put your clothes on," he repeated.

"Kevin," I said. "Do what he says." I could see this getting out of control.

Kevin mumbled and headed for the back seat of the car.

"Oi! Where do you think you're going?" The Eurocop barked at Kevin.

Kevin froze, clearly confused. "Er... To get my clothes?" He pointed at his rucksack on the parcel shelf.

"You can't go in there," said the Eurocop. "That's a crime scene."

"A crime scene?" I was incredulous.

"Littering! Littering's a crime in Devon. Wait here." He headed over to his colleague for a conference. Our cop showed his notebook to the other who continued to direct the traffic without actually looking at it. Much conversation and note taking ensued.

Just as I was feeling the situation was heading downhill faster than a Jamaican Bobsleigh team, I heard the roar of a powerful car engine starting. I turned around to see Simon sitting in the driver's seat of the Police car, hands waving at me. "Get in!" he yelled. Quick!"

Both Eurocops froze and stared at their car. I had a split second to make a decision. I ran with the others for the car and jumped in. We locked the doors as Simon span the wheels and we roared out of the lay-by.

Simon struggled momentarily with the gears then we were racing towards the M5. "I had to do this once before in Varnia," he said with a big grin on his face. "Only then of course it was a winged chariot and I was being chased by the Elvin King's Guard."

Chapter Twenty

I SAT IN THE FRONT passenger seat of the stolen Police car as we sped along the motorway. We passed by Exeter with a surprising lack of pursuit.

"That's odd," I said. "I'd have thought they'd be after us by now."

"They will be," said Kevin from the back. "Only they can take their time. This thing'll have a tracker fitted. They'll know exactly where we are. I expect they'll use the Spy Copters."

Feeling even more paranoid now I craned my neck to take in as much sky as I could. Sure enough, after about twenty miles I caught a glimpse of sunlight flashing of something in the sky behind us. A few minutes later I was able to see it was a blue helicopter gradually closing on us.

"What are we going to do?" I asked.

"We'll just keep going. They won't try to stop us on a busy motorway. They've no need to rush."

We raced up the outside lane, by this time Simon had worked out how to operate the blue lights and sirens. "Woohoo!" he yelled as cars peeled out of our path. "This is way cool. I mean... This beats winged chariots any day."

I continued to scrape the skies around us and eventually noticed two other Police helicopters flanking our position.

"This is hopeless," Tania said. "They only have to wait us out. They know we'll have to stop sometime. I'm never going to get home, I'll be trapped in this insanity forever."

I thought for a moment. What would The Falconer do? He wouldn't just wait till he ran out of petrol and give himself up. If we could only make it to the cottage, there was a chance we could lose them in the doors. But they would stop us long before that. Or if not, as we got out of the car at Tinker's Cottage. We'd never make it from the road to the front door and this thing certainly wouldn't get up the drive.

I hadn't noticed that the motorway in front of us had emptied until it was too late. Two helicopters swooped out of the sky ahead of us and settled just feet above the tarmac, covering the full width of the road.

"Shit!" I heard Simon yell. "Where did they come from? I thought you were watching for them?"

"Sorry," I said. "I got distracted."

Simon showed no sign of slowing down as we hurtled towards the waiting choppers.

"Erm... What are you planning... Simon...SIMON!"

"We're going to fly," he said with a slightly disturbing maniacal laugh.

"Fly?" I yelled. "You do realise this isn't really a winged chariot?. Don't you?"

Simon ignored me and as he shifted direction slightly I saw with horror what he was planning. A raised ramp on the side of the motorway loomed ahead. It was designed to allow police cars a slightly elevated view of the traffic and not as a launch pad.

It was my turn to yell. “Shit!” I hollered as we hit the raised platform and to his credit, he did manage to get all four wheels of the car clear of the ground. Admittedly only for a split second and certainly not long enough to fulfil Simon’s ambitions of an airborne escape over the top of the helicopters. We bounced to the ground feet away from the lead helicopter and the car started a crazy sideways slew towards the spinning tail rotors. I heard a mumbling noise from the back and realised the Pope was actually chanting in Latin. I twisted my head to glance at him.

“Really?” I said.

“Can’t hurt,” I heard as I looked back to the road. Just as we were about to collide with the tail rotor the helicopter twisted ninety degrees and lifted to the sky. Clearly the pilot had designs on seeing the end of his shift in one piece. We hurtled backwards through the gap he’d left and collided with the central reservation. The vehicle stalled but Simon was able to quickly gun it back to life and we headed north again amid a spray of road grit and smoke from the tyres.

“Shame about that,” said Simon as we hurtled up the now empty motorway. “Didn’t work with the winged chariot either.”

We sped past Taunton and Bridgwater then left the motorway for the A39 road to Glastonbury. Just a few miles now, tantalisingly close yet still with no way of making it to the doors and relative safety. The helicopters stayed in escort formation but showed no signs of wanting to interfere again, They had the time advantage and could afford just to wait. The sun settled low behind us and the sky ahead shimmered an incandescent azure under the clear summer evening.

We were about ten miles from Trembly and my mind

drifted once more to thoughts of how would The Falconer deal with this situation. The sign for Shapwick appeared ahead. My cue that our turning was the next one. Shapwick? Suddenly the beginnings of a plan began to form. A lunatic plan. Outrageous, but one potentially worthy of The Falconer himself.

"Turn here," I yelled.

"Where? " Simon glanced around trying to find a turning.

"Back," I said. "Just there." I pointed at the turning for Shapwick just behind us.

"But I thought we were going to —"

"Trust me," I interrupted. "I've got a plan."

I heard muttering from the back seat. The Pope was chanting in Latin again.

Simon swung the car around and we headed for the small hamlet of Shapwick. The sirens bounced off the stone walls of the houses that lined Shapwick's main road as we sped through and out into the country roads beyond.

"Switch off the sirens and lights," I said. "Take it slowly."

Simon did as commanded although somewhat poutishly.

I couldn't see or hear the helicopters but I knew they would be up there. Watching us on their GPS thingies or their infrared doohdahs. Keeping close but not too close. Biding their time.

"Here," I said. I pointed at a track to the right. The entrance was blocked by a large wooden gate with a sign that declared it to be under the sanctuary of the Greater European Society for the Protection of Birds. Shapwick Nature Reserve.

I jumped out of the car and tried the gate. Damn. A huge padlock prevented vehicle access, allowing only walkers through a narrow gap to the side.

"It's locked," I said. "Anybody know how to pick locks?"

"Easy," shouted Simon. "Stand back."

The wheels span momentarily then the nose of the Police car ploughed through the gates. He leaned across and opened the passenger door for me. "You coming or what?"

I climbed in with a slight feeling of bemusement. "Drive very slowly," I said. "As quietly as you can. And no lights."

We eased our way along the track, much to the annoyance of the various twitchers and nature groups who thronged the way.

"Where are we going, Ian?" Tania asked. "This goes nowhere. We'll get stuck."

"The birds," I said. "Watch for the birds."

"Oh God," she moaned. "He's finally lost it. Ian, you are not the fucking Falconer! Do you hear me? Ian?"

"What's happening?" Kevin spoke for the first time in an hour.

"It's Ian," said Tania. "He thinks he's turned into some comic book hero."

The Pope resumed his chanting.

We nudged forwards very slowly as the birdwatchers reluctantly moved out of our way. I scanned the fields each side of the track. Low level movement, like shadows shimmered across the top of the long grass and reeds. The marshlands teemed with life. Sparrows, crows, swallows, geese, tits, pheasants, gannets and huge numbers of seagulls. They skimmed across the marshlands looking for a nest for the night. Thousands of them, probably tens of thousands in fact. Even over the purring engine the noise was intense. The chattering as they called to each other.

"Now!" I shouted.

Simon gunned the engine and hit the lights and sirens. The milling twitchers leapt to one side as we hurtled forwards in a blaze of noise and flashing lights. Instantly on all sides of us the fields erupted into a sea of black as thousands of birds took wing. They left their reed nests and lifted into the sky as one, a huge blanket of wings blocking out the last glows of sunset.

I didn't bother to try to look for the helicopters. I would never have been able to see them through the almost solid wall of birds. But I knew what would be happening up there. Panic. Sheer panic. A flock of startled birds that big would be an impenetrable shield, which if it made contact, would knock the fragile helicopters out of the sky in an instant. The huge variety of birds were as unpredictable as they were beautiful in their swirling. Turning and twisting in the shimmering of an eye there was no way to anticipate their next move. To any pilot caught near them the only sensible solution was to create distance, and very quickly.

We bounced down the narrow track and crashed through the gates at the other end sending the straggling bird watchers running for their lives. Once on the road, Simon killed the lights and sirens and we headed for Trembly, hopefully without our airborne companions. But just to make sure, I took us on another slight detour where I knew a large flock of geese liked to gather in the evening. Another short burst with the lights and sirens and this time a field of white took to the air as the geese broke formation and flew in all directions, confused and panicking. I figured if one of the helicopters had managed to pick us up after the random flocks, the geese might throw them off. The Falconer would have been proud.

We stopped in the lane just outside the cottage and killed

the engine. I got out and listened. The night was settling in and the evening birds were quietening. I could see no lights nor hear the sound of rotor blades but that didn't mean they weren't there. I strained my senses at the darkness. Nothing.

"Let's go," I said.

We left the car like will-o'-the-wisps in the ether and headed up the overgrown drive. Just as we were about ten metres from the door, the sky above us erupted into light and noise. Searchlights raked the ground and dust flew as the thunder of rotor blades thumped the night.

"Stand still!" came a booming voice from above us.

"Run!" I yelled as I made a break for the front door. I hoped it would be unlocked. I'd never been in through this way. I knew Tania was with me as I'd grabbed her arm and was pulling her along. But I knew nothing of the others.

The door was locked but thankfully it opened under my key. Odd how the one key opened every version of the front door. I pushed it open. Two black cats scuttled out between us as we stumbled into a version of Tinker's cottage I'd yet to explore. My hand fumbled for the light switch and the hall flooded with the stark white of an array of halogen lights set into the ceiling. For a moment I was stunned. This was quite unlike any version of Tinker's Cottage I previously encountered. Sharp, modern lines in contrast to the age of the cottage. Polished pine floorboards and crisp white walls set with the occasional token bare stone. I glanced back at the door and the other three stepped in.

"Okay, what now?" asked Simon.

"We have to try to get to my world," I said. "But that's through the patio doors at the back."

"Why didn't we just go there then?" asked Tania.

"Because they are going to follow us and I'd rather they didn't know about the doors. Come on, this way."

We went through the kitchen, a bright chrome and glass obscenity of a place and into the lounge. Here the patio doors stretched the full length of the back wall and as we approached, lights outside glowed and showed us the Japanese garden beyond. The doors slid open under the gentlest of touches and we filed outside.

"Okay," I said. "We go round again. They'll never do that so there's little chance of them finding us."

We ran round to the front of the house. Although I knew this was a different world to the one we'd just left, the one with the helicopters outside, it still made me pause. I peered around the corner, half expecting to see a squad of police cars there, but nothing. All quiet and peaceful. And dark. Oh so very dark. The normal faint glow of the streetlights further down the lane and the slight brightening over the town were nowhere in evidence. This felt off. There was something not right about this world. Surely there should be moonlight or at least stars? But no time to explore. I turned my key in the door and this time we entered a version of Tinker's Cottage that seemed more ancient than any before it. The walls were bare stone. Not the cob stone walls of the other incarnations, no, these walls were continuous stone, as if carved from one solid piece of rock. Or a cave. This could be a cave. I could find no light switch but an incandescent glow gave plenty of light without betraying its source. The entrance hall twisted away to the right and sloped downward slightly. This didn't even seem like a cottage anymore. My hand found the small blue stone in my pocket. I pulled it out. The glow was faint. Fainter than I'd seen it before. Strange.

"Where the hell are we?" Kevin shivered against the sudden chill in the air. The downside to naturism.

"I don't know," I admitted. "Never been here before. This is two steps away from my world."

"What do we do now?" Tania asked.

"We wait," I said. "We wait them out. They'll search the cottage we came into. Hopefully they'll only use the front door as we left it open for them. They might go out the back but they'll most likely search the back by going round outside from the front. They'll want to encircle the building." Secure the perimeter, I thought. Like on Hawaii Five O. That was what they did, they secured the perimeter.

"I need a piss," said the Pope.

"You'll have to wait," I said. "Wait until they decide we've given them the slip and they've gone home."

"This is like the orc tunnels on Golbanio," Simon said. "I wonder how far this goes?" He started down the passage.

"Wait," I said. "We need to stay together."

Simon shrugged and stopped, his hand tracing the shapes in the walls.

We settled down on the floor and tried to relax. I figured a couple of hours would be all that was needed. The police could do a thorough search of Blair World Cottage in that time and they must surely decide we'd slipped away unseen. A couple of hours laying low then I could go round through the cottage twice and I'd be back where I belonged.

"I'm going for a piss," announced the Pope and headed off down the passage.

"Wait," I said. "Just a bit longer."

"You can't negotiate with a bladder my age." He disappeared round the slight bend in the passage.

“I’ll go with him,” Simon said with barely concealed enthusiasm.

“Fine, but don’t be long.” I gave up. They weren’t my responsibility. If they wanted to disrupt the space time continuum by installing a Spiritist Pope into the Goblin Vatican then it wasn’t my problem. I’d explain it to Aunt Flora later. I’d done my best and now they could all just get on with it.

We waited. We waited for ten minutes that became twenty minutes,

“They’re not coming back, are they,” said Tania.

“Looks that way,” I said. “But they’re not my problem.”

“You can’t just leave them.”

“It’s a cottage, “ I said trying to convince myself of that fact as I stared down the strange passage. “Just a cottage. How does one get lost in a cottage?”

“Oh, I don’t know,” Tania’s tone dripped with sarcasm. “How about shoving your one-time lover through a door then abandoning her to the vagaries of an insane universe until she’s convinced she’s lost her mind and nobody seems to believe her and she ends up staring at the walls and screaming?”

I got the impression this was no longer about the Pope or Simon.

“Okay.” I stood and started cautiously down the passage. The walls continued to glow just enough to see where I was going. It twisted slightly to the left and continued its gentle downhill trajectory. I guessed I must have travelled further than the full length of the cottage. I paused. “Hello?” I listened. Nothing. I should just go back and leave them to it. I shuffled forwards a bit more and noticed the passage split in two. Oh, wonderful. “Hello?” I repeated then strained my ears at the silence. Nothing. I stared at the two passages. Were they just different areas of this place or did each lead to yet another universe? Which one? My hand folded instinctively round the little stone. It felt warm. I withdrew it from my pocket and studied it. The glow was brighter, more intense. Very odd. I moved my hand around and noticed the intensity changed as I moved it. Why hadn’t I noticed that before? Perhaps it was the very low light here that made it more evident. I held my hand towards the two entrances and the glow held stable. I turned and held my hand to the passage I had just left, the glow brightened. I was just trying to fathom what this meant when I heard a noise behind me. Running feet. I turned and nearly collided with the Pope as he rushed headlong out of one of the passages.

“Quick!” he yelled. “Get out, quick. They’re coming!”

“Who? And where’s Simon?”

He pushed past me and headed up the passage that led to the front door. A moment later Simon appeared, not quite so panicked but still showing signs of alarm.

“We need to get out of here,” he said.

“Why? What is it?”

Simon followed the Pope while I stood for a moment staring into the passage from which they had just appeared. I saw nothing but I heard a faint sound, like someone slurping tea. It grew louder and I turned and followed the others.

“What on earth is that?” I asked as I caught them up by the front door.

“I’m not sure,” Simon said. “But I need a goblin net and some Witch Bane, preferably picked under moonlight.”

“No problem,” I said. “I’ll just pop down to Tesco’s.”

Simon scowled at me. “I think we should leave.”

“But there are police SWAT teams swarming all over the place out there.” I peeped out of the door to confirm my fears but couldn’t see any Police. But it was so dark I don’t think I’d have been able to see them if they stood two feet away.

“Well, do you want to argue with that thing without some Witch Bane handy? ‘Cus I sure as hell don’t.”

“Simon?” Tania said. “You do know that World of Warcraft isn’t real, don’t you?”

“So some say.”

The slurping noise behind us increased and was now accompanied a snuffling noise. I pushed open the door again. Venture out there with the police possibly waiting to ambush us or stay here and face the tea-slurping snuffle monster?

“Come on.” I pushed the door open. “We can’t stay here.”

We filed out quietly and I closed the door firmly behind us.

The night was absolutely silent and very dark as we felt our way round the walls to the rear patio doors. The lights were still on inside flooding the lawn as effectively as daylight. I crept as close to the patio doors as I could without stepping into the pool of light. A policeman stood in the centre of the room, he appeared to be trying to get his radio to work. I pushed myself back into the shadows. I just hoped that those inside would assume that the outside was being searched by those from the front. The patio doors slid open and my heart tightened as the policeman stepped out and into the garden. We all forced ourselves into a tight bundle against the dark wall, not daring to move.

A flare of light lit the policeman’s face as he held a match to a cigarette. We waited while he stared into vacant space and smoked. The radio crackled and he threw the cigarette into the bushes near us then went back inside, closing the doors behind him. I risked peering through the glass doors. He had just finished playing with his radio then clipped it to his lapel and left the room.

We waited for about thirty minutes before venturing inside. I motioned for the others to stay back but they pushed so close behind me that I felt like I was leading a school outing crocodile.

We crept through the house. Everywhere was crisp and modern. An obscenity of stark lines and with minimalist art chosen for style rather than beauty graced each wall. We checked all the rooms and all seemed empty. The front door was still unlocked and I risked a peep outside. A police car sat in the drive and I briefly wondered how they'd managed to get it there. Two officers sat inside it illuminated by the courtesy light. They were facing the drive rather than the house. I shut the door again.

"It looks like they've decided we're not inside and seem to be waiting outside either for us to come back or a full search team to arrive. Dogs and stuff." Something else I'd learned from Hawaii Five O.

"What do we do?" Tania asked. "We can't stay here."

"We'll wait a bit longer," I said. "At some point they'll wander off to stretch their legs or something."

And so we waited. And waited. But the police vehicle sat stubbornly outside. Probably racking up lots of lovely overtime. Eventually I pushed the door open just enough to slip through. I started as I felt something brush against my legs. A black cat slipped between my legs and disappeared into the garden. No monsters.

"Come on. If we're careful, we should be alright."

The right side of the cottage was bathed in moonlight so we decided to go round the other way. We resumed our crocodile, this time adding our ninja creeping skills, and headed for the rear of the house. All was quiet and no sign of anybody. I unlocked the patio doors and they swung open. I pulled closed the doors and locked them then drew the green curtains. I scanned the room and my eyes took in the welcome sight of my lounge. A white cat nudged at my ankles and made the hungry, pathetic meow. The one that goes with the face that says, 'I've not eaten in a week.'

"I'll find you some food in a minute." I turned to the others. "Make yourselves at home." I glanced at my watch, would Saphie still be up? "I've a phone call to make."

I picked up the phone and dialled. Tania flopped into the large leather armchair with a sigh while the Pope announced he was going in search of a beer and headed into the kitchen.

"Fetch one for me as well," I yelled after him as I waited for the call to be connected. As I thought of Saphie my hand instinctively closed around the little stone in my pocket.

The phone squealed in my ear. I must have misdialled.

"Where d'ya keep your beer?" the Pope yelled from the kitchen.

"There's a case by the back door." I redialled, more carefully this time.

"What back door?"

What back door? Silly old sod. The phone squealed again. That's strange. I resigned myself to trying again in the morning and headed into the kitchen to help the pope find the beer. I stalled in the kitchen doorway. I appeared to be one back door short. My new back door which I distinctly remembered creating myself. My back door, the cause of so much of my recent troubles.

“That’s insane!” I pointed at the blank wall where my door had once been. I ran my hand over the wall just in case my eyes were playing tricks on me. No. There was no door there. Not even an invisible one.

“My door’s gone,” I said. “It can’t be gone. That’s where you came from? You remember coming through that door, don’t you?”

“Not really. But then I can’t remember what I had for breakfast. Did I have breakfast?” He looked around the room. “So, where’s your beer then?

“What? I don’t know.”

I headed back into the lounge. “My door’s gone.” I announced.

Tania stirred in the leather armchair and yawned. “That’s a shame. Never mind, you can get another one tomorrow.” She curled up in the chair.

The leather armchair. The leather armchair that I don’t have. I have a futon. A nice blue futon. I stared around the room again. It was nearly right, but not quite. The curtains were wrong. I struggled to remember what colour my curtains were supposed to be. Blue and yellow stripes. These were green. My hand found the small blue stone and I pulled it clear of my pocket and stared at it. The faint glow more subdued than it had been earlier and I suddenly realised what that meant. All the times I’d watched this seemingly random glowing, meaning dawned.

“Er, guys,” I called. “We’re in the wrong place.”

“Really?” Tania said sleepily.

“And you should be on a futon.” I told her.

My mind struggled to understand. We'd gone through the correct doors. The police car had been outside. They could only be outside the Blair World Cottage. And my cottage was through the patio doors behind Blair World Cottage. I'd drawn the maps and labelled each door with sticky notes. How could that work? I opened the curtains and stared into the darkness and was suddenly struck with a panic that I might never find the way back. Perhaps it depended not just on the door but also on how one approaches it? If that's the case how could I ever hope to find a way through. The stone! I opened the back door and stepped into the garden. Holding the stone in my open palm and feeling slightly foolish, I moved my arm from side to side. The glowing phased as I moved. Glowing brightly as I held it towards the direction from which we had come and darkening in the other direction.

I stuck my head back inside. "We've got to go back around."

General grumbling from inside and I heard the Pope say, "I'm knackered. I'm staying here."

"There'll be beer," I said. "And a futon."

We locked the door behind ourselves and once more did secret creeping between the garage and the cottage. The stone glowed in my hand. We came to the front of the cottage. The police car sat quietly in the dark drive. Two shapes silhouetted in the front.

I held my fingers to my lips and made a completely unnecessary shushing noise. We pressed ourselves tight against the dark wall and slipped around past the front door and back around the other side of the cottage. The stone continued to glow. I had a moment of panic as we passed the place where the kitchen back door should have been but remembered it didn't show from this side anyway. This time the lights were off as we approached the patio doors. I tried to peer inside but could see nothing against the dark. The key turned easily and I pushed the doors open. We filed inside and stood still in the dark, listening. Nothing. I closed the curtains and exhaled the breath I'd been holding since we'd left the front. And relax.

"Nobody move!" a voice boomed. "I'm armed."

Oh, bugger.

The light came on, flooding the room and blinding me momentarily. I squinted into the unfriendly glare. A shape come into focus. A shape holding what looked like a pick axe handle. A shape wearing an green jump suit with an orange circle on the front.

"Eric?"

"Ian?" replied the shape. "You alright? Who's that with you?"

"Eric, meet Tania, you know George, this is Simon and Kevin." I held my hand towards each of my companions.

"Why's he got no clothes on?"

"He's a... Naturist," I said, pleased with myself. Kevin harrumphed a noise of mild approval at my memory.

"Isn't he cold?" Eric stood the pick axe handle against the wall.

"Don't know. We don't discuss it."

"Eric? Is everything alright?" a female voice from the hallway.

"Stay there, Katrina," Eric said. "There's a naked man in here."

Either Katrina didn't hear Eric or her curiosity took over. "Oh," she said as she came in. Katrina was tall and willowy, she wore blue overalls that clung to her figure like silk. Shoulder length dark hair fell untidily forward, concealing part of her deeply tanned face. She gave a coy smile as she studied Kevin.

"You got here out okay then," I said, stating the blindingly obvious.

"Yes. And I've locked all the doors again. Only... erm..."

"Only what, Eric?"

"Only... some other Dopples might have got out. Only a few."

Flora was going to kill me. "How many?"

"Only one or two. Well, thirty one. More or less."

"Thirty one! Who are they?"

Eric shuffled uncomfortably. "They're Dopples of... of... It's a secret." he said with an air of petulance. "He's a big rock star. He's already gone through three livers and five kidneys. It's not right."

I decided I wouldn't tell Flora about those or she'd have me hunting them all down. They couldn't do any harm anyway. Could they?

"I need to close this door," I pointed at the patio doors. "Permanently. Bricks and stuff."

"Okay," Eric said. "I'll make a list in the morning of what we'll need."

"No," I said. "I meant now. We need to close it now," I stared at the doors expecting the full onslaught of Blair World's police force to come bursting through any moment. I glanced around the room wondering if dragging something heavy across the door would do the job. But the biggest item in the room was the sideboard and that was nowhere nearly solid enough.

We headed downstairs and gathered up the leftover building materials from the new cellar. I had to admit Eric had done a beautiful job. Four doors now led from the freshly plastered room. Each door held a large brass lock and a series of deadbolts. I knew that one of the doors led to Eric's world but wondered about the others.

"Have you any idea where the others go?" I asked him as we dragged leftover bricks and timber upstairs.

"No. Don't want to know. Leave that sort of stuff to The Gatekeepers."

We made a fair job of sealing the patio doors, bearing in mind the equipment we had. Part brick, part timber and lots of cement.

"I'll get some more bricks tomorrow and finish it off properly," Eric said. "But that will seal it from the other side at least."

I found a bed, mattress or patch of floor for everybody on which to settle for what was left of the night. I was tempted to ring Saphie again but felt that at two in the morning she probably wouldn't thank me. I settled into a pile of blankets and quilts in the lounge, having let Tania take my bed. I drifted into sleep the moment my eyes closed.

I slept soundly until the noise awoke me. And the shaking. The noise and shaking of somebody shouting at me and tugging my arm.

"You're under arrest!" The shouting cut through the last of my sleep and I forced my eyes to stay open against a sudden glare of light.

"What?" I struggled with words.

"Turn around and give me your arms."

I couldn't quite work out how to comply with that strange

request but the police officer helped me understand. I felt my arms being twisted into a highly uncomfortable position behind me and something cold and hard clamped over my wrists.

"What on earth —" I started.

"Sorry," I heard Simon's voice. "I didn't mean to."

"No talking!"

I twisted awkwardly round in my chair and stared at the scene in front of me. Simon, the Pope and Kevin all sat on the floor, their hands, like mine, secured behind.

A large and decidedly unhappy looking police officer strutted around the room. He picked one of my coats of the rack and threw it at Kevin. "And put that on, you bloody pervert."

A noise upstairs caught his attention. He turned to scan us all. "Nobody move," he instructed and headed for the stairs. I realised Tania wasn't here, that was probably what the noise was.

"I just wanted to explore a bit," Simon said.

I glanced around and my eyes fell on the patio doors. The wood and brickwork that we had used to seal it last night, now lay in a heap all across my carpet.

"I thought they'd all gone," he continued.

"You let them in?" I was incredulous.

"Well, not in as much as... Not on purpose. I just needed to see if it was really a Rock Borer."

"A Rock Borer?"

"If there are Rock Borers down there it might mean there's gold. You see the Kobolds —"

"Simon!" the Pope interrupted. "Shut the fuck up."

The policeman reappeared pushing Tania roughly before him. She fell in a tumble in the middle of the floor.

“Now, nobody move.” He pressed the talk button on his lapel radio. “Hello, Command? This is fifteen two four eight, come in.” He paused whilst he radio crackled noisy static back at him. “Command? Fifteen two four eight. I have...” He glanced slowly round the room. “I have five prisoners for transport.” More static. He turned to us and snapped, “Nobody move or there will be... trouble.” He headed for the front door, the sound of his pleas for assistance becoming fainter as he went.

“Well,” I said. “This is an interesting situation.”

“It will be even more interesting if he steps outside the front door,” Tania said.

“What? Oh, yes, I see.”

“Where the hell is my car?” The policeman thundered back into the lounge. “Command? Command?” He stabbed at the talk button on his radio. “What have you lot done with my car?” He glared at us.

His radio crackled into life. “Hello! Hello! This is Central Dispatch,” a heavy Birmingham accented voice announced. “What is your location?”

That’s odd, I thought. He shouldn’t be able to contact his world from here?

“I’m in...” the policeman stared around the room. “I’m in... I don’t know where I am. Somewhere near Glastonbury.”

“You’ll need to be a bit more specific, mate.”

“Mate? Mate?! Just track me from my radio.”

“Track you? Who the hell do you think we are? M.I. sodding five? I can’t send a cab to ‘Somewhere near Glastonbury’.”

“A cab? I don’t want a cab. I want a police car.”

“You need a sodding Funny Wagon, mate. You’re barking

mad." The radio clicked off and delivered a burst of static into the policeman's ear.

A shadow appeared in the doorway behind the policeman. The shadow resolved into Eric, complete with pickaxe handle. I realised with horror what he intended and shook my head. Eric stared at me and shook his own head. I nodded. Eric looked quizzically at me then swung the handle towards the back of the policeman's head. It connected with a loud clunk and the officer toppled to the ground like Sadam Husain's Statue.

"You've killed him!" Tania squealed.

"He's not dead." Eric crouched over the inanimate policeman and located his keys. "But he will have a bit of a headache."

Eric freed us from the handcuffs and we carted the still unconscious policeman outside. We dragged him round to the front of the house, propped him against the wall then I nipped back inside for an empty gin bottle. "Might not be totally convincing but it will spread confusion." I slipped the bottle in his pocket.

Eric shouted, "Oi!" loudly towards the police car. We slipped behind the wall and peeped round. The policeman in the car seemed blissfully unaware. We repeated the process a couple more times until we came to the conclusion the one in the car was also asleep. One of the Possicats rubbed itself against Eric's leg. He leaned down to stroke it then picked it up.

"This should do the trick," he said, heading for the car. He carefully opened the back door, pushed the cat in, closed the door and ran back to us.

The cat yowled so loudly we could hear from here. The

policeman in the car jumped, startling the cat even more. Instantly the inside of the car boiled in a turmoil of fur and police uniform.

"That seems to have woken him up," I said.

We ran round the back and just as we were about to slip through the remains of the patio doors Simon announced his intent to return to Tunnel Cottage World.

"I can do some good there," he said. "It's what I was born to do. The adventure. You should understand?" He gazed at me as if trying to find a kindred spirit in the world of heroic daring do.

"I don't do adventure," I said. "I have a super-hero for that."

Chapter Twenty-One

SAPHIE BROUGHT THE DRINKS OVER to our table. "Arthur's celebrating the Chinese New Year," she said. "Do you want chicken Balti and chips?"

"I think I'll pass," I said and took the frothing pint of Old Grumbler from her. I placed it on the table and stared at it for a moment. The glass ran with condensation and the dark ale inside bubbled slightly. I was trying a new regime. Pause and think before you drink. I'd read that somewhere. That'll do. I grabbed the pint and half of it disappeared before I replaced the glass on the table. Baby steps, baby steps.

"Busy in here tonight." Saphie took a sip of her wine. "Isn't that Ozzie Osborne over there?"

"You mean that guy talking to Prince Charles? Hmm, you could be right,"

"No, I was thinking about him over there." She pointed to a table by the fireplace. "Him at the table with Keith Richards and Rod Stewart."

The clientele of the Camelot had certainly increased over the last few days. Arthur put it down to his creative menus but I felt it was probably more to do with Eric Three Four Nine. I was going to have to have a chat with him. An official chat. In my official capacity as gatekeeper of Glastonbury One. That was my name for it. The gates had never had names before. Aunt Flora had been very understanding about the mess and said to 'Think nothing of it, dear.' However, there was one small caveat to her generosity. I had to take over the Gatekeeper's job from her until such time as I'd got everybody back where they belonged. She was off to Monaco with Roger and I was to give her a ring when I'd sorted it all out. I had a feeling I'd been conned.

Eric had set up his own building firm and showed little interest in going back. The Pope had given me the slip, although I did receive an eCard from Jerusalem. Which was somewhat worrying. And then there was Kevin. Kevin was currently under arrest for indecent exposure in a public swimming pool. His explanation that covering one random part of his body with a small piece of cloth was just as valid as any other part, so why shouldn't he wear his swimming trunks on his head, hadn't found much favour with the magistrates. He was currently awaiting a psychiatrist's report.

"You staying over?" I asked Saphie. The last few nights we'd spent together and I still didn't fancy being alone in the cottage. I had dreams of the walls opening me up and giant cats coming to draw me back in.

"If you like." She gave a small smile. "We could watch Stargate or something."

"Or something."

* * * * *

Three weeks later I was sitting at my desk looking out of the landing window. All was well with the world. The oak tree was still there right where it shouldn't be and the words flew onto the page. The latest adventures of The Falconer had been well received by my publisher and I'd even surprised Tania by sending a follow up volume three months early.

I paused for a moment. The Falconer had just slipped into a parallel universe where eagles were the dominant species and I was just wondering what their language would sound like when I heard a rattling outside. The end of a ladder appeared at the window. My ladder. The one I had lost several weeks ago when it fell through the window and plopped into another world.

The ladder wobbled a bit as somebody climbed up it. I pushed my seat backwards slightly to create distance between me and whatever monster was climbing my ladder.

Simon's face appeared at the window. He tapped on the glass. I opened the window carefully so as not to dislodge him.

"Simon?"

"You've got to help," he said, an agitated look on his face. "It's the goblins! They've escaped."

The End

Author Note

I do hope you enjoyed this tale, if so, I would be grateful for a few words as a review on your favourite book buying website or Goodreads. Reviews are very important to us authors and I always appreciate them.

Many thanks.

David

~ Find my books and sign up for the newsletter ~

If you would like to subscribe to my Newsletter, just enter your details below. I promise not to sell your email address to a Nigerian Prince or send you adverts for various biological enhancements.

I will however, at entirely random moments, send you a newsletter containing my writing updates, competitions, give-aways, general meanderings and thoughts on the latest Big Thing.

luddington.com/newsletter

Or to find out more about the author

To Follow On Facebook:
facebook.com/DavidLuddingtonAuthor

The Website: www.luddington.com

Twitter: @d_luddington

Other Books From This Best Selling Author

Tony Ryan is bemused. He thought he understood the way the world worked, but now, as a sacrificial lamb of the credit crunch he finds himself drifting... drifting into the clutches of the ever resourceful Pete who could find the angle in a Fairy Liquid bubble... and into the arms of the enigmatic hippy girl, Astrid, who's about to introduce Tony to rabbits, magic caves and the joys of mushrooms.

Charles Tremayne is a spy out of his time. After a long career spent rescuing prisoners from the KGB or helping defectors across the Berlin Wall the world has changed. The Wall has gone and no longer is there a need for a Russian speaking, ice-cold killer. The bad guys now all speak Arabic and state secrets are transmitted via satellite using blowfish algorithms impenetrable to anybody over the age of twelve. Counting down the days to his retirement by babysitting drunken visiting politicos he is seconded by MI6 for one last case. £250,000,000 of government money destined as a payoff for the dictator of a strategic African nation goes missing on its way to a remote Cornish airfield.

Tremayne is dispatched to retrieve the money and nothing is going to stand in his way. Armed with an IQ of 165 and a bewildering array of weaponry and gadgets he is not about to be outmanoeuvred by the inhabitants of a small Cornish fishing village. Or is he?

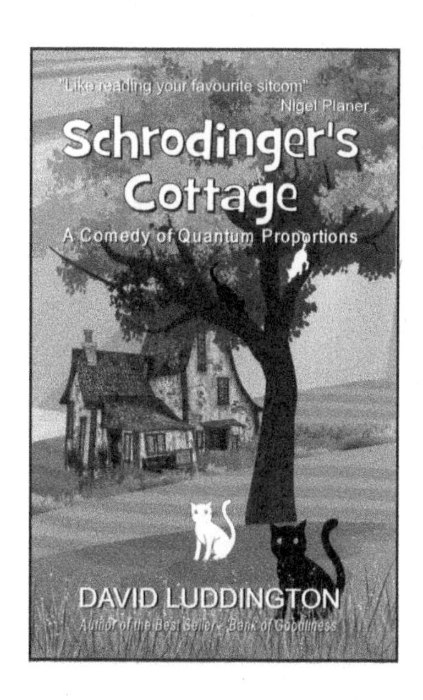

Tinker's Cottage nestles in a forgotten corner of deepest Somerset. It also happens to sit on a weak point in the space time continuum. Which is somewhat unfortunate for Ian Faulkener, a graphic novelist from London, who was hoping for some peace and quiet in which to recuperate following a very messy breakdown.

It was the cats that first alerted Ian to the fact that something was not quite right with Tinker's Cottage. Not only was he never sure just how many of them there actually were, but the mysterious way they seemed to disappear and reappear defied logic. The cats, and of course the Pope, disappearing literary agents, mislaid handymen and the insanity of Cherie Blair World.

As Ian tries to untangle the mystery of the doors of Tinker's cottage he risks becoming lost forever in the myriad alternate universes predicted by Schrodinger. Not to mention his cats.

Schrodinger's Cottage is a playful romp through a variety of alternate worlds peopled by an array of wonderful comic characters that are the trademark of David Luddington's novels.

For fans of the sadly missed Douglas Adams, Schrodinger's Cottage will be a welcome addition to their library. A heart-warming comedy with touches of inspired lunacy that pays homage to The Hitchhiker's Guide whilst firmly treading its own path.

"...And there will be a corner of some foreign field that will be forever England."

Only these days it's more likely to be a half finished villa overlooking a championship golf course somewhere on one of The Costas.

Following an unfortunate encounter with Spanish gin measures and an enthusiastic estate agent, retired special effects engineer Terry England is the proud owner of a nearly completed villa in a new urbanisation in Southern Spain.

Not quite how he'd intended to spend his enforced early retirement Terry nevertheless tries to make the best of his new life. If only the local council can work out which house he's actually bought and the leaf blowers would please stop.

Terry finds himself being sucked in to the English Expat community with their endless garden parties and quests for real bacon and Tetley's Tea Bags. Of course, if it all gets too much he can always relax in the local English Bar with a nice pint of Guinness, a roast beef lunch and the Mail on Sunday.

With a growing feeling that he might have moved to the 'Wrong Spain', Terry sets out to explore and finds himself tangled in the affairs of a small rustic village in the Alpujarras. It is here where he finds a different Spain. A Spain of loves and passions, a Spain of new hopes and a simpler way of life. A place where a moped is an acceptable means of family transport and a place where if you let your guard down for just a moment this land will never let you go again.

Forever England is the tale of one man trying to redefine who he is and how he wants to live. It is a story of hope and humour with an array of eccentric characters and comic situations for which David Luddington is so well known and loved.

"Overall, this is a very warm and funny book. It is filled with wonderful characters and many laugh out loud moments." book-reviewer.com

"Genuinely funny, with many laugh out loud moment..." Matt Rothwell - author of Drunk In Charge Of A Foreign Language

Reading David Luddington is like "Like reading your favourite sitcom." – Nigel Planer

Retired stage magician turned professional mystic debunker, John Barker, finds his sceptical beliefs under fire when he encounters a strange man who claims to be Merlin. After several unsuccessful attempts to rid himself of his increasingly unpredictable companion, John finally relents and agrees to assist in the man's crazy mission, to find the true grave of the mythical King Arthur.

Following a hidden code contained within the text of a soft porn novel, they gather a growing entourage of hippies, mystic seekers and alien hunters as they leave a trail of chaos across the south west of England. When the group comes to the attention of a TV Reality Show producer looking to make a fast profit out of harmless eccentrics and fading celebrities, John decides it's time to take charge and prove one way or the other, the identity of this mysterious person who claims to be a fictional wizard.

"Whose reality is this anyway?" is a warm-hearted tale of what it means to be an individual and to follow one's dreams. With his trademark cast of oddball characters and absurd situations, David Luddington once more transports us into a world where who you are is more important than what you are.

"David Luddington epitomizes the elusive quality of writing that he perpetuates - the British Comedy." – Grady Harp

When ex-SAS soldier, Michael Purdy, comes in front of the judge for hacking the bank account belonging to the Minister for Invalidity Benefits and wiping out his personal wealth, he braces himself for a prison sentence.

What Michael doesn't expect, is to be put in charge of a group of offenders and sent to a remote location in the Sierra Nevada Mountains in Spain to teach them survival skills as part of their rehabilitation programme.

But Michael knows nothing at all about survival skills. He was sort of in the SAS, yes, but his shining record on the "Escape and Evasion" courses was more a testament to his computer skills than his ability to catch wildlife and barbecue it over an impromptu fire. Basically, he was the SAS's techy nerd and only achieved that position as a result of a bet with a fellow hacker.

Facing a stark choice between starvation or returning home to serve out their sentences, the group of offenders under Michael's supervision soon realise that the only way to survive is to use their own unique set of skills – the kind of skills that got them arrested in the first place.

When Shadeys Bank loses yet another C.E.O. to a major scandal, they are desperate to show they've reformed. Who better to present their redemption to the world than a country vicar with a reputation for being annoyingly good?

Reverend Tom Goodman is ousted from his job as a country vicar for allowing a homeless family to stay in the church hall. Meanwhile, a major bank is trying to rescue its image after the latest in a long string of financial scandals.

It seems like the perfect match and Goodman is hastily appointed as the bank's new C.E.O. All they have to do now, is promote him as the new face of Shadeys Bank whilst at the same time, keeping him away from the day-to-day business of dubious banking.

However, Tom Goodman has other ideas. He's not going to be satisfied with being used as an empty puppet for a PR stunt. Unfortunately for Shadeys, Tom is planning on actually making a difference.

And so begins an epic battle of wills. The might of a multi-billion pound bank versus a seemingly naïve country vicar.

No contest.

"Yes Minister meets The Vicar of Dibley."

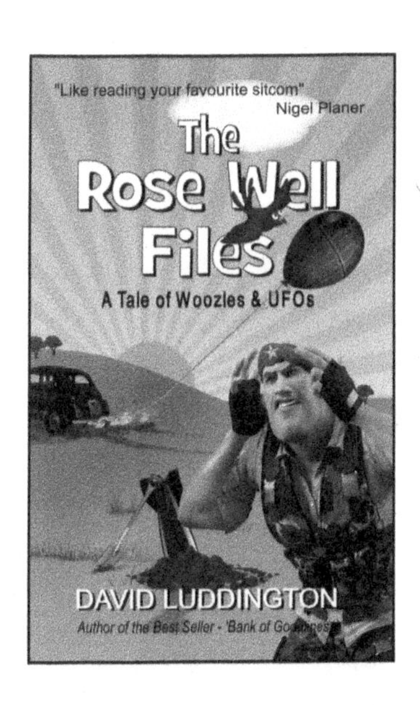

ROSE WELL HOLIDAY PARK NEEDS A HERO.

This once shining icon of the Great British Holiday Camp is dying, and the last residents are more interested in preparing for a zombie apocalypse or fighting off imaginary UFOs than playing Crazy Golf or Bingo.

In addition, a foreign bottled water company is attempting to force a sale so they can seize the last asset of Rose Well Park, the Rose Well Spring. The famous spring water claimed to bestow great health and longevity.

And then there's the bomb.

What Rose Well Park could probably do without, is a hero whose belief in a better tomorrow far outweighs any of his past achievements. But William Fox is all they have.

Armed with nothing more than an undying sense of optimism and a box of books about alien conspiracies, he slowly draws up his plans to make Rose Well Park famous.

"Dad's Army meets X-Files"

Woozle: Noun

A presentation of evidence by citation only. A woozle occurs when frequent citation of publications, lacking evidence, mislead individuals, groups, and the public, and nonfacts become urban myths and factoids.

Printed in May 2022
by Rotomail Italia S.p.A., Vignate (MI) - Italy